PRAISE FOR

"Finely nuanced and exquisitely drawn, *Glas~~~~~~~~~~~~~~~~~~~~~~~~~~~~~~~~~~~~~
after you finish. Kort has masterfully writte~~~~~~~~~~~~~~ ~~~~~~~~ story that
grabs you and draws you into a place where glass isn't the only thing that's fragile.
A must read."

—**Cynthia A. Graham**, award-winning author of *Beneath Still Waters*

"Though weighty in its subject matter, *Glass* avoids enveloping the reader in darkness by two means: the shining narrative and descriptive talents of this debut novelist, and the masterfully authentic rendering of a variety of damaged characters who, however undone they perhaps ought to be, still seek a way not only to help themselves but each other.... [They] insist on our attention and receive our sympathy, even as that sympathy extends out from this author to all of us, the recipients of this gift of irresistible honesty and insight into our human plight."

—**Joe Benevento**, author of *The Monsignor's Wife* and *Saving St. Teresa*

"Kort weaves [the characters'] stories together with beautiful writing, escalating the stakes on every page, driving it to a shocking but deeply satisfying conclusion. You won't find many page-turners in the literary novel genre, but this is definitely one of them."   —**Gary Corbin**, author of the Valorie Dawes Thrillers

"Kate Kort's words are as gentle hands upon the soul of those tormented by past transgressions, and become, in the end, a balm for life's trials."

—**Dennis Young**, author of The Ardwellian Chronicles

"This book is spot on. A reminder of the power of compassion."

—A survivor, counselor, and suicide prevention expert

"Based on the premise alone, I felt drawn to read this book. I'm glad I did; as deep and dark as it was, I really found a lot to like about *Glass*.... The characters all stand out as real people, deeply flawed.... No magic steps in to improve anyone's lot, and everyone just pushes through with what they have. The writing is wonderfully clear and straightforward, and peppered with perfect details throughout. A singular vision, and a remarkable debut!"

—**Eric Henderson**, author of *Stranded in Sunshine*

"This substantial book stays with you, its characters leap off the page and its sustained tension keeps you reading until the very end."

—**Peter H. Green**, author of *Fatal Designs*

"Tense, honest, true.... With Hollywood's sanitized representations of the various types of mental illness, including popular fiction and other media, Kort's *Glass* is a welcome wake-up call.... a great read."   —**Nick Rossi**, *Reading Other People*

"*Glass* is simply a brilliantly written novel.... a story about imperfect people trying to find their way in an imperfect world.... Kate Kort intertangled what we loathe about people with what we love and admire about people...."

—**Brian Simpson**, author of *Island Dogs*

"Kate Kort's edgy but brilliant novel is not a 'feel good' book, by any means. Yet even if there seems to be no light at the end of the dark tunnel Menashe Everett inhabits, there are lessons to be learned there. In the process, Kort's creation becomes an unforgettable character—part Everyman, part tortured soul, and ultimately someone we almost have to root for, despite his flaws."

—**Robert Darrell Laurant**, *Snowflakes in a Blizzard*

PRAISE FOR *TEMPERED*

"In *Tempered*, author Kort revisits the hard topics explored in *Glass*. She has once again created a protagonist that you care about, despite flaws that are not ignored or minimized. Instead of shortcuts or easy answers, she realistically portrays trauma, its aftermath, and the hard work that is required for healing.

"Avoiding cliché endings, she skillfully balances a narrative that is at once gritty and hopeful. It is a book that you walk away from with a new sense of compassion and understanding for those among us who are struggling. Thought-provoking and honest, Tempered is a book you won't want to put down."

—**Cynthia A. Graham**, award-winning author of *Beneath Still Waters*

"As in her previous two novels, Kate Kort takes her readers for an uneasy but fascinating ride with brilliantly drawn characters who are trying, often unsuccessfully, to overcome their abusive pasts. Murray Henderson is someone we root for, even as we question the unhealthy choices he makes. As he tries to create a new life for himself in New York City, the positive potential in new relationships is challenged by the violent responses to life that have become too much a part of his new self. Told with an unflinching realism combined with a sure and lyrical humanity, *Tempered* will keep its readers anchored in a hope for a better life for Murray that in many ways becomes a hope we must hold for us all."

—**Joe Benevento**, author of *My Perfect Wife, Her Perfect Son*

"*Tempered* offers a fascinating character study of a tormented man and the many facets of his recovery. Kort provides an honest, unflinching look at the ways trauma can affect ourselves and our loved ones both.... Kort's novel is an accomplishment. With characters as rich as these, one must wonder if there is potential for a third book—a Murray Henderson trilogy, so to speak. As the narrative so vividly reminds us, there is no easy or absolute end to the effects of the past."

—**Nathanial Drenner**, *Independent Book Review*

Tate Kent

TEMPERED

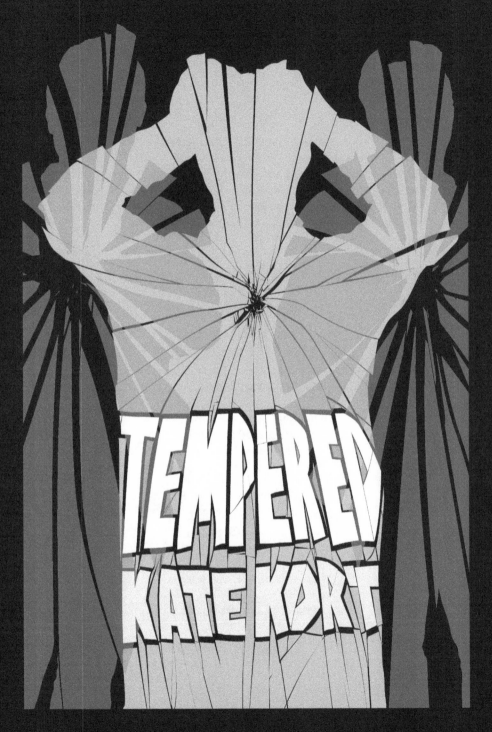

TEMPERED

KATE KORT

Brick Mantel Books
Saint Louis, Missouri

Published by Brick Mantel Books, USA

Brick Mantel
BOOKS

www.BrickMantelBooks.com
info@BrickMantelBooks.com

An imprint of Pen & Publish LLC
www.PenandPublish.com
Saint Louis, Missouri
(314) 827-6567

Print ISBN: 978-1-956897-22-7
eBook ISBN: 978-1-956897-23-4

Library of Congress Control Number: 2022947081

Cover Design: Brent Smith

Printed on acid-free paper.

Acknowledgments

Thank you so much to the people who helped make this book possible. First, Sean Keck, for off-handedly asking if I was working on a sequel to *Glass*. I had never thought of it before, but the wheels started turning after that. Thank you to the amazing writers Randal Houle, Joe Walters, Rankin Johnson, and Gary Corbin for giving such insightful critiques that shaped the final manuscript. Thank you to the wonderful Jennifer Geist and everyone at Brick Mantel Books for believing in my work, and to Brent Smith for producing yet another badass cover. Thank you to the honest, encouraging readers who gave such great feedback: Lisa (Becker) Coad, Tim Anderson, Joe Benevento, Cynthia Graham, Lisa Marsden, and of course the incomparable Ben Kort.

Prologue
CLEVELAND, 1998

I'm still sleeping with the lights on. I thought I'd be done with that by now, but closing my eyes in the dark still feels like hell. Danielle says it doesn't bother her and I guess I believe her. Not much bothers her.

Today is ten years since my father died, so I'm awake at 4:12 a.m., watching the clock tick above the dresser and listening to Danielle breathe. I've never felt as peaceful as she looks right now; I'm sure I look anxious even when I'm asleep.

I get up and go to the kitchen. The light's on there, too. My utility bill isn't pretty, but it's worth not being surprised by whatever lurks in the dark. I hate to be surprised, just like my dad. I open a beer, but I won't finish it. Just a few drinks to slow my pulse. I toss the opener onto the counter, and it slides into a stack of unwashed dishes. It's loud and I wince, but then I remember Dani sleeps through anything.

I move into the living room and sink into the worn gray recliner. It's darker in here so when I glance around, I see shapes I can't place. I rub my eyes and tell myself it's ridiculous for a grown man, nearly thirty years old, to be afraid of the dark. I frown. Maybe it isn't.

My heart skips because there's a pool of blood on the floor, in the corner by the fireplace. I even start to smell it, so I fumble for the switch on the lamp next to me and squint as it fills the room with yellow-tinted light. It's just my T-shirt, wadded up on the floor.

I sigh as I think about the calls I'll get later. My mom. My brother Jake (but not Matthew). John. Maybe Austin. Milestone days get people all worked up. They want to check on you, but the last thing you want to do is talk. It's one of the reasons I haven't told Danielle. She doesn't need to know why I keep the lights on at night, or why I threw away my legal career. I like that we don't have those things weighing us down. Sometimes, with her, I can forget.

Chapter 1
Start Again

I didn't tell John or Austin I was going to New York.

I realize there isn't anybody else I would tell. A few years ago it would have been my mom, but we don't talk as much since she moved out to Chicago to be with Jake and his kids. A few days ago it would have been Dani, but I fucked that up beyond repair. I've tried to call her a few times this week, but she never lets me get past the flustered apology I always open with. Then there's Austin. He won't worry; he's good about giving me space when I need it. But John . . . I trudge forward, staggering under the weight of my bags. I should have called him.

I walk out of the airport, and a strong gust of wind nearly blows me back. I hail a cab right away and heap my stuff into the backseat with me.

I know I packed too much. I'm only here for two days, but I brought a large duffel with about a week's worth of clothes, a few books and toiletries, and a garment bag with my suit. We pull away from the airport and for some reason I feel better.

I was prepared for New York to be loud, crowded, and overwhelming. That's what I'd always heard, and it's true, but I couldn't have predicted my reaction to it. Walking up Sullivan to my hotel, I can already feel my mind calming. I pass a group of older men speaking Spanish. I catch the heavy smell of fried street food as I pass a subway station. I hear the musicians on the corner playing makeshift drums. There are thousands of people in the city block around me, but I don't know any of them. I don't know their neighborhoods or restaurants, and when I see a building or sign, I don't feel the stab of an unwelcome memory.

By the time I check in and shower, I have just enough time to get dressed and find my way to Spodek Law Group. I've never been good with directions, so I double-check my map with the concierge. He has more confidence in my abilities than I do, assuring me I can walk the three blocks with time to spare.

I feel the urge to ask him if I look okay—if I look like I'd fit in there—but he's already turned his attention to someone else. I duck into the bathroom to smooth my hair down and practice smiling in the mirror one more time. My reflection is uneasy, unnatural. It makes me think of an alien trying to impersonate a human. I glance at my watch. I can't put it off anymore.

I push through the heavy lobby door, grateful to be met with the cool October air again. I breathe in, greeted with the recurring relief that I'm no longer in Cleveland.

The next morning, my eyes dart open, already pulsing. The air is now thick and rancid, weighed down by uncovered Chinese food and spilled beer. I turn my head and glance around the room, remembering the details. It'd be better if I hadn't woken up at all.

I catch my reflection in the television, wishing I could bash it in with the curtain rod that hangs above my bed. Would it shatter like a bowl or a sculpture, spraying shards across the room, or just crack into spiderwebs? I narrow my eyes until my vision blurs, not really caring about the answer. I know it won't help.

After all that optimism and unearned confidence, I blew the interview. I failed to impersonate a human. I was sweaty and stuttery, and came off as unreliable. Probably worse. I sit up and look out the window. They didn't even pretend I had a chance—the woman running the interview told me outright it wasn't going to work. And I don't even blame them for giving the job to someone else. A few leaves and bits of stray trash whip past my window. I think about leaving tomorrow. About coming home with nothing.

I walk a few blocks around the hotel, trying to ignore the people rushing past me, all with smug purpose. I zip up my sweatshirt, feeling better without the stiff interview clothes. Maybe I shouldn't be in a job like that anyway. Maybe I'd just feel trapped again.

My mind steadies as I walk. I'm calmed by the people, their anonymity and easy movement, and I start to lose track of everything else. After about an hour, I end up at NYU's campus. I wander the buildings, the green space, the bookstore. It's too depressingly nostalgic, and I think about heading back out when I pass the law library. I pause a moment, but I can't help it. I walk in, just to smell that wonderful air, thick with the clean, earthy scent of books.

I breathe in and my pulse quickens. I scan the room, thinking how lucky these people are that they spend the day here. My hands shake. A thought shoots into my mind. It's a crazy thought, but I walk up to the circulation desk, because I no longer have the luxury of waiting for things to happen. I have the rest of the day in New York, but that's it. And I'm not ready to give Cleveland the victory yet. Three students are busy working, but after a moment the one in the middle, a young woman with dark red hair, calls me over.

"Can I help you?" She's still looking at her computer screen.

"Yeah." I shift my weight, glancing around. "Are there any job openings in the library?"

She looks up. "Student positions?" Her eyes narrow with doubt.

"No, I'm looking for something more permanent."

"Are you a librarian?"

"No, I have a law degree. But I'm interested in anything full time; I don't mind entry level."

She tells me she'll get a staff librarian and walks to the offices behind her. The library is crowded and a line has formed, so I step out of the way and let a few people check out. After another minute or so, I see the student worker emerge, trailed by a middle-aged man with dark shaggy hair and a gray beard.

"Hi," he says, walking out from behind the desk. "I'm Alan Anders, one of the research librarians."

"Murray Henderson," I reply, shaking his hand.

"And you're a lawyer?"

I smile. "I haven't practiced in a few years."

"Still, our openings would be a pretty big step down," he says with a laugh. "You want to tell me how you got here?"

"It's kind of a long story," I begin, appreciative of the casual vibe Mr. Anders is emitting. "I was here for another job interview—a paralegal position at Spodek. I didn't get the job, but I'd like to stay in New York. And the library was about my favorite place in law school."

"Where are you from?"

"Cleveland."

"No kidding?" he says, a wide smile crossing his face. "I lived there twenty years."

"Wow, that's crazy." I flush with relief. "What neighborhood?"

"South Euclid."

"I grew up about ten minutes from there in Cleveland Heights."

Mr. Anders shakes his head. "Unbelievable." He laughs a little to himself, then looks at his watch. "I have a few minutes; why don't you come on back with me?"

Hope surges through my chest and I follow him. I feel like reality is paused with me standing outside the library, waiting for my desperate fantasy to dissolve. Mr. Anders offers me a seat at a conference table and walks to the filing cabinet on the back wall.

He pulls a file and reads for a long time. There's nothing on the walls for me to look at, so I settle for picking at a small divot in the table. I wish I still had on my nice clothes. Mr. Anders pulls another file. And another. Minutes pass. I start to think I should tell him not to worry, that he doesn't have to do this just because we came from the same place, but he pulls out a paper and looks up.

"Okay," he says, "this might be something. How do you feel about Assistant Stacks Coordinator? It's a little bit of everything—organizing reference material, helping us shelve and process, that kind of thing."

I stare at him. "Yeah. That sounds amazing."

"Well, I do need to interview you," he says. "But with a JD you're obviously overqualified." He sets the paper down in front of him. "How long would you want to keep this position?"

"At least a year." I'm not sure where this answer came from, but I mean it.

Mr. Anders nods. "Do you have a while to wait now?"

"Sure."

"Okay." He looks at his watch again. "I've got to get back to work, but we should be able to do the interview in the next hour or so. You're lucky," he says with a smile, "it's a light day."

That evening I collapse onto the bed, exhausted. My temperature rises as I consider what I've done.

I have changed my life.

I have no home. My lease back in Cleveland is up at the end of the month and my address is now the Days Inn on Broadway. In two weeks I need to show up to a job I'd never heard of before today, in a city I've known for forty-eight hours. But I can't think about it too much or I'll start to panic. I'll start to feel like I can't do it alone.

I miss Dani.

She won't take my calls yet, and I don't blame her. I pick up the phone and punch in four digits before I stop. I can't put this on her. I look around the bland, vacant room, and realize I'm not ready to leave everything I need to tell her in a message. I hang up the phone.

I rummage through the bag of groceries I bought at the convenience store a block over and pull out a can of beer. I sit on the bed, leaning my back against the wall, and take a long drink. I just need to relax.

After another hour, I get up enough nerve to call John. I shouldn't have left him to interpret the vague smattering of information I gave Austin yesterday.

He picks up on the second ring.

"Hey, John."

"Murray! Hey, what is going on? Where are you?"

"Well . . ." I trace the phone cord with my finger. "I'm still in New York. I-I might be here for a while."

"Murray," he says, and I can tell he's summoning his patience, "can you please tell me what's going on?"

"I didn't get the paralegal job."

"Yeah, that's what Austin said."

"But I got a different job. Today. At NYU's law library."

There's silence on John's end and I know he's trying to make sense of all this. He's a practical guy, and everything I've done in the past three days has been absurd. "The law library," he repeats. "Why didn't you just come home?"

I try to answer him, but my throat tightens and I can't form the words. *Home.* I shut my eyes against a pounding wave of emotions.

"Murray, are you there?"

The room is blurry when I open my eyes. I blink, once again taking in the unfamiliar hotel room. "I'm sorry," I say after a moment. "I fucked everything up."

"What do you mean?"

I open my mouth, wanting to say it, but I can't. Shame stalls my voice and I can't admit to the man who has been a father to me for the last ten years that I'm even weaker, more selfish, more dangerous than I was the day we met.

"John, I have to call you back." My voice wavers. "I'm sorry, can I call you tomorrow?"

There's a pause. "Sure," he says, and I wish I could see his face because I can't read his voice.

I hang up with him and glance at the empty beer cans on my nightstand and the digital alarm clock next to them. I'm tired and should get to bed—get away from my destructive thoughts. But I don't close my eyes for another two hours, after I've finished the six-pack. And when I do sleep, I dream of Cleveland Heights.

Chapter 2

Anniversaries

Cleveland, Five Months Earlier

Most Sunday nights I made it to The Velvet Dog. Somehow it was still my favorite place in Cleveland. I glanced down like always toward the basement as I walked up to the front door. Chase was waiting. He still dressed up for poker night; that night he was wearing a shiny blue dress shirt and ironed khakis.

"Hey, Murray. Did John come with you?" He glanced at his watch.

"No, he said he'd be a few minutes late."

"Did he sound all right to you?"

"What do you mean?"

Chase rubbed his gray-blond beard and looked away. "I think he's really feeling down. I mean, next week will be ten years since Ash—"

"I know," I broke in. My father and Mr. Everett, gone in the span of two weeks. How could I forget.

"I just wish I could help."

"You run the poker game," I said, managing a smile. "That helps. Believe me."

"I hope so."

We walked to the back of the club, to the usual table. The place hadn't changed at all in ten years, which was comforting as well as unsettling. On the wood-paneled walls hung the same nostalgic Cleveland photos; the same dim lights littered the ceiling like kitschy stars. The floor was still sticky. It wasn't long before the door opened behind us and I turned, relieved to see Austin. Sam was right behind him and they seemed to be joking about something. Good. Austin could use a laugh.

Sam gave Austin a devilish wink, like he had more to say but it wasn't meant for us. Sam was the youngest in the group until I joined. He just turned forty but still reminded me of a cocky college freshman.

He hopped the bar and began fixing himself a drink. I walked over to Austin.

"I'm glad you made it," I said, trying to gauge his mood.

He hadn't been shaving and his eyes were heavy, but his smile still seemed genuine.

"Thanks, Murray. I tell you, though, it's going to be a hard week."

"You mean about Mr. Everett?"

He nodded. "Ten fucking years." He looked around, but Sam was still at the bar and Chase was focused on shuffling at the table. "I still can't believe it, you know? It feels like we were all just at his funeral."

"Yeah. I think about that day all the time."

Austin put his hand on my shoulder. "Sorry, kid. I shouldn't complain. I know this is all harder on you."

I shrugged, ready to tell him it wasn't that bad when Sam called out to us.

"What'll you have, guys?"

"Gin, splash of tonic," Austin replied. He leaned down to brush something off his jeans, and his thick silver hair gleamed under the bar lights.

"Any beer's good for me," I said, moving to the table and sitting down next to Chase. "Thanks, Sam."

"You bet."

He brought the drinks over as John rushed through the door, cursing as he tripped over the front step.

"Chase," Sam said, with apparent restraint. "The goddamn step."

Chase poured pretzels into a bowl. "It's on my list."

John swept his light brown hair out of his eyes and adjusted his grip on the bag he was carrying. He was getting on toward fifty but had always looked young for his age. And there was an energy he radiated—a contented aura I often found comforting.

Sam went back to the bar. He grabbed a bottle of vodka and held it up. "John?"

John nodded and smiled, sinking into the empty chair next to me. "Sorry, guys. I'm sorry I'm late."

"No problem," Chase said. "Haven't even dealt yet."

Austin asked Chase a question about contract work around the bar, so John leaned in close to me.

"You doing all right?"

I smiled. "I think so."

John gave me a look, like he wanted to believe me but couldn't. "I tried calling you last week. A few times."

"I know." I rubbed my neck. "I'm sorry about that. I just didn't want to think about it."

"Yeah, I get it."

"But I was wondering, maybe . . ."

"Yeah?"

"Can we talk after this? Go to Clevelander or something?"

John nodded. "Of course."

"Thanks." I looked down, embarrassed I said anything at all, but relieved he'd said yes. I noticed his bag again. "What'd you bring?"

"Oh, yeah." He reached down and brought the bag up onto the table. "Guys," he said, motioning for Austin and Chase to stop their conversation. Sam looked up from his drink. "I found something I thought we should look at."

My stomach twisted. I wasn't going to like it.

He brought out a book, *The Complete Baseball Record Book* from 1987, and pulled several folded sheets of paper from between its pages.

"A few weeks before he died, I asked Menashe to give me feedback on a short story of mine. I'd just started writing and didn't know what the hell I was doing. I used some of the therapy exercises he'd given me to start, which is how I began writing about my time in Vietnam." He unfolded the papers and smoothed them out on the table. "Anyway, I thought he'd forgotten about it. He had enough on his mind."

John frowned and I already felt my stomach begin to churn.

"But he didn't forget," John continued, emotion softening his voice. "He returned this book to me a week later, and I didn't think anything of it. But I went to look something up a few days ago, and my story fell out of its pages."

"What did he say?" Chase asked.

"I thought he'd mark it up. But he didn't write anything until the last page."

John flipped to the back and I saw there was a lot of writing under the last line of John's story. I recognized Mr. Everett's handwriting and my muscles tensed. How many times had I seen him scribbling notes on his yellow legal tablet? John took a breath and started to read.

> *"John,*
>
> *Sorry I don't know shit about this. I'm a horrible writer. I meant to give you something helpful, but once I started, I realized you don't need me at all. What I can tell you is, I know you've changed since you started writing. Your head is clearing. You're determined. And your heart's in it. I wish mine was. I'm sorry I haven't helped you as much as I wanted.*

Your success has always been your own. I really appreciate how you gave this a shot, though. It always made me feel better to have my best friend around. Anyway, whatever happens, please keep writing."

John wiped his eyes and looked around the table. He did way better than I could have, reading that, but now he was close to breaking down. I used my sleeve to wipe my own eyes, then I turned to him.

"He knew," I said. "He knew what he was going to do."

John nodded and Austin rubbed his face with both hands.

"Why couldn't Ash just level with us?" Austin muttered. "We would have understood, right?"

"I don't think that's how it works," Chase said. "He was in so much pain. He prob—"

"No," Austin barked. "Don't tell me how it works, Chase. I've been there, remember? No, he didn't trust us. He didn't trust anybody."

I glanced at Sam. He was looking down, playing with his chips. This must have been pretty uncomfortable for him. He got to know Mr. Everett, but he was never a client. He never saw that side of him.

"I just wish . . . ," John said. "I wish I'd found it before he died. Maybe I would have understood what he was thinking. You know, I could have helped him."

Stopped him.

"What else is in there?" I asked, indicating John's bag. A thick uneasiness rose in my throat.

John smiled as he once again reached into the bag. He pulled out a new bottle of Ten High whiskey. "I thought we could all take a shot for our friend."

Chase went to the bar and came back with five glasses. Austin was looking sick now, too, and I knew he wasn't ready to feel all this. He'd worked so hard not to. Chase filled the glasses and passed them out. He looked up.

"Should we say something?"

John gazed into his glass. "How about, we'll never forget the man who brought us all together. We'll never forget what he worked for, and all he gave up." John lifted his glass and the rest of us followed. "To Menashe."

We all murmured the same and knocked back the whiskey with resigning force. It was harder than I was used to and burned the back of my throat. But it was nothing. This pain was nothing.

Chapter 3
Rahmi

By my third day of searching for an apartment, I can no longer focus. The ads and flyers are running together and all I can think about is every morning the Days Inn sucks another hundred dollars out of my savings. But once I find a place, I can feel like I'm really here. Like I'm moving forward.

I'm late to meet this guy about his two-bedroom place on Bleecker Street, so I end up running the last three blocks. The old building is beautiful, red brick with black fire escapes zig-zagging up the sides, and somebody yelling down from a window to her friend on the street, just like in the movies. The location is great; I could walk to work in about ten minutes. But I won't get my hopes up yet.

I'm standing on the street, panting, realizing I'm not sure if the doorman will even let me in, when a young Middle Eastern man jogs out of the building. A good-looking guy, tall and well built with black hair and a faded Mets T-shirt. He's wearing rectangular glasses with thick black frames. He looks around, then his eyes settle on me.

"Hey, are you Murray?" he asks, out of breath as well.

I nod.

"Sorry, I hope you haven't been waiting long."

"No, I just got here." I smile. "This is a great building." I wish my T-shirt wasn't sticking to me with sweat.

"Oh, yeah," he says, squinting up at it. "Want to take a look at the place?"

"Sure. And you're Ronnie?"

"Rahmi. With an 'm.'" He laughs and I think he must get that a lot.

"Sorry, I guess I heard you wrong on the phone."

"No problem," he replies, waving for me to follow him. "Come on in."

We take the elevator to the fourth floor. It's mirrored, and on the way up, Rahmi points to my baseball cap. "Are you from Cleveland?"

"That's right."

"Nice. Drew Carey, right?"

I laugh. "Yeah, he really put us on the map."

We get out and walk down the hall until Rahmi stops at number 429. He turns the key and apologizes for the mess, but as he opens the door, the place looks quite clean.

He grabs a soda from the fridge and offers me one. His hand shakes a little as he holds it out, and for the first time I get the idea he's nervous.

"Thanks." I take the soda and follow him out of the kitchen. I'm still sweating, and I can't get Dani's voice out of my head. She's telling me it looks pretty easy—starting all over again without her. I shake my head. It's not like that.

"Well . . . ," he says, looking around, his thumb jittering against the can. "This is the living room."

I smile because it's clear he's not used to doing this. "It's nice."

"It's also Grace's room," he continues, showing me how the couch folds out into a bed. "She doesn't have much stuff, so it works out." He points behind me. "And that was the kitchen, right there. It's got the normal stuff: fridge, electric stove, microwave. No dishwasher, though."

"That's all right." I follow him down the small hallway to the bedrooms. He's whistling a little, but I don't think he realizes it.

"This," he says, tapping on the first door. "Is Jemma's room." He gives me a look. "We don't go in there." He opens the next door. "This is my room. Pretty small," he says, "but not bad." Rahmi steps in to give me a better look. I take in the room. I don't think I've seen such a well-organized place since I lived with my mother.

"Would you do all my cleaning, too?"

He laughs. "Maybe we could work something out."

We check out the bathroom, tight and crammed with toiletries, before walking out to the living room again. Off to the left is an office nook, about the size of the bathroom.

"This," Rahmi says, pulling over a screen partition to shield it from the rest of the apartment, "could be your room."

My eyes sweep over the space. "Think I could fit a futon in there?"

"Oh, yeah," he says. "Absolutely."

I'm self-conscious now because I can feel him still watching me and I'm not sure what else I should say. Out of the corner of my eye, I see him smoothing his hair back, then he moves into the kitchen, letting me look around, I guess. I try to take it all in, imagining life in six hundred square feet with three other people. I glance again at Rahmi, busying himself at the kitchen counter, and my heart beats a little faster. I take a few gulps of soda and meet him back in the kitchen.

"Should we go over some of the details?"

"Sure."

"Are you interested so far?" he asks as he sits down at the table. He offers me a chair and I sit, too.

I nod. "Yeah."

"Awesome. Well, you'd be the fourth roommate. We've got Grace; she's twenty-one and a full-time student at NYU. She's a nice girl, kind of a goof, but fun to hang out with. Uh, let see," he says, taking a drink. "There's Jemma; I think she's about twenty-five. Now, she's something."

"What do you mean?"

"She's really private, so I don't have a lot of details, but, well ... most of the time she's not even here—I have no idea what she does. She's got kind of a goth vibe going. She's serious, angry, but won't talk to you much."

"Okay." I guess I can handle that.

"Then there's me." He shrugs. "I'm thirty-three, work part time at my family's restaurant, and go to BMCC."

"BMCC?"

"Oh, sorry. Yeah, it's Borough of Manhattan Community College. I'm working on an English degree, but it's slow going. I guess I'm easily distracted." Rahmi smiles and his eyes meet mine. "As far as the living situation," he continues, glancing down, "I'm pretty neat and organized—as you noticed—and I don't like a lot of noise at night, that kind of thing."

"That sounds good to me." I pause. "What's the rent?"

"Well, you and Grace pay less, since you don't have your own rooms." He squints at the ceiling. "That would put you guys at three-fifty a month. Jemma and I would be five hundred."

I'm working out the numbers in my head and Rahmi's watching me.

"Does that seem doable for you?"

I nod. "Yeah," I reply, getting excited. "That should be fine."

"Great." He sounds relieved. "So, you want to tell me about yourself? I mean, you seem pretty normal, but it's not necessarily a deal-breaker if you're not." He leans back in his chair.

"Boring is more like it." I rub the side of my neck, trying to think of what to say. How much to say. "Well, I'm twenty-nine, and from Cleveland. I went to law school out there and practiced for a while, but it wasn't for me.

I was working as a file clerk for a law firm until I came out here, which was ... man, I guess about a week ago now."

"Did you come out for a job?"

"Yeah." I smile. "But I didn't get it. It was a paralegal job at Spodek. But after they turned me down, I didn't want to leave. So, I walked around the city and ended up at NYU. I passed the law library and got the crazy idea of asking them for a job. It worked."

"Wow," he laughs. "That takes some guts."

"No, I've been stupid," I say, shaking my head. "I was really lucky they had this position. I mean, it's entry level, but I think it'll let me stay in New York." I pause. "I'll definitely be able to pay rent."

Rahmi smiles. "I'm not too worried."

Chapter 4
Unsettled

I open my eyes. Yellowed ceiling tiles hover above me. I don't remember where I am. It feels wrong and my wrists jolt, like an electric shock. Sometimes that happens when I go off my antidepressants; it's part of the withdrawal. But that's not it this time, and my heart pounds because there are strange shadows on the wall.

"Rahmi?" I call.

But I hear John's voice drift from one of the shadows. His voice is distant and he tells me not to come back to Cleveland. He says things are better now that I'm not around. I sit up and try to tell him I'm sorry for how I left, but he's gone. The shadows are still there, though. I hear Dani's voice and I try to figure out which one is hers, but then I realize she's not a shadow. I turn around and she's sitting on the floor behind me. Her lip trembles and her eyes won't look into mine.

"I'm sorry," she says. "I'm sorry I didn't ask you to stay. Come back home."

My stomach twists because I recognize what she's doing. A self-defense apology. I never thought I'd be on the other side of one.

"Danielle, I—"

But before I can finish, Rahmi comes in and turns on the TV. It's loud and I can't remember what I'm trying to say, so I turn around and call to him to turn it down. I turn back and Dani's gone. The shadows are gone.

I open my eyes again, my heart still pounding.

It's the ceiling tiles, yellowed like before, but the early morning light coming into the room is soft. There are no shadows. I sit up and move the partition to the side so I can see more of the apartment. Someone's in the kitchen—Grace, I guess—making coffee. She's wearing an oversized T-shirt and plaid flannel pajama pants. I take a breath and rub my eyes, still haunted by Danielle's image.

I stand and stretch my arms, my back sore from sleeping on the floor. I must have a pained expression on my face when I enter the kitchen because Grace raises her eyebrows, then hands me the cup of coffee she'd just poured for herself.

"Thanks," I say. "Sorry." I frown, unable to fight my way out of this haze. "Sorry to be here already, I . . . I'm Murray. I guess Rahmi called you about me?"

"Yeah." She takes a drink and shrugs. "Fine with me. I'm Grace." She smiles when I still stand there, unmoving. "You need to drink that coffee, though."

"Do I look that bad?"

She nods toward the mirror by the front door. "Like my seven-thirty class the morning after Urban Bourbon."

I glance at my reflection. "Yeah, I don't know what that is, but I see what you mean." I sit in one of the rickety kitchen chairs and take a long drink. I rub my shoulder, wincing. "I need to get a bed today."

Grace pours a second cup of coffee and sits across from me. She has an effortless beauty about her: clear, dark skin that glows even first thing in the morning, and a smile that's already melting my nervousness. "So, how're you liking New York so far?"

"It's great," I say, watching as she twists a strand of thick black hair around her finger. "Different, for sure. I hope it's not just a honeymoon thing."

"Well, let me give you a little warning now that you're here," she says with a glance down the hall. "Rahmi loves to play tour guide with new people. He's going to offer to take you to all the overcrowded bullshit destinations you can handle."

"Really?" I hadn't expected my roommates to do much of anything for me. I imagine the two of us walking around the city, Rahmi pointing out the sights. I narrow my eyes a little. "He did this for you?"

Grace rolls her eyes. "Yep. I tried to tell him I grew up about an hour away in Trenton, but he was already in the zone and didn't want to hear it."

"Well maybe he was just, you know, interested in you."

She laughs and shakes her head. "I don't think so." She gets up and puts her cup in the sink, then grabs an orange from the counter. "You should have seen him when he joined this study group," she says, sitting back down. "He found out three of the guys were from out of town, so he got them to scrap the studying and go to Coney Island for the day. It's just how he is. You'll see what I mean."

I smile and steal a glance down the hall, which reminds me. Jemma. "And what about her?" I ask, nodding toward her room.

"Oh, Jemma?" Grace discards a scrap of orange peel on the table. "That girl's a big fucking question mark. She's always going out at night, sleeping all day, she won't say more than three or four words to us if we do run into her. Rahmi and I are always trying to guess what she's up to, but it's probably better that we don't know."

I nod. "Makes sense." I'm about to ask her another question when she glances at the clock. It's 7:10.

"Shit," she says, scooting her chair back with a painful grating sound. "I've got to get to class."

"Sorry," I say, "I'm sure I've thrown off your routine."

"Yeah, thanks a lot, new guy." She smiles, then walks down the hall to get ready.

I lean back and continue drinking, wondering what time Rahmi gets up, and if I'll even meet Jemma today. I hope not.

"All right," Grace says, coming back into the kitchen a few minutes later, "I'll see you, okay?" She hoists her backpack up onto her shoulders and walks to the door.

"Sure." I nod. "See you."

"You know," she says, turning back around, "I can show you around sometime, too, if you like. Not Rahmi's touristy bullshit, but the good stuff—restaurants, clubs, whatever you like."

"Thanks," I reply, my face getting hot. "I appreciate it."

She heads out the door, and as soon as I'm alone, uneasiness creeps back in. At first I think it's just the newness of everything, but then I see my crumpled blankets in the corner and remember: Dani. I'm unsettled because the last time I heard her voice she was crying, and the last time I saw her face she couldn't even look at me. I want to know she's okay, but I can't call her. She's done, and I have to accept it.

I open a few drawers in the kitchen until I find a spiral notebook. It looks like they've been using it for grocery lists. I tear out a blank sheet and take one of the pens from the back of the drawer. My blood is coursing now because I'm doing something. I can reach her, even if that's it. Even if it's the end.

I start to write. It's coming out disjointed and frenzied but I have to get something down. When I'm through, I lean back in my chair and read it. I cross out a line. I shake my head and cross out another. And another. Hot tears burn my eyes as I crumple the paper and slam my fist against the table.

I hear movement down the hall, so I slip the crushed letter into the pocket of my pajama pants. I sit up straight, holding my empty coffee cup like a prop, expecting Rahmi to come down the hall into the kitchen, but it's Jemma. I assume it's Jemma; we haven't actually met yet. She's only about five feet tall, slender, with dark eyes and thick black eyebrows, bleach-blond hair and a style I can only describe as high school punk. Her deadpan expression lowers to full-fledged disappointment when she sees me sitting at the kitchen table.

"Hi," I say. "I'm Murray, the new roommate."

She looks down at my hands and I realize I'm tapping my fingers against the cup I'm holding. I stop.

"So, what's rent now?"

"I'm sorry?"

"With you. What's the new rent?"

"Well"—I look past Jemma, needing a break from her bored stare—"I think Rahmi said five hundred."

She shrugs and opens up a cabinet. She pulls out a handful of granola bars and heads back down the hallway without a word. When the door clicks shut, I bring my letter out again. The crumpled ball is damp from the sweat of my hands. I stand and walk over to the trash can, burying it under yesterday's garbage.

Chapter 5

Getting Out

CLEVELAND, FOUR MONTHS EARLIER

It was almost midnight. Danielle had gone to bed an hour ago, but Austin and I sometimes talked until one or two in the morning. He took a long drink of beer, his fifth, then set it on the kitchen table.

"You still didn't answer my question," he said, a smile twitching on his lips.

"About Dani?"

"Yeah. Why aren't you telling her anything? I mean, I get it; I don't tell people shit. But you guys seem to like each other."

I shrugged, searching the worn table for answers.

The truth was, she did know some things about my past. She knew my father was very violent. She knew he was a police officer who was shot and killed ten years ago. She knew I had been seeing an amateur therapist, Menashe Everett, to try to deal with some of my problems. She knew the therapy was unorthodox: smashing glass artwork in the basement of a nightclub. She knew I'd had five relationships before her. She knew two of them were with men. Nothing I'd said put her off. But for some reason, I didn't want to go any further into it.

"I guess I'm not sure where we stand. She likes things casual. Like, she doesn't mind if we see other people, she doesn't mind if I ask her to spend the night or not. She's not very committed. I don't think she'd want to hear about that kind of stuff."

"You think she doesn't care?"

"I don't know. She never reacts strongly about anything. Maybe she doesn't."

"Geez, kid, and that's all right with you?"

I shrugged again. "She's only twenty-four; I think in a couple of years she'll get more serious."

"You want to wait around for that?"

"I like her. And I don't have anywhere else to be."

Austin tilted his head a little. "Fair enough." He leaned back in his chair and cracked open another beer.

"I'll drive you home later," I said, indicating his drink.

"Thanks, Mur."

I nodded. He was the only one who could call me Mur without it bothering me. My dad used to call me that sometimes, and it was usually like a punch in the gut to hear it, but with Austin it sounded different. Like he made it up on his own.

"So, how'd the week go for you?"

He groaned. "Fucking awful." He put his beer down, grimacing like something stung. "I write in this journal, you know, that Pastor Jim has me do. But I think it makes it worse. It makes the dreams worse. Everything's right there." He slapped his hands together. "All the vivid bullshit."

"You had more dreams this week?"

He nodded. "Ash was in nearly all of them. He's in Vietnam with me all the time, now."

"Does he help you? Like, in the dream does he try to help?"

"He usually gets killed doing something stupid." Austin laughed, then rubbed his eyebrow. "I'm sorry, it's not funny. It's always scary as hell at the time. I feel like I have to look out for him there, but I never can protect him."

I frowned. "I'm sorry."

Austin shook his head. "I know you're in the same boat."

"I guess."

"You get any sleep this week?"

I lowered my eyes. "Not much."

Austin sat back. "I know it's bad right now," he said, "but this anniversary shit is almost behind us. And remember, I'll always be here if you need me."

I looked up. I didn't expect it to hurt to hear him say this. I thought back to his last suicide attempt, six years before. I was the one who'd found him, found the pills, lying in the bathroom of his scuzzy apartment. He'd told me the same thing at Mr. Everett's funeral—that he'd be there for me—but he almost wasn't. And I couldn't do this without him.

"Austin, can I tell you something?"

"Sure."

"I've applied for a couple of jobs. On the East Coast."

"Oh, yeah? What kind of jobs?"

"Nothing big, just paralegal and legal assistant jobs. I mean, anything's a step up from file clerk."

"How many jobs are we talking?"

I paused. "Eleven."

Austin laughed. "Man, you really want to get out of town."

"I haven't told John," I continued, my voice hushed in a guilty whisper. "I haven't told anyone."

"What kind of shot do you have?"

"Not great. My job history's pathetic. I just want to feel like I'm doing something, you know?"

"Yeah, I know."

"So, should I tell him? Or Dani?"

Austin shook his head. "Wait till you hear something. No use in riling anybody up. If I know John, he'll give you a hard time at first, but then he'll come around."

"I guess so."

"And as far as Danielle," he said, leaning forward, "that might give you the answer you're looking for about your relationship."

I nodded. "Thanks, Austin. I doubt it'll even come to that."

Austin shrugged. "Maybe not. But maybe this is your shot."

"To move up?"

He laughed. "To get out."

Chapter 6
The Jemma Problem

After three weeks, I'm finally settling in. It was jarring at first, waking up in a makeshift room the size of my closet back in Cleveland, navigating the three other personalities I'm now living with, learning a new city and a new job. But the chaos here isn't sinister; it doesn't find its way into my dreams. And the pull of my old life is starting to weaken.

It's Tuesday and Rahmi, Grace, and I have just finished dinner. There's no sign of Jemma, as usual.

"We've got to do something about her," Grace says. "She's going to get us all in trouble."

Rahmi frowns. He's not going to agree. We've been talking off and on for days about approaching Jemma. It's clear she has a drug problem, and whatever she's on, it's getting worse.

"I've told Jemma, though," Rahmi says. "I told her she can't bring that shit in here. She seemed fine with that."

Grace shakes her head. "Something's different." She glances over toward Jemma's room. "I don't mind checking things out."

Rahmi gets up and clears the dishes. "It doesn't even matter," he says. "She's got that big lock on the door."

"Oh, I could pick that."

I smile. Grace is still so young, so funny and quick and innocent; it makes me sometimes wish I could get back there. But then I remember my life at twenty, or even at ten, and I understand there's nowhere in the past I want to go.

"I'm with Rahmi on this," I say, getting up and moving with the others to the living room. "If she's got something illegal going on, we don't want to be involved."

"Surprise, surprise," Grace says, giving me a sly smile. "I guess I have to take care of things myself."

Rahmi shrugs, collapsing onto the couch. "Up to you, just leave me out of it when Jemma finds out."

"Deal." Grace is already pulling out her backpack and rummaging around.

"This could put you in legal trouble, too," I say as she digs, but she's set on it now.

"Don't worry about me." She comes up with a Swiss army knife and two bobby pins. She goes to the front closet and pulls out a wire hanger. "One of these ought to work," she mutters, heading down the hall toward Jemma's room.

I sit next to Rahmi. "You working at the restaurant tonight?" I ask him.

"No, thank God." He stretches. "I've got a paper to write, but that's about it. You?"

"I might go take a walk. Still trying to get familiar with the city."

"Oh, that reminds me," Rahmi says, leaning forward and giving my leg a light smack, "there's another place I need to show you."

"Yeah?"

"Aha!" Grace shouts from the hallway. "Got that bitch open."

"Oh, geez." Rahmi sighs.

"Yeah." I rub my palms on my jeans. "So, what's the place?"

He perks up again. "Oh, the cathedral. St. Patrick's."

"A cathedral?"

"Yeah. You're Catholic, right?"

"That's right." I think I mentioned it in passing one of my first days here. I'd never have expected him to remember.

"Well, it's a huge landmark anyway, but might be up your alley in particular."

"That's really nice. Yeah, I'd love to go." I smile. I don't need to tell him it's been a decade since I was inside a church.

A minute later we hear Grace closing the door and refastening the lock. She comes over to us and her face is serious. "You guys, she's got some kind of shit in there, but I don't know what any of it is."

"What did it look like?" I ask, leaning forward.

"Bottles of these white pills, like circles," she says, curling her fingers to show us the approximate size. "I also found some purple ones, blue ones, and some needles."

Rahmi groans. "Jesus."

"I mean, you use needles for stuff like heroin or cocaine, right?" Grace puts the hanger back and sticks the knife and pins in the front pocket of her bag.

"I guess," Rahmi says. He turns to me. "You have any experience with this, Murray?"

I shake my head. "Sorry."

"Let's just talk to her about it," Grace says.

Rahmi raises his eyebrows. "You want to tell her you went through her room?"

"No, but we knew even before that. I mean, we've got to get her to keep it somewhere else, right?"

"Yeah." Rahmi gets up from the couch. "I've got to write this paper, guys. Let me think about it, okay?"

Grace and I nod and Rahmi makes his way to his room, closing the door behind him.

Grace turns to me. "You're with me, right, Murray?"

I shrug. "You're right that we don't want that stuff here, but ... I mean, right now we're all guilty of constructive possession."

She smiles. "I forgot you were a lawyer."

"It's hard to turn off."

She looks past me for a moment. "I thought about law school at one point."

"Really? What happened?"

She shrugs. "I knew I couldn't handle all the reading."

I laugh. "So you're taking the easy way out with med school."

"Something like that. And whenever things get hard, I imagine my mom telling me there aren't enough brilliant Black girls in medicine, and then I usually find some motivation."

"I bet." I glance at her books on the coffee table. "You'll be a great doctor." She smiles and I look down. I clear my throat. "Same story for me, really. I always told myself there should be more white guys practicing law."

Grace laughs. "Brilliant white guys?"

"No, just white guys."

Grace is about to respond when the phone rings. She walks to the kitchen to answer it, and I check my watch again. It seems the phone was for her, so I grab my jacket and wave to her, pointing to the door to indicate I'm going out. She smiles and waves, then goes back to her conversation.

Chapter 7
Roger
Cleveland, Two Months Earlier

Chase came bustling in the front door of The Velvet Dog, holding his briefcase and a few giant bags of chips.

"I forgot I wanted to bring these," he said, walking over and letting it all collapse onto the table where I was sitting. "You guys go through the snacks like nothing else."

Chase went to the back for something, and Sam and John walked through the front. John was trailing behind a bit, looking glum, like he'd been hoping for another minute or two alone. Sam, as usual, seemed oblivious and made his way to the bar. The Velvet Dog was Chase's place, but Sam, who'd spent the past few years as a hotel bartender downtown, had always taken over drink duty on poker nights.

Sam didn't ask that night, just took his best guess as to what we wanted to drink, which he said kept things interesting, and brought the drinks over to our table. I tried to ask John if he was all right, but it was hard to be discreet with everybody there, and he just ended up nodding with a half-hearted smile.

The guys settled in, and I was wondering if Austin was going to make it when the front door flung open, and he charged inside.

"This is absolute bullshit!" Austin bellowed, holding up a piece of paper in his clenched fist.

My heart jumped and I stumbled to my feet, nearly tripping over my chair. I took a few steps back, looking to the others. They were alarmed, but nobody else moved. Austin rushed to the table and slammed the paper down.

"It's un-fucking-believable! That piece of shit!"

"Austin," Chase said, taking the paper. "Sit down, will you?"

My hands trembled and I worried Chase shouldn't try to handle Austin, but I remembered he was used to dealing with unruly bar patrons.

"Let me read it." Chase read the paper to himself before passing it to John. Austin sank into a chair and rubbed his face with both hands. Sam got up and went to the bar, mixing Austin a drink.

"I've seen it," John said. "I saw it on my way over." He put the paper at my place. "You should come look at it, though, Murray."

I realized I'd backed ten feet away from the table. My eyes shifted to Austin. His head was down, resting in his hands, and his leg jittered. I moved back and took my seat. The paper, now crumpled, was a flyer. Nice quality, thick and white, with bold type. I read it to the group.

"'Destroy with joy at Roger's Smash Space.'" I glanced at Austin. "'Sessions begin at one hundred dollars for fifteen minutes. We provide the gear, you bring the energy.'" There was an image of shattered glass and a baseball bat. The address was in Moreland Hills. That was a nice neighborhood.

"Is that Roger Maldonado?" Chase asked.

I forgot he knew who all Mr. Everett's clients were. As his landlord, Chase was the one who had found Mr. Everett the morning he died. He found out about the museum. He read all our files. And Roger was memorable. He sought out the glass for fun, not therapy. But when I met him at Mr. Everett's funeral, Roger told me he'd started going as a real client. That he actually needed it.

John nodded. "That's my guess."

"Of course it's him!" exclaimed Austin, who'd been quietly fuming. "That asshole is making money off Ash's therapy."

"But it's not really doing any harm," Chase said, taking the flyer back. "Maybe somebody will get some relief from it."

"It wasn't meant to be like this," John muttered. "Not out in the open. He's not going to get to the people who need it."

"He's not trying to help people!" Austin yelled, rising from his chair. "He's just a rich asshole trying to cash in on the museum." He looked at all of us. "I'm going for a walk," he said, storming off to the front of the bar and out the door.

I looked at John and he raised his eyebrows.

"I understand where he's coming from," Sam said after a moment. "I mean, I never saw Ash in that way, so I don't want to speak for you guys, but it seems like a pretty shitty thing Roger's doing."

John touched my shoulder and I flinched, still on edge. "You okay, Murray?"

I nodded. "I'm not sure what to think of it yet."

"Sure."

After a few more minutes, we moved on, had another drink, played a few hands of cards, but I couldn't focus. I kept wondering if Austin would come walking back in, but as it got on toward eleven, that was a long shot. We talked about a little of everything—Sam's new girlfriend, John's writing, the work Chase needed to do on his other clubs—but I knew John's mind was still on Roger's new place, just like mine.

We ended up dispersing a little before midnight. Sam left first, which was unusual, but I was sure he sensed our declining moods. John and I said goodnight to Chase and walked out together. I told John goodnight and started to head toward the bus stop when he called me back.

"Murray, wait." He walked toward me. "I wanted to ask you in there, but ... are you okay? I mean, about Austin?"

I smiled, embarrassed. "Yeah, I just, you know. Sometimes his temper ..."

"I know." John nodded. "I'm sorry."

I looked down. "No, it's stupid."

When I raised my head, John was watching me. His expression was hard and sad at the same time, and I knew what he was thinking. I tried to come up with something else to say before I turned back to the bus stop when he came forward and hugged me. It surprised me, but I felt pressure in my throat and a sharp stinging in my eyes when I realized how much I needed it.

I couldn't leave it alone. I hoped I'd get used to the idea after a few days, but I couldn't get it off my mind. I wondered if Roger knew what he was doing to us. He put those flyers in our shitty neighborhood, right on Mr. Everett's old street. Nobody here could afford what he was selling; it was a rich kid's luxury. I didn't know what he was getting at, so that Saturday morning, I grabbed a flyer off the post near my apartment and took the bus to Moreland Hills.

I got off at the intersection of Som Center and Jackson and walked the last few blocks to the building. It was trendy, as I expected. The outside resembled a complex of industrial-style loft spaces, but the inside must have been gutted. The windows were covered. I shielded my eyes, wondering how many safety precautions Roger took designing this place.

I rang the bell and a woman on the intercom asked what I was here for. I told her I needed to talk to Roger about an appointment and she buzzed me in. The first floor appeared to be for storage. Hundreds of giant cardboard boxes lined the walls and were stacked in the middle of the open basement space. I walked up the narrow stairway and opened the door at the top. The second floor could have been a spread in *Architectural Digest.* Chrome light fixtures, glossy wood paneling, top-of-the-line finishes. The open space served as a waiting room, with leather couches and chairs and a slick modern receptionist's desk. Down the hall to the left were several rooms, all with their doors closed. Behind the front desk was an office with frosted glass windows. Somebody was in there, sitting at the desk.

"Hi," the young woman greeted me. She couldn't have been older than twenty. "You wanted to talk about an appointment?"

"Yeah." I nodded. "With Roger. Is he around?" I glanced behind her.

"Oh, I can help you with that." She pulled out a thick binder. "What days are good for you?"

My temperature rose. This was already harder than I wanted it to be. "Actually, I need to talk to Roger. I, well, I know him. We've known each other a long time."

"Sure, of course." She picked up the phone and after a few seconds the frosted figure behind her answered.

"Mr. Maldonado, I have a friend of yours here. He'd like a few minutes with you?" She covered the phone with her hand. "I'm so sorry, what was your name?"

"Murray Henderson."

She told this to Roger but now I was certain he wouldn't remember me. And he never knew my last name.

"Okay. Thank you." She hung up the phone and smiled at me. "You can go on in."

I did my best to hide my bewilderment and walked back.

Roger was still sitting at the desk, staring at his computer, tapping hard at the keyboard every few seconds. He didn't acknowledge my presence, and as I moved closer I saw he was playing some kind of game. He pounded a few more keys in desperation, then looked up, smiling.

"Got 'em." He stood up. "You ever play Duke Nukem 3D?"

I shook my head.

He must have been close to forty, but he looked younger than I did. His black hair was still thick, though shorter than I remembered it.

"You should." He smiled again. "What did you say your name was?"

"Murray." I paused. "Do you remember me?"

Roger sat in his leather office chair and indicated that I should take a seat in the armchair behind me. He watched me for a moment. "I'm sorry, I don't."

"Okay." I took a deep breath. "We met ten years ago, at a funeral. For Menashe Everett. We sat next to each other."

Roger frowned. "You knew Ash?"

"Yeah, I was seeing him," I said, my patience eroding. "Just like you."

"Huh. Has it really been ten years?"

My hands squeezed into fists. "Yeah."

He peered at me again. "I'm sorry, that day was kind of a blur for me. I can't place you."

"It's okay." I rubbed my eyes. "That part's not important. The thing is, my friends and I, we saw your flyer. About this new place."

"Friends?"

"Yeah. We were all Mr. Everett's clients."

"Okay." Roger nodded. "Well, we're already scheduling a few months out, but I'd like to make this work since you were at the museum, too. I can offer you guys regular spots every week if you're all right with fifteen to thirty minutes. I know Ash gave people the whole hour, but since it's more for entertainment here, I've found that's plenty of time. And if you all sign up we can work out a discount."

It took me a second to comprehend he was giving me a sales pitch. I was glad Austin wasn't there.

"Roger," I began, willing myself to contain my anger. But I realized I had no idea what to say to him. I didn't think I'd have the confidence to stand up to the man who exploited Mr. Everett's life's work, but now that I was there I just wanted to kill him. "Roger," I repeated. He was looking at me expectantly. "Can I see a room?"

"Sure," he said. He stood up and led me to the door. We turned right down the hall of rooms, and he opened the first door on the left. "This might look familiar to you," he said, smiling.

I walked in and had to stop myself from crying out.

He'd set up the place exactly like Mr. Everett did. He had the same stainless-steel tables, the same bare light bulbs overhead. The pieces were just like ones Mr. Everett would have chosen—all large vases and sculptures, all clear glass. In one corner he had the baseball bat and hockey gear, waiting for the first client—or whatever Roger called them. Everywhere I looked was a memory from the museum. My heart raced and I heard Mr. Everett's voice.

How many rooms, Murray?

I heard the shattering glass. Adrenaline shot through my arms and pounded my temples.

My eyes welled with tears and I turned away from Roger, but I couldn't help it: I started to cry. I never thought I'd see a place like this again. Not without him. I shook I was crying so hard, and I heard Roger come toward me. I spun to face him.

"Roger, you asshole!" I shouted, wiping my eyes with my sleeve. "Don't you get it? This is sick!"

Roger took a step back. "Murray, what did you expect? You came to use this place, right?"

"I came to find out what the hell you were thinking. This was never supposed to be for fun."

"But people do think it's fun. Lots of people. I've got appointments booked through January."

"Congratulations."

"Aw, Murray, come on," he said. "There's no harm done, right? Ash had a great idea; I'm just keeping it going."

"How can you forget what he did for you?" My voice was rising again. "He would never have wanted you to start this place."

Roger shrugged and walked around the pieces, still calm. He seemed like a different person from the man I met at the funeral. "I'm just making a living," he said. "It's well within my rights to start this business. I understand you're not happy about it, but that's not my problem."

"I'm a lawyer," I blurted. "I can check into your permits. Any kind of code violation and I can have you shut down."

"You don't think I checked all that shit out?" Roger laughed. "Jesus. It's Ash who was running a piss-poor operation, down in that basement." He rubbed the side of his face. "You know he even punched me once? Not much of a professional."

"Good," I replied, even though I didn't believe him for a second. Mr. Everett wouldn't hit anybody.

"Well"—Roger sighed, indicating the door—"if you don't plan on signing up, I guess we're done here."

I nodded and pushed past him out the door. I ignored the receptionist who told me to have a good day, and rushed down the stairs, needing to get out of that place.

Chapter 8
Outside of Therapy

I had to run a few errands on my way home from work, so I'm later than usual. In the lobby I glance at my watch and decide to take the stairs rather than wait for the slowest goddamn elevator in existence. Rahmi and Grace usually eat dinner early with me on Tuesdays and I feel bad if they're waiting.

I burst into the apartment, already talking.

"Sorry, guys," I say, tossing my bag down. "I didn't think I'd be this long—"

"They're not here," Jemma says. She's sitting on the couch, reading.

I jump a little when she speaks, but she doesn't take her eyes from her book. "Oh, hey, Jemma. How's it going?" I try to sound casual, but this is only the fifth time we've spoken and she scares me.

She looks up and her eyes are red under thick mascara. "Which one are you?"

I laugh but she doesn't even smile. "Murray." I clear my throat. "From Cleveland, remember?"

She turns back to her book.

"Do you know where they went?" I ask. "Rahmi and Grace?"

Jemma puts her finger down on the page where she left off, looking up with exasperation and letting me know my conversation is not welcome. "There's a note," she says, pointing to the counter. "They're not going to make it."

I can see she's ready to leave, and I should let her. But something about her antagonism is familiar. The effort she's putting in to maintain that hard stare. Her raw, red eyes. She's in pain. I run a hand through my hair. I usually avoid these kinds of situations. When I was in trouble, I wanted to be left alone, too. Or I just assumed I didn't deserve anyone's help. But the way Jemma's glowering at her book makes me wonder what might change if more people stuck around when things got hard. I let my bag fall onto the kitchen floor and walk into the living room. Jemma's doing her best to ignore me, but I sit in the recliner next to her.

"What book is that?" I ask, tilting my head to see better. She doesn't answer. "*The Chrysalids*," I mutter, squinting. "Any good?"

She closes the book and looks up. "What are you doing?"

Her watery eyes glare at me, and I think she must have been crying rather than shooting up before I came home.

"I just feel bad," I say, "I haven't said much to you since I moved in."

She rolls her eyes but I look down and see that her thumb is vibrating on the cover of the book, causing it to rattle against the title page.

"Did the Indian guy put you up to this?"

I frown, but she lets out an annoyed sigh before I can answer.

"I really don't give a fuck who lives here," she says.

I nod. I guess that's something. "Are you from New York?"

She's looking away from me now, but shakes her head.

"Oh, yeah?" I'm encouraged I got an answer at all. "Where are you from?"

"Listen," she says, her eyes snapping back to meet mine and her cold voice wavering, "I don't know what this is about, but you need to stop." She looks toward the door like she might need an escape. "I don't want to be friends."

"Okay." My stomach sinks. "I'm sorry."

Before I can apologize further, she stands up, collects her book, and trudges down the hall to her room. I came on too strong and now I doubt I'll see her in the living room again. I rub my forehead. I make the same mistakes over and over. I sit back in the recliner, surprised at how bad I feel.

It's midnight before I see anyone else. I've moved to the couch, so I'm slumped there, watching *NewsRadio* reruns, when Rahmi walks in. He smiles and comes over to join me, but I can tell he wasn't expecting anyone else to be up. I offer him a beer and we sit in silence for a while, spacing out at the television. He drums his fingers on his leg every so often and can't seem to get comfortable on the couch. At the commercial break I turn to him.

"Is everything okay?"

He runs his hands through his hair and looks a little embarrassed I mentioned it. "It was just a long night at work."

"Oh, I'm sorry." I pause. "What happened?"

He laughs. "You don't want to hear this stuff."

I shrug and click the remote, turning off the television. "This was at the restaurant?"

"Yeah. But I've got to warn you," he says, holding up a hand, "there's a lot of family bullshit in this story."

"Sure. I can handle it."

"Well, to summarize, my parents told me my sister doesn't want me at her wedding."

"Your sister? Why?"

"She and I, we used to be really close when we were kids. Like best friends." His voice darkens. "The last few years, she hasn't wanted anything to do with me."

I frown. "What happened?"

Rahmi drums his fingers a little faster. "She's older than I am—ten years older. She remembers life in Turkey. My parents kept a traditional home, and that's how she grew up. When we moved here, I was only three but she was almost fourteen. My parents relaxed a little, they let us assimilate to American culture, but Seda never could. She stayed like my parents. That's how she's most comfortable."

"But you were still close?"

He nods. "She protected me. We explored the city together when I was a little older. She'd take me to baseball games, or to the park. All the touristy stuff. But . . ."

I wait for Rahmi to continue, but he can't seem to find the words. Maybe he regrets telling me all this. "So, what changed?" I ask gently.

He lets out a long breath. "About five years ago, I let her in on my big secret—that I'm gay."

I nod. I'm not surprised, but I never like to assume. I've been burned that way before. "So, she doesn't approve?"

He laughs. "Hardly. I knew she wouldn't be happy, but I thought at least she'd come around after a few weeks. I thought she could help me tell our parents. But here we are, five years later, and Seda still won't talk to me. And I never did tell my parents."

"She never told them?"

"No, she's worried for their health."

"Geez." I sigh. "I'm really sorry."

"And this wedding," he continues, his voice catching, "in my mind, it was supposed to be a turning point for us. I thought I'd be able to talk to her at the reception, and capitalize on that warm, fuzzy place she'll be in." He blinks a few times. "I'd tell her, 'Hey, you know this wonderful feeling you have of being with the person you love? I just want that for myself.' I mean, how can that be bad?" He takes off his glasses and wipes his eyes with his sleeve.

"It's not bad," I say. "It's not bad at all. I guess she's just not ready to hear it."

He nods. "You know what she told my parents? You know why they think we're not talking anymore?"

I wince. "Oh, no. What?"

"She told them I'm on drugs. That I was getting out of control and she couldn't help me anymore. That's why they have me work so much at the restaurant—they want to keep an eye on me."

"That's fucked up."

"Yeah."

He closes his eyes and exhales slow, deep breaths, like he's meditating. It appears to settle him.

"I hope someday she'll come around," I tell him. "She's missing out if she doesn't."

"Thanks." Rahmi cracks his knuckles and stands up. "Jesus, I need another beer. You?"

"Sure."

He pops the caps off in the kitchen and walks back over to me, collapsing on the couch. He hands me one. "Okay," he says, "it's your turn."

"What?"

"You owe me a fragment of your family's bullshit." He takes a long swig. "Anything."

I study his face. "You serious?"

"Yes, I'm totally serious." He wipes his mouth with the back of his hand and smiles. "Come on, I feel like I vomited my whole toxic history and I need a little reciprocity here."

"That's nice. I forgot you were an English major."

He shakes his head. "No stalling. What've you got?"

As I call to mind the various details I could share with Rahmi, my hands quiver and my temperature rises with embarrassment. *Make something up. Just make something up.* I take a few deep breaths. I focus my eyes on the bottle in Rahmi's hand and try to remember this is not a therapy session. This is not a police report. I'm just sitting with my friend at one in the morning, having a drink.

"Oh, man," he mutters. "You must have something good."

I understand the longer I draw this out the worse it will be, so I look at him and shrug. "My dad used to hit me. It . . . well, it got pretty bad. He put me in the hospital a few times."

"Fuck," he says, putting a hand on my shoulder. "Man, I'm sorry. I shouldn't have made you do this."

"It's okay. I could have made something up if I wanted to."

He nods and squeezes my shoulder a little before releasing it. "I am sorry, though."

"Thanks." I look down at the bottle in my hands. "It's nice to tell someone. I haven't really done that, outside of therapy."

"Oh, yeah? I've thought about giving therapy a try sometime. Did it help you?"

"It did." I smile. "But it wasn't easy."

"Yeah." He takes a long drink of beer. "That's kind of what I'm afraid of."

I shake my head. "You would do fine." I try to give him a reassuring pat on the leg, but then worry it was too much. Too forward.

Rahmi's watching me now, but I can't read his face.

Maybe he wants to say something else but is too worn out to come up with the words. He reaches his hand out, slowly. He touches my face, and I don't move away. I move a little closer to him because I understand what's happening. I understand this is what I need right now. He looks relieved, like he expected me to reject him. Bright red heat creeps up my neck to my face, and I'm sure it's noticeable. I start to say something to break the silence and explain my awkwardness when he moves all the way in, kissing me powerfully. And for once, I don't think. I let go. I relax. I let all the bullshit roll off of me and I get a glimpse of freedom. I feel like myself again.

Chapter 9
Old Patterns
Cleveland, One Month Earlier

A few weeks after my talk with Roger, I got a call from the Spodek Law Firm in New York City. They wanted me to come interview for a paralegal job the following week.

I hung up and my body trembled with the kind of excitement I hadn't experienced since I got into law school. My writing jumped all over the page as I marked the day on my calendar. I breathed in, waiting for my temperature to lower. The time I'd spent obsessively building up my savings was about to pay off; I'd need plane tickets, transportation, food—

I smiled. This was something I wanted, and I hadn't allowed myself to acknowledge that before now. I wanted to make choices that weren't just reactions. I wanted to feel like I was moving forward. I wanted to move up. And I wanted to get out.

Before Danielle got home, I decided not to tell her yet. It would be better when I had some time to sit with it, to work out how to approach it with her. But when she walked in the door, my excitement got the better of me. She could see it, too, that something was different.

"Hey, Murray," she said with a suspicious smile. "You look like you were waiting for me."

I laughed. "Yeah. I guess I was."

"What's up?" She tossed her purse onto the counter and grabbed a soda out of the fridge. She cracked it open and looked at me.

"Well, I just got off the phone ... This guy at a law firm in New York wants me to come out for an interview. For a paralegal job."

Her eyes widened. "Murray! What?" She laughed and tucked her long wavy hair behind her ears. I could see her trying to work it out. "I didn't know you were looking for another job."

"Yeah. I didn't want to say anything before—you know, I didn't think anyone would be interested."

"Of course they are!" She ran over and hugged me. "And New York? That's crazy."

"Yeah," I said, pulling back. "It is crazy." I watched her as she walked back to the counter.

"Wow," she said, shaking her head, "I just can't believe it. I'm really happy for you." She took a drink. "When's the interview?"

"Next Thursday."

"That's soon."

I nodded, unsure of how to continue. "Dani ... they might offer me the job."

"I know." She smiled. "I bet they will."

"New York is pretty far away."

She shrugged. "Same time zone."

I couldn't tell if she was making a joke, but my face flushed. "So, you'd stay here? If I got the job?"

She laughed and leaned her back against the counter. "Hell, I don't know. It's a lot to think about right now."

I frowned. "Sure."

My eyes burned as I watched her go to the pantry for the barbecue chips she liked. She walked back and started telling me about this customer she'd had to deal with at the drugstore today, crinkling open the bag. She interrupted herself to offer me a chip. I shook my head, glaring at the cheap silver rings on her fingers. Always so relaxed.

I guess I'd gotten my answer. She wasn't offering to go, and she wasn't asking me to stay. She wasn't even telling me we should break up. This could have been the biggest turning point in my life and all I knew was I evoked no feeling at all from her.

There was so much I wanted to say but I didn't know where to begin. She was still talking but I couldn't follow her anymore. My head was pounding and when I looked down, I saw my hands were clenched into fists. That same old tension was building inside me and I had to leave. I mumbled something about going out, but I must have looked upset because she stopped me.

"Murray, wait," she said, stepping between me and the door. "Are you all right?"

"I just need some air."

She touched my shoulder and peered at the side of my face. "Your ears are red." She withdrew her hand. "Are you mad?"

A pang of guilt cut through my anger. Dani and I had only fought a few times over the previous year we'd been together, but she knew enough to recognize the signs. I looked past her toward the door. She was still in my way.

"Is this about the job?" she pressed.

I took a breath and fought down the churning bile in my stomach. We should have done this a long time ago.

"It just doesn't seem like you care much, about what happens." My voice was hard and strained. I needed to leave.

"Of course I do," she said. "I'm happy for you."

The blood slammed against my temples now. "But what about us?" I demanded, my voice rising. "Do you care if we break up or stay together?"

"Murray, you just told me about this. You have to give me time." She glanced behind her, like maybe she was thinking of leaving, too.

"But you do this with everything!" I shouted. "You never fucking say what you want! Do you really not care?"

"Will you calm down?" She crossed her arms. "That's not true."

"Then just stop!" I exclaimed in a rush of adrenaline. "Stop acting like everything's so goddamn casual!"

She took another step back from me. "That's not what I'm trying to do," she said. "I just like to have options."

I shook my head. She was treating me like I was crazy. I'd wanted her to have one honest moment with me, and she couldn't even do that. My breathing came fast. I closed my eyes and ran my hands through my hair. They came back shaking. I opened my eyes and Danielle was watching me.

"I'm going out for a bit, all right?" she said.

She sounded unsure. As usual. For some reason that pissed me off more than anything.

I pushed her, thinking I'd move past her out the door.

She wouldn't even look at me.

I was invisible. I didn't matter.

I tried to slow everything down and even out my breathing, but a terrifying rage rose to the surface. I'd let it build too long, and now I just wanted it out of me so I could feel some relief.

"What the hell is it going to take?" I yelled at her. The brief, harsh echo of my voice made me tremble. "What can I do to get a fucking reaction from you, Dani?"

I shoved her harder, into the wall.

She started crying.

That did it. My head started to clear and I stared at her, finally seeing her. I heard a distant voice in my head, telling me I was weak, that I deserved what was coming. I ran back to the kitchen sink and threw up. I didn't know what to do. Dani was sitting on the floor, crying, and it was because of me. I'd had over ten years behind me, but now I was back to zero. Less than zero. I walked toward her, unsure of what to do. I knelt and cleared my throat, ready to say I was wrong, but when she looked up and saw how close I was, she cowered away. Now I felt as bad as I'd ever had, and I couldn't be there any longer. I managed to stand then stumble out the door, leaving Dani still on the floor.

Chapter 10
The Best Apology

The air is cold, reminding me I need a winter coat. The one I had—warm and waterproof, unlike the worn jacket I'd hastily brought to New York—is sitting in a storage unit on Euclid Avenue. I used my last paycheck from my old job to hire a company in Cleveland to put all of my things from the old apartment into storage. I forget a lot of what's there, but I miss some of it. I tell myself all the time I'll be back soon, but in reality I'm not so sure.

I walk east, toward the university. I pass my Laundromat, my convenience store, my ATM—all these places I already feel a certain ownership over. There's a line out the door again at Nisi, this fancy Greek place, and I walk slowly to hear bits of conversation from the people waiting. *You have ten lighters on the nightstand and can't keep one in your pocket?* I turn left on LaGuardia, skirting NYU, and stop at an empty payphone booth. I pump in the change and dial John's number, ready to finish the conversation still haunting me.

"John," I say, grateful he picked up. "It's Murray."

"Murray, hey, how are you?"

"Pretty good. Getting settled."

We've had a few superficial conversations since I bailed on him, and I'm sure he thinks that's all he'll get now.

I hear a metallic clanging in the background. "Sorry, I'm organizing a few things," he mutters. "So, are the roommates working out?"

"Yeah. They're pretty great."

"Good."

I pause. "John? I'm sorry I didn't tell you before, about coming here. I messed up."

"Hey, I know it's hard," he says. "Are you . . . are you okay now?"

The question makes my eyes burn and my stomach twist all over again. "I don't know."

"So, tell me. What's going on?"

I don't respond. I can't.

He laughs a little. "Come on, we used to be able to do this. Just pretend you're back home, sitting around with me and Austin."

I wipe my eyes with my sleeve. "You're right," I say. I take a breath. "I guess, I just felt like I had to leave. Like something was going to explode if I didn't. I couldn't stop thinking about Roger and his new place after I went down there." I shake my head. "I wish I hadn't seen it at all. And all those memories of Mr. Everett and my dad coming up at the same time, it's like, I was suffocating, you know? Everywhere I went, there was another terrible memory." I pause and he's silent. But I can't quit now. "And I had a huge fight with Dani, right before I came out here. She didn't seem to care whether or not I moved away, and I got upset." Tears well in my eyes again. "I just, I couldn't be there anymore."

"Did you and Dani break up?"

I nod. "Yeah."

"Did you hurt her?"

He says it so quietly, but the question is still like a knife to my chest.

I pause, blinking hard. "I pushed her. I slammed her into the wall."

"Fuck, Murray," he says under his breath. John rarely curses, so I feel even worse.

"I know."

There's silence for several seconds and I have the urge to put my hand through the wall of the booth. To hurt myself. To do anything to get away from this feeling.

"You've got to get a handle on this," John says. "This is not who you are."

"I know." But in the very back of my mind, I worry that this is exactly who I am. And maybe that's why it's so hard to keep covering my mistakes. "You're right."

John doesn't say anything for a while.

I try to pretend, to imagine I'm sitting with him at his kitchen table, like we've done so many times before. I can see him frowning, searching for the right words, the right way to tell me I've ruined everything.

"You need to do this," he says. "See this thing through in New York."

"Really?"

"Yeah. You should give it a shot. You were right to get out of Cleveland. I know all that tension was just building up." John's voice is still hard. He's mad at me.

"John, I'm sorry. I should have told you all this before. I should have had a better plan—"

"It's okay," he breaks in. His voice isn't any softer. "But I need you to do something."

"Sure."

"Find a counselor. You need to get help managing your anger."

"I will." My stomach churns. "You should know, though," I say, "I've been trying to call Dani, to tell her I'm sorry. She doesn't want to hear from me yet, but ... I know how badly I messed up."

"Good," he replies. "The best apology you can give her is to never let it happen again. To anyone."

"Okay." I nod, resigning myself to do what he says. To follow through, for once.

"Okay."

I sense he's going to hang up, but I can't end things like this. I shake my head and try to bring myself back. "Is Austin doing okay?" I ask.

"When's the last time you talked to him?"

"A few days ago, I guess."

"How did he sound?"

"Not good." I narrow my eyes at the police car speeding past me, lights flashing. "He sounded depressed. And angry."

John sighs. "He's about the same, then. He's been in a bad way lately."

"About Roger?"

"Yeah. He's fixated on that place. He keeps riling himself up with these rants about how horrible it is, and he can't let it go."

I nod. I wish I could be there with them. "How has his drinking been?" I ask, even though I already know the answer.

"About what you'd expect," John says. "I tried to get him to go talk to his pastor, but he's not even leaving his apartment these days."

I lower my head. "I wish I could help, but he doesn't want to talk to me."

"I know he's shutting us out more, but I'd keep calling him. I think it does help."

"Okay."

More clanging. "All right, Murray, I'd better get back to this. Thanks for calling, though." He pauses. "It's good to hear your voice."

"You, too."

The words I want to say stick in my throat, so I hang up the phone and lean my back against the booth.

After a minute I walk out and head west on Third, not ready to go back home yet. I think about Rahmi and Grace, how they never seem to let pressure get to them. I think about Jemma, and what kind of darkness she must be living in. I walk past a few broken bottles, their glass shards scattered into the street. It feels like everyone's dealing with life better than I am, but I don't know another way.

Chapter 11
Mr. Bremer

I work a half day on Wednesdays, so instead of going back to the apartment, today I walk a block in the other direction toward the student health center. On the third floor I find the university health services for faculty and staff offices. I take a deep breath and walk into the main office, up to the front desk.

"Hi," I say to the student working reception. "Can I make a counseling appointment?"

"Sure," she replies, looking up from her computer. "Have you been here before?"

"No, I'm new to the school."

She looks up my name on her computer and prints several pages of forms for me to fill out. She clicks through the counselors' schedules and tells me I can come in next Friday at five-thirty to meet with Janet. I'm not thrilled about having to wait so long, but I start to tell her that will be fine.

"Hold on," she says, squinting at her screen. "It looks like Lamar had a cancellation this afternoon. Lamar Bremer." She checks her watch. "He'll be back from lunch in twenty minutes and has an opening after that. Are you available now?"

"Yeah," I say, flustered. "Sure."

"Great." She fastens the forms to a clipboard and hands it to me. "Bring these when he calls you back."

As I take a seat and flip through the papers, I realize these forms are just like the ones Mr. Everett had me fill out all those years ago. I smile. He did know what he was doing.

I fill out the forms, wondering what kind of person Lamar Bremer is. I tap the pen against the clipboard. In a way, I'm glad I can get the awkward first appointment over with today—it's always my least favorite—and for the first few minutes of waiting, I'm calm. But when it's getting close to time for Mr. Bremer to be back from lunch, my leg jitters and my hands sweat as

I flip through the campus magazine. I could reschedule. John would understand. He knows how hard it is to start over, to trust another person like that. I stand up and toss the magazine back onto the table, ready to go over and tell her I'll take the spot next Friday, when Mr. Bremer opens the door. It must be him because he walks in with such confidence, like he's been doing it for years. He's tall, thin, and wearing a suit. He's bald, seemingly by choice rather than genetics, and his dark skin is peppered with small acne scars. He's younger than I am.

I sit back down and avoid his eyes. He's not expecting anybody, so he doesn't look at me. He says hi to the receptionist and she motions him over. She murmurs about the change to his schedule, gesturing to me and making me turn back to the magazine I've picked up again. They talk for another minute before Mr. Bremer walks over to me.

"Murray?" he says with a welcoming smile. I nod and he shakes my hand. "I'm Lamar Bremer. Why don't you come on back?"

I stand and follow him to an office down the left hallway. It's nice for a university center, and I notice his diploma on the wall. He has a master's in social work from here. I'm not too hung up on credentials, though.

I sit in a soft armchair opposite his desk while he looks through my forms.

"So, Murray," he says after a few moments, causing me to start, "you have a lot going on right now." He laughs a little, still sifting through the papers.

"Yeah." I crack my knuckles. "I've made some changes, I guess."

"I'll say." He sets the forms aside. "First, though, let me tell you a little about myself."

I nod, relieved we're not diving in yet.

"I was born and raised here in New York. Just a few blocks that way." He smiles and points out the window. East, I think. "By the time I got to high school I wanted to go into social work. Both my parents are counselors, and it's a need in our community that I knew wouldn't be going away. So, I got my bachelor's in psychology and MSW here at NYU, and I've been counseling teens and adults for the past three years." He reaches back for my forms and gets a curious look that lets me know we're done with the easy part. "I saw something about your education that struck me," he says. "Do you mind if I ask you about it?"

I shake my head, pretty sure where this is going.

"You have a law degree, and you could practice," he says, focusing on the top form, "but you've been working the past three years as a file clerk. Does that even require a college degree?"

My face reddens. "I'm not sure." It does not.

"Did you ever practice law?"

"I did, but not for very long. It wasn't something I could handle, I guess."

"Handle?" He cocks his head a little, and I wish I'd chosen a different word.

"It was stressful," I say, trying to be more careful. "Sometimes the details of the cases . . . they were hard for me to deal with."

"And this was criminal law?"

I nod.

"Okay. Well, I guess I'm getting a little ahead of myself," he says, uncapping a pen. "You wrote down that you're here to talk about anger. Is that right?"

"Yeah. It's something that comes up every few years. I can't seem to get it under control."

"Can you say when it all began? Was there a specific incident?"

"No." I squint past him out the window. "It's really been all my life. As early as I can remember." I take a breath. "I mean, no specific incident, but my childhood wasn't great. I know that's part of it."

"Have you been in therapy before?"

"I wrote it down on there." I point to the forms on his desk.

He smiles. "I know. Some of it I'm still going to ask you, just to get it out there."

I nod. "Yeah, I saw a therapist for the first time a little over ten years ago, for about four months. I saw three or four others after that, but only for a few months each."

"Okay." He studies me. "How much do you want to talk about your childhood?"

I laugh. "I get to decide?"

"For now."

"Can we skip it, then?"

"Sure." Mr. Bremer shrugs. "Can you tell me about what triggers your anger?"

I think back over the past few months. I try to swallow, but my mouth is dry. I'm at the place I fear most in therapy: I have to show the ugliest side of myself, the moments that make me look like absolute scum. "I'm sorry, Mr. Bremer." I gaze down, unable to find the words.

"Nothing to be sorry about. And please, call me Lamar."

Call me Ash.

"It's worst when a lot of things add up," I say. "Then something comes along and ends up being the last straw."

45

He nods. "Did you have a 'last straw' in Cleveland? Is that why you left?"

"I feel like I had a few of them."

"Talk to me about that," he says, leaning back in his chair. He hasn't written anything down yet, but maybe he doesn't like the way it looks. Maybe he knows it scares people and makes them withdraw. He'll probably fill the pad when I'm gone.

"Well," I say, "the tension had really been bad for me a few months ago. It was around the time of a kind of anniversary: ten years since I'd lost a good friend to suicide, as well as ten years since my father died."

"Wow," Lamar says, raising his eyebrows. "That's really tough."

I nod. "And at the same time, something did happen. Another guy in town, Roger, he'd been a friend of his, too—"

"A friend of whose?"

"Of my friend who killed himself."

"Okay." He's writing now. "And what was your friend's name?"

"Menashe."

"All right," Lamar murmurs. "So, Roger is a guy you know in Cleveland, who had also known Menashe. Did I get that right?"

I nod.

"Okay, so what happened with Roger?"

"He started a business," I say, as evenly as I can. "He took my friend's idea, which was supposed to help people, and he's using it just to make money."

"What kind of a business?"

"I don't think I can talk about that."

"Sure." He's really writing now. "And this was the last straw?"

I nod. "The first one."

"Did you confront him?"

"Yes."

"And you lost control?"

"Yeah." My heartbeat runs away from me as I picture the scene with Roger. "I went down to his new place—his business. I tried to keep it together, but I exploded at him. I called him an asshole and said he was exploiting Mr. Everett, forgetting all he'd—"

"I'm sorry," Lamar breaks in, frowning again. "Who's Mr. Everett?" He's looking at his notes.

"Oh. I mean Menashe."

"Did you always call him that? It seems pretty formal for a friend."

46

I smile. "He didn't want me to, but I could never break the habit. He was older than I was—about twenty years older, I guess."

"Okay." He nods. "I noticed you did that with me, too. You called me Mr. Bremer."

"Oh? I don't remember."

He smiles. "I might be younger than you." He flips through my forms. "Yep, says here you're twenty-nine." He looks up. "You've got three years on me."

I shrug. "I guess it's just how I was taught. And you're kind of like my doctor, so ..."

"So, someone in this kind of position you'd address more formally?" he finishes for me.

"Yeah, I guess." I'm not sure why we're spending time on this.

"But still in your mind you call your friend Mr. Everett," he says, almost to himself. "How long did you know him?"

"About four months."

"Oh, so not that long."

My face heats up. "It didn't have to be a long time. We got very close."

Lamar's watching me carefully now. Maybe this was a bad idea. "You're starting to feel it, right?" he asks.

"What?"

"I see what you did with your hands, there." He points to my lap.

I glance down and unclench my fists. I don't remember doing that.

"And it looks like you're flushing a bit."

His acknowledgment only makes it worse. I'm aware now, and I can see my jittering leg is also giving me away. "Do something for me, okay?"

"What?"

"Close your eyes and picture a good time you've had. Any good time. While you're doing that take five long, deep breaths, then open your eyes again."

I feel like an idiot, but I do it. It takes me a few seconds, but I think about the day I was admitted to the bar. A couple of my friends from law school took me out that night. I breathe and open my eyes again. Lamar is still scrutinizing me.

"I'm going to suggest you have strategies like this to calm you down when you feel those physical signs." He pauses. "Did you realize you were getting angry?"

I clear my throat. "I felt warm, and I knew I was getting frustrated. But I didn't know I was doing that with my hands, and I didn't feel my leg jittering."

"Okay. It's important you practice being aware of what your body does when you're ramping up. You'll have way more success working through your anger if you can recognize it early."

"But thinking about something else isn't working through it," I say, frowning. "It's just a distraction."

"Absolutely," Lamar replies. "But those strategies are only to help the physical symptoms subside. Once your body is calm, you can look at what's making you angry."

"Okay."

"I want to apologize. I didn't mean to belittle your friendship with Menashe by saying you hadn't known him very long."

This takes me by surprise and my eyes burn. I don't know what to say. I hadn't expected to talk about Mr. Everett at all today. I nod but I can't look at him.

"Should we go back to Roger? I interrupted you before."

I nod again. "Sure."

"How did he respond when you yelled at him?"

I take a moment to recall. "He stayed calm," I say. "He told me he wasn't doing anything wrong—that he was taking a good idea and running with it."

"So, he didn't get worked up at all."

"Right."

"Did that calm you down?"

I shake my head. "Pretty much the opposite. It made it worse."

Lamar writes a few things down. "You kept yelling?"

"For a little longer, I guess. Then he asked me to leave."

"Did you break anything? Try to hurt him?"

"No."

"All right." He pauses as he finishes writing, then looks up. "What was the second straw?"

"We have time for that?" I ask, surprised. I've been watching the clock and half an hour has just passed.

"Oh, yeah," he replies, glancing at his watch. "I do a full hour for the first appointment." He sees my stricken expression. "Is that okay with you?"

I check my watch against the clock. "Yeah." I thought I was getting a reprieve from what was coming; now I'm in the sickening middle of it.

"Can we talk about the second straw?" he asks again. He flips to the next page of his notebook, having filled the previous one.

I nod. "It was a fight I had with my girlfriend." I pause for him to ask a question, but it seems he wants me to continue on my own. "I had been asked to interview out here—I'd just gotten off the phone before she got home. She didn't even know I'd been applying for jobs. I wanted to see if there'd be any interest first."

"And what's your girlfriend's name?"

"Dani—Danielle."

"And she's your age?"

"Twenty-four."

"Okay." He's writing. "Sorry, please go on."

"Anyway"—I rub my forehead—"when I said I might be moving to New York, I expected some kind of reaction, you know? I thought she'd either jump on board and want to come with me, or want me to stay in Cleveland."

"Or want to end things?" Lamar says.

"Sure. I would have understood that. But she didn't seem to care what would happen. She likes things casual."

"So, you lost your temper?"

"Yes. I yelled. I told her I wanted a clear signal from her about something."

"How did she take that?"

"I hadn't lost my temper that suddenly before. It caught her off guard."

"You scared her?"

I sigh. "Yeah." I look back up at him, remembering something. "But you know what?" I say, pointing at him. "I tried to leave the apartment. When I felt myself getting out of control, I tried to leave. But Dani saw something was wrong; she didn't want me to leave like that."

"Sounds like you're trying to blame her for losing control." Lamar says this with a sympathetic smile, but it still makes my stomach drop.

"No. I just want you to know, I saw it coming and I did try."

"That's good," he replies, "but you need to understand it's a pretty small leap from that to 'I'm sorry, honey, but if you'd only let me leave the apartment, I wouldn't have had to hit you.'"

I stiffen in my chair. "I never did that."

"I'm glad to hear it," he says. "What did you do?"

"What do you mean?"

"You said you wanted to leave the apartment, that you were getting agitated. You yelled and it was starting to scare her. So how did it end?"

"She was calm," I say. "It highlighted the whole problem, that she doesn't care enough to get upset or to let me know what she's thinking. That just made me more frustrated."

"Like with Roger," Lamar remarks.

"What?"

"You said when you confronted Roger, he was calm and that made your temper worse. It's like you're slighted when no one else reacts to a situation as strongly as you do."

I try to process this but my mind is too flustered. "I don't know."

"It's okay." He waves his hand. "I was just thinking out loud. I'm sorry—go on."

"I needed to get her to react to something," I say. "Everything was building up so much in me: the stress from the anniversaries, from this thing with Roger, now having to interview in New York. I—I just lost it."

"But you didn't hit her?" He sounds doubtful.

"No. But I did push her. Pretty hard."

He looks past me for a moment, like he's trying to put something together. "Then what happened?"

"She started crying. I didn't know what to do, so I left. I threw up, then I left."

Lamar writes for a few seconds. "You didn't mention violence on your forms."

"I wasn't sure how much I was going to tell you."

"Murray," he says, putting down his pen, "I'm sure being here is extremely difficult for you. But we need to make sure this kind of thing doesn't keep happening. To you, or the people you come in contact with."

"I know." I'm looking down, waiting for him to say something else, but he doesn't. I raise my eyes and he's still watching me. "I know," I repeat. "You're right. Everything you said is right."

He doesn't look satisfied but lets us move on. I get the feeling he doesn't think I can handle much more probing, so we finish the hour working on more of his decompression strategies. At two o'clock I get up to leave, and he rises as well, shaking my hand.

"It was nice to meet you, Murray," he says. "Would you like to make this regular?"

He sounds hopeful, like he does want to see this through with me. I look around the room, the bright New York office with encouraging posters of students getting help for their depression and addictions and toxic relationships. I look back at Lamar, an obviously talented counselor not yet put off by my train wreck of a life.

I nod. "If you think I can be helped."

He smiles. "I know it."

I leave the university and walk straight home, drawing my jacket around me and muttering fragmented thoughts to myself. When I get there, I'm alone but I don't know how long that will last, so I yank open the kitchen drawer and pull out a pen and paper. I've waited too long. I sit at the table, staring down at the piece of paper, and start to write.

> *Dear Danielle,*
>
> *I want to tell you how sorry I am, but now that I'm writing this, I realize just how many things I'm sorry for. I'll start with the worst: how I acted before I left for New York. I'm so sorry I pushed you and yelled and was all-around horrible. There's no excuse, so I won't try to give you one. Please just know I'm sorry, and I hope you're okay.*

My heart is beating so fast I'm sweating. I stand up and walk to the sink, resting my hands on the sides just in case. I take a few slow breaths, then splash my face with cold water. I can't even write an apology to Dani without making everything about myself. My reaction, my pain. I sit again, disgusted with how weak I am, but more determined now. I want to do this right, for her.

> *And I'm sorry I tried to force you to give me an answer about the job. I wanted an instant decision and that wasn't fair. There were a lot of things I did that weren't fair. I never really let you in, and I'm sorry for that. I should have told you more about what I was thinking, and I should have asked you more, too. I'm sorry I never said much about my life before us, because looking back, that could have made a difference. I'm sorry I never let us be a team.*

I read back the words. I haven't truly acknowledged them before now. I blink back tears because I understand that things could have worked with Dani, I just didn't let them.

> *I hope you're doing all right now. I think about you a lot, but I'm also coming to understand that it's over. I'm sorry I called you so many times. I didn't think about how bad that would be for you, and it was selfish.*
>
> *I want only good things for you, Dani. Maybe now you can find them.*
>
> *Murray*

I sit back, frowning at the paper. I'm not sure what I expected, but it wasn't this. I feel sick and exposed sending this out into the world, but I have to. I fold it and stuff it into an envelope, where at least I can't reread it forever. I address and stamp the envelope, then walk outside to the mailbox before I can change my mind.

Chapter 12

Austin's in Trouble

A couple of weeks later, John calls me at the apartment. It's nearly nine o'clock at night, and Rahmi and I are watching TV on the couch while Grace sits in the recliner, pretending to study but laughing at all the jokes on the show. When the phone rings, she jumps to get it like she was expecting it to be for her but soon calls me over to take it.

"Hello?"

"Murray, it's John."

I turn my back to the living room, my stomach dropping at the coldness of his voice.

"What's wrong? Are you okay?"

"Listen," he says, "I need you to come back."

My vision jumps. Sweat is already stinging under my arms. It's not like John to be dramatic. Whatever it is, it's real. "What is going on?"

"It's Austin," he says. "He was arrested."

"What?" I glance over my shoulder and see Rahmi's looking at me, so I smile to show him everything's all right. I turn back around, my heart hammering. "He's in jail? John, what did he do?"

"He's not in jail anymore; I paid his bail. But he goes to trial in a couple weeks." John sighs. "He's been harassing Roger. Stalking him, pestering him to shut his business down."

"Has he even been talking about Roger with you?" I break in, confused. He hadn't mentioned Roger to me in over a month.

"No. I think that's why he was pulling away from us. He didn't want to let us in on what he was doing."

I rub my eyes and lean against the counter. It must be bad. When Austin hits a breaking point, it can be catastrophic. "So, what happened?"

"Well," John says, "he ended up getting drunk the other day. He rode the bus down to Roger's place and confronted him. Roger tried to give him the same defense he gave you, and Austin beat him up."

"Shit," I whisper.

"Yeah."

"How bad?"

"A fractured arm and a black eye were the worst of it. He's lucky; Austin can do a lot more damage."

I slump into a chair at the kitchen table. I'd hoped Austin was getting past all this, but he was just getting worse. And keeping it all to himself.

Rahmi walks into the kitchen. He sits in the chair across from me, quiet and frowning. I give him a weak smile.

"I'm not sure I should come back."

"He needs you."

"He needs me, or he needs a lawyer?"

"Murray, we are his closest friends," John snaps. "I shouldn't have to tell you that."

I shake my head. He's right. "I'm sorry," I say. "I know."

"The problem is he's scared shitless right now," John continues, "and it's making him lash out at anybody trying to help him." He pauses. "I just don't know what to do for him anymore."

I close my eyes. "I'm sorry," I say again. "Of course I'll be there."

"Okay," he says, letting out a long breath. "Thank you."

"I've got two personal days," I say, watching as Rahmi gives me increasingly confused looks, "so I can be there Thursday morning and stay through the weekend. Is that okay?"

"Yeah, that'd be great." He pauses. "We really have missed you, Murray."

"Thanks." I fight the emerging tremor in my stomach. "I've missed you, too."

Chapter 13
Jail Time

John picks me up at the airport in Cleveland a little after nine a.m. I'm startled by his appearance; John usually looks so put together. I walk over and hug him, but continue to steal glances, trying to remember why this feels familiar. His hair is tangled and unwashed, pulled into a hasty ponytail. His khaki pants are wrinkled, and his eyes are glazed. The first thing he says to me—"Are you okay?" in his tired, miserable voice—jogs my memory. I haven't seen him like this since Mr. Everett's funeral. The day we met.

"I'm okay," I assure him, hoisting my bag up on my shoulder. "How about you?"

He laughs. "Sometimes with Austin, it's like having another kid."

"Is he back at his apartment?" I ask as we walk away from the gate.

John shakes his head. "He's at my place. He's been so depressed with all of this . . . I didn't want him to be alone."

"Yeah." I nod. "That's nice of you."

"So," he says, slowing his pace when he realizes I can't quite keep up with him, "I hope you don't mind, but the only spot left is the couch. It'll be kind of a full house."

"No problem. I really appreciate it."

"And I want to say," he continues, in a serious tone that makes me wary of whatever's coming next, "I hope you can go easy on Austin. At least at first. I know he messed up and this will bring out the lawyer in you, but what he needs right now are his friends."

"Sure." I'm surprised John thinks of me that way. I'm usually at my weakest with him and Austin.

We walk out of the airport. The sky is bright gray and it's snowing. There's already an inch on the ground. John looks at me critically.

"Is that your coat?"

I sigh. "Yeah."

For the moment, it's quiet back at John's house. His daughters are at school and his wife is working at the hospital. We trudge in through the laundry room, stomping the extra snow from our shoes before taking them off. I go in first, walking into the cheery yellow kitchen while John hangs up his coat. Austin sits at the table, drinking a cup of coffee. He looks the same as I remember, better than I expected. He stands when he sees me.

"Sorry I dragged you back here, kid," he says. He walks over and hugs me. His grip is strong.

"No. I'm glad to see you."

Austin nods and sits back down. John comes in and puts on more coffee while I join Austin. In some ways, it's like our old Wednesday nights together. But I can tell John's a wreck.

"You want anything in it, Murray?" he asks, pouring two cups.

"Black's fine. Thanks."

He brings them over and they rattle against the table as he sets them down.

Austin turns to me. "So, Mur, tell me about New York."

It's not an invitation, but rather a command. His gravelly voice is stern, like he knows we have other things to talk about but needs the distraction. I glance at John, who shrugs a little. There is pretty much Austin doesn't know, since he'd started avoiding my phone calls, so I go ahead and fill him in. I tell him about my work at the law library, my roommates. I tell him Grace reminds me a lot of Sam, which makes him smile. I tell him about my therapist. I feel like I'm talking too much, but every time I try to wrap things up, Austin asks another question. John's right: he's scared.

I indulge him for another ten minutes or so, but John's starting to look sick, so I clear my throat. "I think we should talk about you for a bit."

He looks upset for a moment, but then he turns to John. "Guess this is it."

John nods. "Tell him what happened."

"All right." Austin moves his cup aside and rests his arms on the table. "This is the thing. I tried to let it go after we saw Roger's flyer. I talked with Pastor Jim about it, tried the heavy bag, I even got this book on meditation." He adjusts his baseball cap and glances at me. "And I'm sorry I kept you guys in the dark. It's just, talking about it seemed to make everything worse."

I nod.

"So, I decided to go see Roger. I thought I could explain why opening that place was a shitty thing to do."

"You thought he would listen to that?" I ask, wondering if Austin's reasoning had been the same as mine.

Austin shrugs. "I guess I wanted to try. But honestly," he says, shaking his head, "in the back of my mind, I knew what would happen. I mean, if you couldn't hold it together talking to Roger, what chance did I have?"

I lower my head, my mind racing. "How did it escalate?" I ask.

"Not how you'd expect. I came in and told him this was a shitty thing to do to Ash, and to all of us. He was an asshole right off the bat because he thought you put me up to it, after the run-in you had with him."

I nod and swallow against the knot in my throat. "I believe it."

"But then Roger said he remembered me," Austin continues, his voice growing hard. "He said he'd see me at the museum sometimes, if he was early for his session. He got this mean, nasty kind of smile, and said I always looked crazy, like I was out to kill somebody." Austin looks over at John and I understand why he told me to go easy on him. "I swear, Murray, it was like he was trying to get me to lose it." He leans back and takes off his cap, tossing it on the table. His thick gray hair is messy underneath. "He said when he heard Ash had killed himself, he didn't believe it. He said he thought of that crazy guy he'd seen at the museum. But I was already seeing red by then. It was too much." Austin clears his throat, but his voice is still as gruff as ever. "So, yes, I went after him. I could have killed him, but in the middle of pounding him I got a better idea. I grabbed some papers off his desk and found a room."

"One of the glass rooms?"

"Yeah. I wanted to destroy it, but not in the way he wanted. I didn't touch any of the glass. I went to set the papers on fire, but my lighter jammed. Roger ran in after a minute, yelling at me. I'm sure he'd already called the police. So, I got out of there."

I sit for a moment. John grips Austin on the shoulder as he gets up to grab his cigarettes. I attempt to sort through possible strategies, but this is a mess.

"Come on, Mur," Austin says. "Is it that bad?"

"Well . . . ," I say, my eyes darting toward John. I think he's giving me a look, but maybe it's just my imagination. "Let me tell you what I notice."

"Okay."

"The good thing is, you didn't start a fire."

"Yeah."

"What's going to be a challenge is the fact that you beat him up pretty badly. He needed medical treatment."

Austin frowns but doesn't say anything.

"The other thing is the trial."

"What about it?"

I drum my fingers together.

"It's all right, Murray," John breaks in. "Whatever it is, you can say it."

"I just don't think this is going to look very good to a jury. I mean, we're your friends. We know what kind of person you are. But the prosecutor will focus on specific parts of your past. Violence, suicide attempts, alcohol, that kind of thing." Austin sits a little straighter. "John and I can be character witnesses, but I don't think it will make a huge difference."

"What about treatment, though?" John asks. "Isn't it good that he's sought out counseling and this church group for support? I mean, he's working to get better."

"Sure, but it's all going to emphasize that he's got a problem in the first place, and needs a lot of people to try to control it. That's how they'll spin it, anyway."

"We're already coming from behind," Austin grumbles. "I mean, you've seen Roger. He's a good-looking rich kid. He'll send in a slick, expensive lawyer, flash a smile, and call it a fucking day."

"Maybe not," I reply.

"Well, there's got to be something," John blurts out, banging his coffee cup down on the table and causing me to jump. "Roger was provoking him, right? Taunting him?"

I start to stammer a response when Austin interrupts. "Any sympathy for being a veteran?" he asks.

"Yeah," I say, glancing at John. "I think people will respond to that."

"So, what's the bottom line?"

"Have you talked at all with a lawyer?"

Austin shakes his head. "Not yet."

"I can't say exactly, but aggravated assault could give you some jail time."

"How much?" Austin asks, his leg vibrating under the table.

"Depending on the prosecutor, they could seek up to five years."

"Fucking hell." Austin looks up at John, whose gaze is focused on the table.

My chest burns. I can't tell if I feel worse for John or Austin, but I wish I could give them some good news. It's my fault Roger reacted the way he did. It should be me losing sleep over a five-year sentence, not Austin. I take a long drink. The least I can do now is the last thing I want to.

"What do we do?" John asks after a moment.

"I need to go talk to Roger," I say.

"What?" John coughs a few times. "No. I'm not having you go back there."

"What do you want to say to him?" Austin asks.

"Our best shot," I explain, "is avoiding trial altogether. We need to convince Roger he doesn't want a court battle, and Roger will have to convince the prosecutor to drop the charges."

Austin frowns. "Sounds like a long shot."

I nod. "It is. But let me try. I'll think about what to do today, and then I'll go see him tomorrow."

They look at each other and I can see Austin trying to persuade John.

John looks at me, his face serious. "Can you handle this?" he asks.

I nod. "Yeah."

But I don't know. I might fall apart, or fail to get Roger on board. It turns my stomach to think about going back. But I know Austin. I know how much he cared about Mr. Everett. To hear the things Roger said to him, I'm surprised he didn't kill him. And I also know, if Austin goes to jail, he'll most likely die there.

Chapter 14
Power Play

I've been in Roger's waiting room almost an hour. I know he's punishing me. I glance toward his office, squinting my eyes to make out his shadowy figure behind the desk, on the phone. Always on the phone. I shake my head. He's trying to intimidate me, wear me down before we even meet.

"Murray Henderson," I hear him say with a laugh, nearly twenty minutes later.

I look up and he's standing in his office doorway, motioning with his good arm for me to come back. The other is in a sling. He looks polished, as always, but the skin around his left eye is a deep purple fading to green, and his jaw is swirled in similar colors. I sit in the same chair as before, as anxious and angry as I'd been then. But I've got a better idea of why I'm here now, and I remind myself to stay calm for Austin.

"Pretty ballsy coming back here," Roger says, sitting down in his leather desk chair, "after everything your friend did. I figured you were in on it."

I frown. "What does that mean?"

"You put him up to it. You found somebody crazier than you and had him do what you couldn't."

"Austin's not crazy." I focus my eyes on Roger's computer monitor while I breathe. "And I didn't tell him to come down here."

"Okay." He smiles.

"I want to talk about the charges against him," I say. "Not as a lawyer, just as his friend."

"Sure." He brings out a file of papers from a cabinet under his desk. "You want to talk about the assault? Let's hear it."

"I think it's bullshit."

"Wow," Roger laughs, tossing the papers on his desk. "I did not expect this approach."

"From what Austin told me, you provoked the assault."

"You're going to blame the guy who got pummeled? Pretty heartless, Murray. Especially for you."

I study Roger's face. There's something sinister about the way he's watching me now. But it's like his power play in the waiting room; he thinks he can intimidate me into leaving him alone. "Your injuries were minor," I say. "I think you should drop the charges."

I catch him taking a drink during that last part, so he coughs and sprays water across his papers.

"You're crazy," he says, still coughing. "Why would I drop the charges?"

"You and Austin don't have anything against each other, personally. I don't think there's a reason you'd want to see him in jail." I pause, but he doesn't say anything. "If we covered your hospital bills, and got you some extra money for pain and suffering . . . maybe we could avoid court altogether."

Roger is silent and I can't tell what's on his mind. He leans forward, drumming his thumb on the desk. I can see now he has two small cuts under his left temple. "It's not enough," he says.

My stomach sinks. "Why?"

"Because you can't come into somebody's business, beat the shit out of him, and expect to walk away."

"Austin isn't himself right now," I say. "He's still dealing with a lot of trauma."

"Aren't we all?"

"His PTSD will get worse in jail. His depression, anger, all of it."

"You should have thought of that before you put him up to it. Or you should have given him a more foolproof plan."

"I told you, I didn't put him up to it."

"I guess it makes sense," he continues in a low voice. "You've done some pretty messed up shit, right?"

I don't understand where Roger's going with this, but my hands are sweating. My pulse has picked up, and he's looking at me strangely again.

"I keep trying to picture it," he says. "I keep trying to picture you doing it, but I can't. I mean, shooting somebody? You don't seem the type."

I'm dizzy now, and the light in the room dims a little. "What are you talking about?"

"I did some research after you came in last time. And more after Austin attacked me. I know you shot your father."

Blood slams against my ears. "It's not a secret."

"No," Roger agrees. "This is more my own curiosity. I'm just wondering why."

I swallow hard. "If you found a police report, you already know."

"There's usually more to it than that."

I rub my face with my hands. *Why is he doing this?* "I'm not talking about this with you."

"Fine. Keep your charges."

He comes around and sits in the chair opposite me. I don't like him this close. He has more small cuts—one on his neck and three on his forearm. His eyes are serious.

"I don't get this," I say, my voice shaky. "You'll drop the charges if I talk to you?"

He shrugs. "Maybe."

I sit, watching him, struggling to pull in ragged breaths. "Okay," I say after a moment. "If you want to know, it was self-defense. He had beaten me for years, and this time he was going to kill me. He wouldn't stop. Okay?" I throw my hands up. "Satisfied?"

Roger frowns. "And what about the glass? Did that contribute?"

"What?"

"Did your time with Ash make you want to do it? You know, did it rev you up?"

"No." I wish he wouldn't mention Mr. Everett. "I didn't want to do it at all."

"Okay. Did it help you, though? The glass, I mean."

"Roger," I say, meeting his eyes, "are you thinking of making this place into therapy?"

"I don't know, maybe," he replies dismissively.

"I don't think that's a good idea."

He doesn't seem to hear me. "But did it help?"

"Yeah," I say, unsure of how much I want to share with him. "It helped me recover old memories."

"Really? Like repressed stuff?"

"Yeah."

"And they came back to you while you were in the rooms?"

I nod. He doesn't seem as evil now. It feels like he's doing research—like he's actually interested.

"Did you have any more sessions after you killed your dad?"

I suck my breath in. "Can you not say it like that?"

"Sorry."

"No, I didn't. I was in the hospital for a while, and after that . . ."

He nods. "I know." He seems to soften. "There wasn't much time."

"Yeah."

Roger looks thoughtful for a moment and I hope he's done with this.

"Okay, Murray," he says, leaning forward and gingerly resting his arms on his knees, "this is what I'm thinking: I will get the prosecutor to drop the charges against Austin."

I hold my breath, waiting for it.

"You need to pay a pain and suffering amount that we work out together."

I nod. Chase and Sam will probably help out, too.

"The other thing is, I want to be able to ask you questions sometimes, about how things went for you at the museum. Will you agree to that?"

I narrow my eyes at him, trying to understand what's behind all this. I don't believe he's looking to help people; that's not Roger. I'm sure the end-game centers on himself. With the pressure off Austin, though, it doesn't matter. "All right," I say. "It's weird, but all right."

"Okay," Roger replies, holding out his good hand. "I'll call you when it's done."

I shake his hand. There's another cut on the edge of his wrist.

Chapter 15
Departure

"**A**nother beer for my friend, Murray the lawyer!" Sam shouts as he refills my glass at the bar. I smile. If I'd known he was going to do that, I would have gone to get it myself. Chase walks behind my chair to get more pretzels and squeezes my shoulders as he passes. Austin's laughing with John, his eyes bright and his smile easy. He calls for Sam to bring him another gin and tonic.

"What time do you want to get to the airport tomorrow?" John asks, leaning forward to retrieve the little planner out of his back pocket.

"My flight's earlier than I thought," I say. "Is ten o'clock okay?"

"Oh, sure," he replies, writing it down. "Should be fine."

I focus on my cards, avoiding his eyes. I don't know why I can't just tell him I need more time alone—that I can't settle my mind on a two-hour flight. He'd understand that.

"Think you'll be back this summer?" Chase asks as he stacks his chips.

I watch him for a few seconds, unsure. The guys are all looking at me now. "Yeah. I'm sure I will."

Sam laughs. "I'll be the next one you've got to bail out." He takes a long drink of his rum and Coke. "So keep yourself sharp."

I smile. "You bet."

"No." Austin puts his arm around my shoulder. "This guy," he says, with a hazy lilt to his speech, "has things to do. Big things. We're gonna stay out of his way."

My face reddens and Sam starts to tell us some lawyer joke he just remembered, but ends up jumbling the punch line. Austin tries to help him out but gets it wrong, too, and they both collapse in laughter.

"Okay," Chase announces, "I know this is a celebration, but—Austin and Sam, time to switch to coffee. Everybody else," he says, pausing to look around the table, peering into our eyes to gauge our lucidity, "one more drink each. I'm tending now."

Sam groans, but goes to get the coffee set up while Chase clears away some of the bottles. John, sitting to my right, checks his watch again. I wonder if he wants to leave.

"Is it getting late?" I ask.

"Not really. I guess I'm just getting old."

"Well, it's been a crazy few days."

He glances past me toward Austin, who's trying to explain why his three tens should beat a flush.

"We should get him home soon," John says in a low voice. "He's having a good time now, but ..."

I nod. "I know."

"Okay."

We finish out the hand, then I stand up and tell the guys I've got to get some sleep before I head back tomorrow. I almost say "head home," but I catch myself. John would have been hurt and Sam never would have let me hear the end of it. Chase and Sam are still talking, so Austin, John, and I push the heavy front door open and step into the swirling snow. I glance back and take one more look at the sign for The Velvet Dog, unlit on its night off, hovering above the vacant basement apartment.

I wake up early and stumble to the bathroom. Everyone's still asleep. It's freezing, and I look up to see the register has been shut off to save heat. I turn the water on and stare into the mirror while I wait for it to warm up. I look ten years older than I am. My eyes give me away—their hard lines and dark circles. And it's not as noticeable, but my blond hair is going gray, especially at the temples. I study myself with curious distaste. I'm no longer lanky and awkward like I was as a teenager, but I still look weak. My eyes give that away, too.

The water's warm now, so I wash my face in the sink. My hands come back shaking, dripping water down the cabinet and onto the floor. I glance around in a panic, my chest on fire. I focus on the mirror again and hear Roger's voice in my head, saying I'm a hypocritical piece of shit for telling him about morals and ethics after what I did. He says I should have shot myself instead.

I cover my eyes and focus on the blood pounding in my head. My slow, deep breaths aren't working. I sink to the floor, leaning my back against the wall. I blink and try to remember Austin, the fact that he won't languish in some dirty prison cell, or worse. But I can hear the glass shattering now. I can feel the smooth body of the baseball bat, and I wish I were holding it now.

I crawl to the toilet and throw up. It's still there—the rush of adrenaline I'd get during a session. Goddamn Roger. I just wanted to be past all this.

I check my watch. It's too early to call Rahmi. I get to my feet and once again wash my face. I take a drink from the faucet. I dry myself off and glimpse my tired, ragged reflection again. I slam my hand against the countertop. This isn't how it was supposed to be.

Austin's still asleep when John and I set out for the airport. I figured he would be, so I told him goodbye last night, as best I could in his state. He was emotional, and hugged me for nearly a full minute. I told him I'd call him when I got to New York, and he said he was never going to forget what I did for him.

John's quiet as he drives. He looks years younger than he did when he picked me up on Thursday. He's showered and slept well; he's combed his hair and his clothes are clean. I look out the window as we drive down the plowed highway, thinking about what I'll do when I get back. What I'll say to Rahmi. John's still silent as we near the airport—not upset, it seems, just content to be still—but I'm running out of time. I suppose we're about ten minutes away, and my heartbeat picks up because there's something I still need to say to him.

"John," I begin. I have to clear my throat because my voice is hoarse from not talking. "I've been seeing somebody, in New York."

He looks at me in surprise. "Really? Like, romantically?"

"Yeah." I nod. "I didn't plan it, or anything, and I was meeting with my counselor out there before it ever—"

"Murray," he stops me, smiling, "it sounds like you're apologizing. You don't have to explain. I'm happy for you."

"But I know you were disappointed," I say, surprised to hear my voice waver. "I know you thought it was a bad idea. And I don't want to end up hurting anybody else, either. I really don't." I glance at him but he's not reacting. "It's just been nice, you know? Having somebody there."

John nods. "How often do you see Lamar?"

"Every week."

"And you've been keeping your temper with her?"

"With who?"

"Your girlfriend."

I smile. "It's actually my roommate, Rahmi."

"The guy from Turkey?"

"Yeah."

"Oh, all right." John glances in the rearview before he takes the exit. "Sorry, I shouldn't have assumed."

"It's okay. And yes, I've been keeping my temper with him."

"Good."

"Lamar says I should let him in more, though," I say. "There's just a lot of heavy stuff I'm not sure I want to put on him."

"Yeah. How long have you been seeing him?"

"About seven weeks."

"And how much does he know?"

"Well . . ." I scratch the back of my neck. "He knows pretty much about my childhood, and he knows about the therapy with Mr. Everett."

"But not about what happened with your dad?"

"Right." I look down. "Something like that can really change things."

"I don't think so," John says, shaking his head. "I think anybody you like this much has to be a pretty good person. And a good person won't see any of it as your fault."

"There's no way to soften it, though," I say. "I wish I could take the shock out of it."

"I know. It's not an easy thing to hear. Just let him have some time with it. Don't push him for a response if he needs to process."

"Okay." I nod. "Thanks."

"You know you can still talk to me, right?"

I turn to him. "Of course."

"I just—I know I worry a lot, about everything, but I didn't mean to be so hard on you."

I shake my head. "I needed to hear it."

"But I made you think you had to keep the most important thing in your life from me for seven weeks. I'm sorry for that. I just want you to know, you can always talk to me."

"Thanks. I will."

We sit in silence for a minute before John turns to me again.

"Have you told Austin?"

I laugh. "No. I think he's more comfortable when I'm dating girls."

"Yeah." John smiles. "But you don't need to worry." He looks over at me. "You know that, right?"

I nod.

He pulls the car up to departures and puts it in park. I get out and open the trunk to get my bags. Leaving will be harder than I thought and I'm hoping John doesn't say anything too sentimental right now. It won't take much to break me.

"Hey," he says as I come back around. He's standing at the front of the car. "You'll call me when you get in?"

"Of course."

"And you've got everything you need?"

I smile. "I think so."

"All right," he says, squinting up as a plane flies overhead. "I guess I have to let you go, then."

I set my bags down by the curb and give him a hug, immediately feeling the sting in my eyes I'd been dreading. I tell him goodbye and grab my things, heading toward the turnstile doors. John waits until I'm in the building before starting his car and driving away.

Chapter 16
Little Relief

It's seven-thirty before I make it back to Bleecker Street and lumber into our apartment. I've just thrown my bags down and closed the door when Grace yells to me from the living room.

"Your boyfriend has been insufferable." She turns back to the television. "Will you just take him with you next time?"

I smile and toss my coat on top of my suitcase. "That's not a bad idea."

"Seriously," she says, turning to me again, "I didn't think he was going to make it. Every other minute it was something like, 'Oh, we can't go to that restaurant, it's one of Murray's favorites,' or, 'Hey, turn off *Drew Carey*, it makes me miss him,' or, 'Don't use Murray's coffee mug, that—'"

I laugh. "Okay, I get it." I collapse into the chair across from the couch. "Anything new with Jemma?" I nod toward her door.

"She's being extra weird again," Grace says. "Yesterday I ran into her in the hallway and she glared at me, like usual. She passed me and I turned around once I was almost to the corner. She did this fast knock on a door, somebody opened it just a crack, and she shoved an envelope inside."

"Which room?"

"Four-twelve."

"Do you know who lives there?"

She shakes her head. "She still has drugs here, though. Rahmi found a pill in the bathroom she must have dropped. We were waiting till you came back to decide what to do, but . . . I mean, we have to get the police involved."

"Yeah." I rub my face with both hands. "That's going to suck."

She nods.

I sigh and look down the hallway.

"How was your trip?"

I blink and turn back to Grace, bringing my mind back. "It was good," I say. "Glad to be back, though."

She starts to say something, but we hear keys jangling outside the door. She raises her eyebrows at me.

Rahmi opens the door and says hi to Grace, then sees my stuff on the floor.

"Hey," he says, smiling as I come out of the living room. "Welcome back."

"Thanks." I give him a hug and breathe deeply. "I missed you."

I step back. Grace is watching us, smiling.

"I'm going to put my stuff away," I say, rolling my eyes at her. I pick up my suitcase and Rahmi grabs the other one.

"Goodnight, you guys," she calls.

Back in Rahmi's room—our room—I can see it's going to be a challenge to fit the clothes I brought back. I misjudged how little space there was here.

"We'll make it work," Rahmi says, watching me mentally reorganize the closet and become more and more frustrated. "Come here for a second."

I toss a garment bag aside and go sit next to him on the bed.

"How was Cleveland?" he asks, taking my hand.

I'm not sure what tipped my emotions, but for some reason I start to cry. I didn't see it coming. I'm worried this will scare Rahmi, but he just puts his hand on my back and doesn't say anything. I can't stop and now I'm hardly able to take a breath. In the back of my mind I know this should be humiliating, that I'm a grown man, but Rahmi's watching me with such kindness that I stop worrying about it. After a minute I'm able to catch my breath, but I won't be able to explain. I can't make sense of anything.

"I don't know what to do."

"About what?" Rahmi's voice is smooth and low.

I shake my head. "I just wanted to move on, you know? I thought I could get out of Cleveland and forget. Start again. But . . . I don't think I can ever really get out."

"What happened with Austin?"

"Roger dropped the charges. Or he will."

"Really?" He frowns. "But that's great."

"It is," I say, "but . . ."

Rahmi takes my hand again. "What is it?"

My blurry eyes blink him back into clarity. "There's something I need you to know."

"Okay."

"Remember what I told you, about my dad?"

"Yeah." I see his jaw tense.

"Well, in college, when I was seeing Mr. Everett, it was because I couldn't remember anything." My heart's thudding in my chest now and I falter. I'm revealing too much. "I mean, I knew I had this anger and this anxiety," I say, staring at my hands, "but I didn't know what was behind it. It was there, in the museum, that I started to remember."

"So, your dad . . . ," Rahmi trails off. "He had changed?"

I nod. "He'd gone to anger management, then my mom took him back."

"But you didn't remember that?"

"No." I look down. Rahmi doesn't want to hear all this. I sound crazy. "I only remembered how he was when he came back."

"Geez. I didn't know that could happen."

I take a deep breath. "But when it all came back," I say, "I didn't want to go home. I told Mr. Everett I couldn't go back. But he said I should talk to him, at least. Try to reconcile."

"Did you?"

"I tried." My voice lowers, and my hands are shaking now. "But we ended up arguing. I called him an asshole and he punched me. I tried to stand up for myself, but that made it worse. He just let go on me."

Rahmi holds my hand a little tighter.

As hard as it is, I look at his face. "Rahmi," I murmur, "I got his gun, and I shot him."

Rahmi's expression doesn't change.

I wait for it to sink in, but he doesn't move. I feel horrible, like I'm confessing to the police and they doubt everything I say. I feel like a murderer. But I keep talking. I can't take it back now, anyway.

"I gave him so many warnings," I continue, starting to cry again. "I didn't want to do it at all. But he wasn't ever going to stop." I wipe my eyes on my sleeve. "He died. He died that day because of me."

Just as my worry increases because Rahmi's still not saying anything or nodding or even moving at all, he wraps his arms around me. He breathes in with his face pressed against my head and holds me like I might crumble if he lets go. Maybe I will.

After three or four minutes, he lets go. I look at his face and see he's been crying as well. He runs a hand through my hair.

"This is why you need the lights on at night?"

I nod.

Rahmi shakes his head a little. "Murray, I don't know what to say. I can't believe that happened to you." He grabs the tissues from the nightstand and hands a few to me. "I'm glad you told me, though, and that you trust me. I want to do whatever I can to help you."

71

It's the nicest thing he could have said, but for some reason I don't feel better. I feel worse.

"That means a lot," I tell him.

His eyes are still cloudy, and troubled.

"It's all right, though," I add, "if you need some time with it. I know it's hard to hear. I've had ten years with it and it's still hard."

Rahmi nods. "What's hard for me is now I have a better picture of what your life was like before," he says. "I feel like I know you pretty well, and it must have gone against every part of you to do something like that. I'm just glad you don't have to deal with your father again."

"Thanks." I rub my sweaty hands onto my pants. "I was worried you'd think of me differently."

"If anything, I'm even more impressed you're a functional member of society." He smiles, but sadness lingers behind it.

It will take him some time; I understand that. And I wish his words were true, but every day I feel like I'm slipping further back into dysfunction, smothering all the torches that once lit my path.

Chapter 17
Pseudotherapy

I'm on edge the next two weeks, expecting Roger to call. About a week after I'd left Cleveland, I heard from John and Austin that the charges were dropped, but nothing from Roger. Every time the phone rings my veins jolt, because I'm sure this is it. But it's usually Greg calling for Grace, sometimes Rahmi's parents guilting him into working more hours at the restaurant, sometimes John or Austin.

When he does call, though, I'm glad. I'm tired of losing sleep over this and I just want to know what he expects. I want to get it over with.

I'm walking in the door after my session with Lamar when the phone rings. I'm not in a great mood because Lamar, rather than congratulating me on getting Austin off the hook, was wary of my deal with Roger and convinced Austin would have more violent outbursts down the line. I let my bag fall to the kitchen floor and grab the phone on the third ring.

"Hello," I say. I rub my forehead with my other hand.

"Wow, Murray," Roger replies. "Did you know it was me? You already sound pissed."

"I always think it's you," I say, more annoyed than I expected. "What took you so long? Is it like the waiting room—you're just trying to punish me?"

He laughs. "You're over-thinking this. I'm a busy guy. And I've had some legal shit to deal with, remember?"

"I remember." I pull a beer out of the fridge and sit at the table.

"Anyway," he says, "I've been keeping some notes, just random thoughts and questions as they come to me." He pauses and I picture him sitting at his desk, dividing his attention between me and Duke Nukem. "I thought we could do about twenty minutes today. You know, see how it goes."

"How many times do I have to do this?" I demand, unable to keep the disgust out of my voice.

"What?"

"How many times do I need to talk to you before we're even?"

"Let's see," he says, sounding annoyed himself. "How about one week for every punch I took from Austin? That seem fair?"

My hands clench but I refuse to let him get the best of me.

"So, what, two weeks then?"

He laughs. "Six, my friend. Want to see my medical records?"

"No, thanks."

"So, we have a deal?"

"You want to talk every week for six weeks?"

"Well . . ." He pauses and I can picture him smirking. "I was thinking twice a week."

"Oh, come on," I say. "That's bullshit, Roger."

"Is it? Without this deal your friend would be going to jail. I think it's the least you can do."

I sigh and scratch my fingernail over the top of the table. "What about once a week for nine weeks?"

"Murray," he says with amusement, "what are you afraid of? The hard part is over. You just have to let me in on your experience."

"So you can make money?"

"No."

"Then what? What are you getting from this? It's sick."

I don't hear anything on his end for a few seconds and I'm worried I went too far and ruined the deal. I close my eyes. I know I sound unreasonable. What he's asking for isn't so bad; I just can't stomach doing it with him. Roger's become a sore point, and combining him with lengthy discussions about my past sounds excruciating. I open my eyes. And he tells me the hard part's over.

"Okay," he says. "Let's try once a week. Maybe I'll get what I need in nine weeks."

What I need.

"All right." I frown. It's not like Roger to give in on anything.

"Good." He punches a few computer keys, then rustles some paper. "Okay," he mutters. "So, how many sessions did it take you to first feel something?"

"Feel something?"

"Yeah, like, to know it was going to help."

"Well," I say, my stomach pitching, "I mean, I felt different right away. After the first session."

"That soon?" He sounds skeptical.

"Yeah. It wasn't just the glass, though. It was Mr. Everett." I blink a few times. It's always hard to remember him, and know he's gone for good. Our time together was a bright spot in my shitty life, and I can see now just how valuable that was. Having Mr. Everett—the one person who knew the worst about me but still cared—who knew I could be better—wasn't just comforting, it was lifesaving.

"Right."

"But you were seeing him, too," I say, confused. "You told me something like five years, right?"

"Sure, but that was just for fun."

"Until the end. You were going for therapy at the end."

"I've got to tell you," he says, "it's a little annoying that I have no memory of you from Ash's funeral, but you seem to remember every detail of our conversation."

"Yeah, it is annoying. I guess that day just meant more to me."

"I was also on Vicodin a lot back then." More typing. "So, there's that."

"What exactly do you want to know?"

"Everything," he says. "How did you get relief so fast? What did you do in the rooms? What did you think about?"

"I didn't get relief that fast," I tell him. "I felt different, and I knew it was something I wanted to do again, but I was still a wreck."

"Okay."

"I wasn't comfortable at first. I had to work up to it. When I had my first room, I was scared. It felt wrong, destroying everything. But each time got easier, and soon I didn't even think about it. I thought about everything else."

I close my eyes. Flashes of light fill my vision. The bare room. The dots of blood on my shaking hands. Mr. Everett offering to help me up.

"But if you uncovered repressed memories while you were there, what were you thinking about? Why did you start going in the first place?"

It's a fair question, but I have to fight the urge to tell him it's none of his business. That if he seemed to care even an infinitesimal amount for Mr. Everett and his museum, I'd be much happier to share the details about my life. But I remember Austin, and where he'd be.

"I started," I say, "because I was angry and anxious, and I didn't know why."

"You couldn't get help from a real therapist?"

"What the fuck does that mean?"

"You know what I mean," Roger replies. "Ash was a great guy, but he wasn't a doctor. Not even close. I'm just wondering if you tried other therapy before you went to him."

"It's complicated," I say, digging at my already shredded cuticles. "I didn't want my parents to know I was seeking treatment. I saw a counselor at my university, but she's the one who recommended Mr. Everett. Her brother had seen him. And I couldn't have afforded to go anywhere else."

"She thought you needed something different."

"Yeah."

"And how long did it take you to recover your memories?"

"Until my last session. About four months."

"Okay," he murmurs. I get the feeling he's writing, and it's making me nervous. "I'm going to assume these were memories about your father."

"Right."

"So, what, he just didn't like you?"

"Why are you being such a dick?" I snap. "You think that's helpful?"

"Whoa, calm down. I'm trying to understand where you're coming from."

"This isn't relevant."

"Come on, Murray," he says. "You think we're going to go nine weeks without getting into this stuff? I need all the information I can get so I can figure out why the glass helped you."

And not me. I guess that's what he's trying to say.

"All right, fine." I lean back and sigh. "One thing I remembered was him breaking my arm."

More papers rustling. "Why?"

"He needed to be in control, always," I say, taking a fast guzzle of beer and hoping to slow my racing heart. "And kids don't always stay in line."

"You seem like somebody who'd follow the rules, though."

"Not always."

"He was a police officer, right?"

My muscles tense. I'd forgotten about the report. "Yeah, that's right."

"So maybe he also brought that mentality home with him."

It doesn't matter that he's trying for once to be helpful or that he's right; hearing Roger propose theories about my family dynamic is making my skin crawl.

"Roger," I say, "let's talk about the glass."

"All right." He coughs a few times. "You had issues with anger and violence, right? So, Ash thought you'd be a good fit for his therapy because you already had destructive tendencies?"

I see Mr. Everett scribbling on his yellow legal pad, occasionally staring past me with a pensive frown as he searched for the right words. *Destructive tendencies.* That fit me perfectly, but it wasn't what he saw.

"No." I shake my head. "No, that wasn't it at all. I mean, I don't think anybody knows if the glass will work for them until they try it. It could have easily gone the other way for me."

"Yeah." He sounds a little disappointed.

I take a slow breath. "How many counseling sessions were you able to have with Mr. Everett before he died?" I ask.

I know this crosses a line, asking Roger about his personal life. It means we're in this together, and I'm not sure I'm ready for that. But I can tell he's hiding something, too, and it's such hell to live in the shadows that I wouldn't even wish it on Roger.

"Not many. Maybe three?"

"Okay," I say, rubbing my eyes. "Roger, I think that's what you're missing. I mean, the glass was intense and different, and it helped, but I wouldn't have gotten anywhere without Mr. Everett. He knew what was going on before I did. And he never made me feel like I was crazy."

"Hey, listen," Roger says sharply, "I appreciate the thought, but you just let me collect the information, and I'll figure out what to do with it, all right?"

"Fine."

"Okay." A drawer slams in the background. "I think that's good for today."

Chapter 18
Go Home, Denver

I refuse to go to JW Market on Sullivan, even though it's close and Rahmi swears by it. He's addicted to their deli sandwiches, but I never understood the draw, and everything there is overpriced. So, I walk a little farther to shop at the Grab&Go on Sixth. I'm there today because it's my turn to get the basic groceries for the week.

It's a Sunday afternoon, cold and gray, and I rub my hands together to keep warm as I peruse the milk selection. Grace likes whole and Rahmi likes skim, so I get two percent because that feels like a compromise. I'm nearing the end of the aisle, on my way to find peanut butter, when I hear a familiar voice. A familiar, angry tone. About halfway down the aisle across from me is Jemma, even more foreboding in daylight, with crazy spiked pigtails and enormous black combat boots. She's arguing with some guy, backing him into the rows of chips even though she must be a foot shorter than he is. Her words are hushed and desperate.

The guy is maybe ten years older than Jemma and looks normal. He's dressed for a nice office job, sharp haircut, no piercings or tattoos that I can see. He's losing patience, though. He's shaking his head and rolling his eyes while she continues to hiss something at him, then he grabs her wrist. It's so sudden I jump a little. He's serious now and he must be squeezing her pretty hard because her eyes are widening and she's telling him to stop. My heart's thudding now because I have to help her. I set my basket on the floor and walk down their aisle, ready to do something, though I'm not sure what, when he lets go and she runs off. He's still there, pretending to scan the chips. Jemma's already out the front door, so I run after her, bumping my shoulder into the guy as I pass.

"Jemma, wait!" I call as I push through the front door of Grab&Go.

There are lots of people on the street, but she's easy to spot. I sprint ahead until I catch up with her.

"Jemma," I say again, out of breath. "Are you all right?"

She turns around and her eyes are red and glowering. I can tell she's already wiped them because there's a smear of mascara trailing from her eyelid up to her temple. She scowls at me.

"Leave me alone."

"Is that guy going to bother you again?"

"What the fuck? Are you stalking me?" She fumbles in her pocket, then pulls out a cigarette. "Just fuck off."

I watch as she lights the cigarette with a shaky hand. She turns and walks back down the sidewalk. Again, I run after her.

"Jemma, wait. One more thing."

"What?" she snarls, spinning back around.

I gesture to the store. "Did you need something from there?"

"No." She takes a drag. "I was supposed to get paid, and now he needs more time."

I nod and she shakes her head.

"Just go home, Denver."

I smile. "Cleveland."

"Whatever."

I study Jemma's ratty clothes—a gray plaid shirt that looks like a worn hand-me-down, the patched-up combat boots, and what I'm pretty sure are the same dirty black jeans I've seen her wearing every other time we've crossed paths. She doesn't keep any groceries in the kitchen at our apartment, so I don't know if she's unable to buy food, but she looks like she's lost weight. And her hands won't stop shaking.

"Do you need some money?" I ask. "You know, until the guy can pay you?"

She had been in mid-turn, ready to leave again, but that stops her. She narrows her eyes. "Not in a million years."

"I'm just trying to help."

She lets out a short scornful laugh and leans in close. "Don't make me into your goddamn project," she says in a low voice. "I don't like you, and I don't need your money."

Jemma turns and walks away before I can respond, but I don't know what I'd say anyway. It feels like she's heard it all before. I watch her for a minute, then turn the other way, back to the Grab&Go.

Chapter 19
Murray Surprises Rahmi

Rahmi's sister is getting married today. We've all felt it, this past week, the tension and heaviness as Rahmi slogs around the apartment, sometimes mumbling bits of conversation but mostly working on school and watching television. The restaurant has been closed for the last few days and will be for two more, but sometimes it seems he'd be better off working, with fewer idle moments to think about how his only sister abandoned him.

I get up before Rahmi and slip out of our room, closing the door behind me. Grace is already at the kitchen table, drinking coffee and doing homework. We're often the first ones up, and have similar morning routines. We like coffee first thing, so we see each other the way we are today, in flannel pajama pants and wrinkled T-shirts, with disheveled hair and groggy eyes. I pour myself a cup and tell her hi, then head toward the living room to give her space to work, but she stops me.

"You can come sit," she says, closing her book. "I need a break."

"What are you working on?" I ask, moving back to the table and sitting down.

"Biochem." She sighs. "It'll all be worth it, though, right?"

"Well, for me, yeah. I'll be coming to you with all my mystery rashes."

She smiles and tosses the book into her bag, then goes back to her coffee. I take a drink, my mind returning to Rahmi. Grace pulls her long, voluminous hair into a ponytail, watching me. "So, today's the day, huh?"

"Yeah." I glance back toward our room. "I wish I could make it easier for him."

Grace gets up and pulls a box of Froot Loops off the top shelf. She sits back down, eating the cereal out of the box.

"You guys should go out," she says, crunching. "Take his mind off it."

"Yeah. You're right."

I'd actually been trying to think of something to do for him all week. I'm not very good at being romantic, and I'd hate to make his day worse. I tried to surprise Dani once when we were dating. It was her birthday and I made reservations at a new Spanish place downtown. I got us lost on the way, then sideswiped a parked car while illegally U-turning. We were so late we lost the reservation and ended up eating at the Arby's down the street.

"It doesn't have to be hard," Grace is saying. "Take him to a nice restaurant. What's that place he likes so much?"

"Shuka? Yeah, I thought about that."

"You could see a movie. You know, nothing too serious."

"Right." I nod. "I'll have to see what kind of mood he's in."

She gives me a look. "Sad bastard is going to be the kind of mood he's in," she says. "It's been his mood all week."

I shake my head. "It makes me crazy, what Seda's doing to him."

"I know. But you can't change her mind. And after today, he can move on."

"Yeah, I hope so." I rub my forehead.

"So, what about you?" Grace asks, stuffing her hand back in the cereal box. "You've got brothers, right?"

"Right . . ."

"Are they cool with you being gay?"

I laugh, but I shouldn't be surprised. Grace likes everything out in the open. And she's one of the few people I don't mind discussing this with.

"Well," I say with a smile, "I'm not exactly gay—I date girls, too. And I was dating only girls when I lived at home."

"But they know you're into guys, too, right?"

"One of them does. I don't talk to my oldest brother."

"Oh, yeah?" She leans forward a bit. "What happened there?"

I still smile, but I can't let this go much further. "He's not a very nice guy," I say. "There's a lot we don't agree on."

"Okay." She nods. "I'm sorry to hear that."

"Thanks." I reach over and grab a handful of Froot Loops. "But my other brother, Jake, he's great. Totally supportive. We're just not as close as we use to be. Same goes for all of my family, I guess."

Grace sets aside her cereal box and places her hands on the table in front of her, like she's got a lot to say on the subject and I'm about to hear it, when we hear a door close down the hall. Rahmi trudges into the room without glancing up at us, then makes his way to the living room where he collapses on the couch. I get up to pour him some coffee.

"I'm going to go take a shower," Grace says.

I nod and she walks the long way around the room, behind the couch, squeezing Rahmi's shoulder before disappearing down the hall. I take the two cups over to the couch and sit down next to Rahmi, handing him one.

"Thanks," he says, still staring into space.

"You want some cereal?" I ask, gesturing to the box still on the kitchen table.

He shakes his head.

I glance around the room, wanting to say something that would help. "It's supposed to snow later," I say. "Maybe we could take a walk in it."

"Sure," he replies. He takes a drink of coffee and gives me a halfhearted smile.

"Do you have much homework this weekend?"

"Not really. Just some reading and a short research paper."

I nod. "That's good."

"You know what's funny?" he asks suddenly, with a disdainful laugh that lets me know it won't be funny at all. "The guy Seda's marrying isn't a traditional match. He's not anybody my parents would have wanted for her. He's a Catholic Midwestern white guy."

"Hey, you've got one of those," I say, attempting to make him laugh or at least smile, but he just shakes his head.

"The hardest part is she believes she's right. She thinks I'm the unreasonable one."

"I know. But it's not true. And maybe she'll understand someday."

"Maybe."

I touch his arm. "I'm really sorry."

"Thanks." He slumps against the back of the couch.

I feel such sickening pain for him, and I wish there were anything I could do. I survey the drab, dimly lit apartment, depressing in its own right, with nothing much to distract but homework and television. I look out the window at the gray sky, the cold, severe buildings, and people swarming around in knit hats and heavy coats. I get an idea, and glance over at Rahmi, wondering if he'd go for it.

"What?" he asks, giving me a wary look.

"We should go out. Get a change of scenery."

"Where?" He doesn't sound thrilled.

"We could go to lunch first. Maybe Shuka?"

"I don't know. I might not be up for it." He frowns. "And what do you mean, 'first'?"

"Well, I want to go somewhere else after, but it's a surprise."

"A surprise?"

"I'll be honest," I say, trying to gauge his degree of aversion, "I don't have a great track record with these things. Others tend to suffer when I plan surprises, but . . . I think you should trust me."

He smiles a little. "Are you going to know how to get there?"

"I might have to look at a map, but I'm pretty sure it involves the D train."

He turns away, but I can tell he's still smiling. "Okay," he says finally, facing me again. "I guess I'll trust you."

We hold hands to the subway station, and I try to make Rahmi laugh as we ride to Shuka, but his mood has deflated again. He tells me we should go somewhere else if there's a wait, but that would only make things worse. As we walk up to the front door, though, I'm encouraged to see few people in the lobby, and we end up getting seated within about ten minutes.

As Rahmi mopes through lunch, I have the disheartening thought that coming here, to his favorite restaurant, on such a difficult day, might ruin it for him forever. I catch his eye and smile.

"You want another drink?"

He looks down at his empty glass and shrugs. "Sure."

I flag down the waiter and order another beer for Rahmi and another rum and Coke for me. I push the thought out of my mind.

After lunch I check the map at the subway station. I was right and all we have to do is take the D train to the last stop. Rahmi doesn't even pay attention as we get on and find a seat. After a few stops, though, I get him talking about one of the books he's reading for class, and he perks up.

We ride the last ten or fifteen minutes in silence. I look out the window as we pass an old car wash, empty warehouses, sickly-looking trees, all against a dreary gray backdrop. I glance at Rahmi. This was a bad idea. He's watching the young man lying down on the bench across from us, asleep. The boy next to him, maybe ten or eleven, is reading the graffiti on the walls while his mother sorts through an accordion file of coupons.

When our stop arrives, only a few people are left to get off the train. Rahmi's still preoccupied as we walk through the tunnel, down the stairs, and out of the station. We finally reach the street and the cold wind hits us with brutal force. It appears to jog Rahmi out of his thoughts, and he looks around. I can see he's confused, but I can't imagine he doesn't know where we are. Even I recognize it.

"So . . . ," I say, smiling. "What do you think?"

I gaze up at the Ferris wheel. It's impressive, but I assumed it would be lit up. I frown. And moving.

Rahmi laughs. "Coney Island? In February?"

"Sure," I say, lowering my eyes to meet his. "I mean, it's cold, but it'll be great. You like the rides, right?"

He starts laughing again, a tickled, genuine laugh, but this time he can't stop. He tries to say something a couple of times but can't catch his breath. I look around, coming to understand. It's so good to see him happy, though, I don't even care that I've done something stupid. I start laughing, too.

"Murray," he says after a moment, his eyes sparkling with tears, "you didn't know they close it in the winter?"

"I thought New Yorkers didn't care about weather." I look up again. "Really—all winter?"

Rahmi makes an incredulous face like I'm going to set him laughing again, but he opens his arms and gives me a long, unyielding hug. "You're just the cutest," he says. "Yes, it's closed all winter. For, like, seven months, actually."

"That's too bad. I wanted to go on those rides."

"You think people want to ride the Cyclone in twenty-degree weather?"

I shrug. "Maybe if they weren't such pathetic babies."

He smiles and takes my hand. "We can still walk along the boardwalk."

A few snowflakes are already swirling around the frigid air as we walk east toward Brighton Beach. There are still plenty of people out, but most of them appear to be hurrying to a destination, rather than meandering around for fun. We pass the kitschy shops and food stands and attractions, and Rahmi's telling me stories of when he'd come here as a kid. For a moment I worry again that I'm spoiling memories for him, but his voice is light and his eyes are warm, and I realize he's having a good time sharing his past with me.

We don't make it to Brighton Beach for about an hour because we stop at all the sights along the way. We're both freezing—we each have a good coat, but neither of us has gloves, and Rahmi's old hat isn't much better than a thin sweatshirt hood. We stop in a little Greek place that claims to serve great falafel, but we're still full from lunch, so we both order coffee. We settle into a small booth and I smile at Rahmi, blowing hot air into my chapped hands. He smiles back.

"I'm sorry," he says, "for being such a drag earlier. I got caught up feeling sorry for myself, I guess."

"Nothing to be sorry about. None of this is easy."

"You made it a lot easier," he remarks as the waitress sets down our coffees. He takes a drink, wincing like it's stronger than he expected. "Now

I'm starting to think about getting through it—like maybe it doesn't have to follow me for the next five years."

"That's great."

"Thank you," he says, his expression serious. "Your attempt to ride roller coasters in February is exactly what I needed."

I laugh. "I have a feeling I'll be hearing about this for a long time."

"I'd bet on it." He leans back against the torn vinyl booth.

We stay for another fifteen minutes, talking and drinking coffee. I'm guessing Rahmi's in no hurry to get back outside, either; the snow is coming down hard now, and the wind off the Atlantic is whipping it into fleeting white tornadoes.

"Should we catch the subway down here?" I ask. "There's another station, right?"

"There is, but we should walk back the way we came."

"You want to walk another mile up the boardwalk?" I point to the window. "In that?"

Rahmi gives me a look. "You realize if you had your way we'd be on the Wonder Wheel right now?"

"Is that the Ferris wheel?"

"Yep." He stands up and zips his coat, then pulls his hat down over his head. "Come on, we can get another coffee to go."

"All right," I say, unable to help smiling.

I'll have to tell him sometime how many of our days started out hard for me, too. That he's the one who always pulls me out when I'm not sure anything can. We push out the door, bowing our heads to meet the rushing wind. He takes my hand and it doesn't even matter that we'll be hypothermic by the time we reach our apartment. Maybe I have a future in surprises after all.

Chapter 20
Under Control

"I'm glad things are going so well," Lamar says, but I can tell he's not getting on board yet.

"Yeah," I say. "And the job's working out. There's this big event at the library next month: Pro Bono Week. It's a lot of work, and my boss is already a wreck about it, but everything's going well. I feel like I'm living here now. Not just killing time until I fail and have to go back home."

"You were expecting to fail?"

I almost answer right away but stop myself. It feels like a trick question. I glance around the room, its formal, professional appearance—like Lamar's—sharply contrasting my own raggedness. I guess I never did move beyond the schlubby indifference of my teenage years. Looks just weren't something I could afford to dwell on. I scratch my arm under my sweatshirt and pretend like I can't feel Lamar watching me.

"There were so many moving parts," I finally say. "Even if the job ended up working out, something about the apartment could fall through. Or I'd miscalculate my budget and run out of money. Or they'd need me back in Cleveland."

"John or Austin?"

I nod. "It's stupid, though. They're the ones who have always taken care of me."

"But they needed you when Austin was in trouble," he reminds me.

"That was pretty crazy, though. A one-time thing."

Lamar shrugs and crosses his arms. He's not behind his desk today. He's sitting in the upholstered chair across from me. It feels more casual, but he still has his notepad with him. "If they did ask you to," he says, "would you go back? For good?"

I think for a moment. "I don't know. I mean, they're my best friends. And Austin ..."

"What about Austin?"

"There aren't a lot of people who understand what he's going through. John and I get it, though. I get the anger, John gets Vietnam."

"But I bet that's hard—being around him when he's angry."

"Sure." I nod, a few memories flashing through my mind.

"Really hard, I'd imagine." He taps his pen against the notepad while he watches me. "Has he ever gotten violent with you?"

"Austin? No. I mean, he's yelled and hit tables and walls and things like that, but he's never been mad at me. Not like that. And sometimes I can help him through it."

"Do you ever worry you'll be in the wrong place at the wrong time, though? That he'll take his anger out on you if you happen to be in his way?"

I open my mouth to speak but can't form the words. I don't want to say anything against Austin, but I've thought about it. I lived nineteen years with a man like that and sometimes I worry a part of me might seek that out again. But then I feel sick and ashamed because Austin's not like that. He's not like that at all.

"Should we move on?" Lamar's looking at me and I'm sure he's already written down everything he inferred by my silence, so I nod.

He frowns and looks through his notes. He flips page after page like he's trying to find something, but it must have been several weeks ago. Finally, he looks up. "Murray, why did you go see Roger, after the flyer came?"

"Roger?" I ask, confused. "Because he started the glass place. You don't remember?"

"I do." Lamar smiles. "I'm just trying to get a little more specific. So, you went down there because you were angry?"

"That's right."

"But at the poker game a few days before," he says, checking his notes again, "you said you weren't sure how to feel about it. You couldn't think it through because of how Austin was reacting."

"Sure, but after a couple of days it started to bother me."

"Were you pretty angry as you rode down to see Roger?"

I stare past him, thinking. "No," I say. "It wasn't until I saw him, and the place."

"Okay." Lamar nods. He writes a few quick notes on his pad. "Can I tell you what I think is going on?"

"Okay."

"I think you spend most of your mental and emotional energy trying to keep people from getting upset."

I'm not sure what he's getting at, so I wait for him to continue.

"I think," he says, leaning forward, "you went to see Roger because you were trying to avoid any more outbursts from Austin. He really scared you that night with the flyer, and maybe you thought you could take care of things with Roger yourself, and fix the problem for Austin."

"That's not what I thought I was doing."

"I know," Lamar replies. He turns back to his notes. "That's the major one, but I see small examples of it all over. You asked Austin to tell John you'd moved to New York. And with Rahmi, it seems like whenever he gets upset about his sister, you try to distract him."

"Hey," I snap, the heat rushing to my ears, "I was being a good boyfriend. You think it's bad that I don't want him to be in pain?"

"Not at all," Lamar says. "But we've talked about a lot of things in here. And I've noticed again and again that you're unable to handle negative emotions. It's not just that you want Rahmi to overcome his pain, it's that you can't handle being around it in the first place."

"That makes me sound like a selfish asshole," I mutter.

"I don't mean it to," Lamar says. "It's nothing wrong with you, lots of people do it, but it's exhausting living on the defensive like that. Letting other people's emotions carry so much weight."

"So, every time I think I'm helping somebody, I'm just trying to help myself?" I didn't mean to sound bitter, but at the hardness of my voice Lamar pauses and looks at me.

"Every time you think you're helping somebody, you are helping somebody," he says. "I just want you to feel less fear while you're doing it."

"I wasn't feeling fear."

Lamar folds his hands in front of him. "When Rahmi talks about his sister, do you ever feel your heart rate increase?" He raises his eyebrows. "Do you heat up, even sweat? Do you watch him for signs he's getting too upset? Does your stomach bother you?"

I don't answer and he leans back.

"How about when you have to give bad news to John or Austin? Or telling your boss that your work is going to be late?"

I lean back as well and cross my arms.

"It makes sense," Lamar says. "In childhood you were conditioned to fear negative emotions. They're unpredictable. So as an adult, you react to that negativity, doing your best to calm things before they turn violent." He holds up his hand when he sees I'm going to protest. "Even if you *know* violence won't occur in a situation, it's your instinct preparing you for the worst case."

I sit back again and sigh. I'm not sure why this is upsetting me. Objectively, it doesn't seem that noteworthy to hear I'm motivated by fear, but now my insides are churning and my mouth is dry.

"So, what do I do?" I demand. "How do I fix it?"

"It isn't like that," he says, shaking his head. "You're looking for an off-switch that doesn't exist. You want so badly to get away from these difficult feelings that you're willing to trade long-term progress for temporary relief."

"Okay, fine," I reply, shifting in my chair to stop my leg from jittering, "how do I get long-term progress?"

Lamar narrows his eyes at me like he's trying to make sure I'm ready for what he's about to say.

"You need to stop thinking of yourself as the guy with the anger problem." He lets out a breath. "You need to stop believing there is some defect inside you that takes over when you have an outburst. I know you feel like you have no control sometimes," he says, "but that also gives you a way out of the responsibility of owning your actions. You are in control. You don't have to let that fear turn into anger, and you certainly don't have to let that anger turn into violence."

I don't like the way this sounds—like I'm doing it on purpose. I look up and the clock says we still have ten minutes, but I can't talk anymore about it now. I'll say everything wrong. And whatever Lamar says, I'll take it badly.

"Can we do this next week?" I ask.

He nods. "Sure." He glances at his watch. "Do you want to talk about anything else?"

I shake my head. "I need some time," I say, standing up.

I sling my bag over my shoulder. I mutter a goodbye and trudge out the door I'd felt so good walking through only a short time ago. It doesn't take long and it doesn't take much.

Chapter 21
The Same Mistakes

I'm agitated, and pissed at Lamar, so I'm glad to walk into the apartment and find it empty. I take three beers from the refrigerator, mumbling to myself about young show-off counselors as I make my way to the couch. I drink the first one in no time, and feel a little better as I turn on the television and pop the cap off the second. I try to think about what Lamar was saying, but I can't focus with the soap operas blaring, so I click the power button and close my eyes.

I breathe.

I finish the second beer and open the third.

I use my anger as an excuse.

I'm trying, but I can't see what Lamar sees and it's making my breath come faster. My face heats up and my head pounds. It's so easy for him, the way he judges my life. The way he ingests a few key details and spews out a diagnosis. I open my eyes. Must be nice.

My hand shakes as I grab my beer off the table. I take a slow drink, no longer even trying to control my building rage. I set the bottle down, hard. Lamar is so full of shit. I wipe my mouth with my sleeve. He doesn't know me. He thinks I'm trying to get out of taking responsibility, but he's wrong. I don't have to see him; it's not like I've been ordered to. I'm trying to get help, and he's just making it harder.

I take another long drink. And he's been out of school, what, two years? Three? What the fuck does he know?

This time I slam the bottle down. The bottom breaks, and beer glugs out onto the table. I watch it flow, not doing anything to stop it. My eyes sting and I know I'm moving backward. I look at the rest of the bottle still in my hand. I smash it into the table, as hard as I can. I'd forgotten this feeling: power combined with weightlessness. It satisfies something at my core. The two empty bottles fall over from the reverberation, so I pick them up, too.

I slam one down even harder than the first. Then I do it again. I lift my left hand and it's bleeding. I'm not sure what I expected, but I see the blood and start crying.

My dad used to say if blood is the worst thing you see, be grateful. I know now he must have been picturing his friends in Vietnam—guys who were killed in front of him. And sometimes it helped. It made sense when I fell off my bike, and when I got hit in the face with Matthew's football. It even made me feel better when my sled careened into a tree. But when he broke my nose for scratching his car, or when I failed to be invisible after a long shift, and his wedding ring left a crescent-shaped scar below my eye, those words felt more like a jeer. *Be grateful. I could do so much worse to you, kiddo.* Maybe that's what he wanted me to remember.

I wipe my eyes, leave the shattered mess for now, and walk to the kitchen sink. I run cold water over my hand until enough blood washes away for me to see the glass shards embedded in my skin. I pull them out and wrap my hand in a dishtowel. It's better than I thought. I walk back to the living room, glancing at the clock. I should be alone for a few more hours. I can clean this place up and no one will know. Like it never happened.

The bleeding has slowed, so I put a few Band-Aids on the cuts and use the dishtowel to start cleaning. I slide the beer and glass off the coffee table and into the trash can I brought in from the kitchen. I scrub the table with soap and water, trying to get that heavy smell out of the air. I crawl around the floor on my hands and knees, determined to find every last shard of glass, even though it's impossible. Some have even scattered across the room, in the nook where Grace now sleeps. I get out the little handheld vacuum and scour the floor, every few seconds rewarded with a rattling sound. But it's not enough. I run my hands over the carpet. I don't want anyone stepping on this shit weeks later. I pick up a few crumbs. I need them to be gone, all of them. Erased. Like it never happened.

I lift my head and sit up on my knees. My vision's cloudy but I'm putting it together. That's what he's saying. I rub my forehead. Lamar. He said losing control gives me a way out. If I set aside my knee-jerk, fuck-you reaction, I start to see it. My pattern. I want to flip my shit, then pretend like nothing happened. I want a satisfying release without its logical consequences.

I put the vacuum away and slide down onto the couch. My anger's gone, replaced by burning nausea. I bury my face in my hands. I'm sick. But even thinking that is part of my problem. Just like Lamar said. I think I'm sick, defective, hosting a toxic black shard of my father's DNA, and I can separate myself from it. It's no longer my fault. I look up and blink to clear my vision. I still can't see the plan. I can't see any way to get from my selfish bullshit to long-term progress. And I don't think this is what Lamar signed up for.

Chapter 22
Police Mentality

I fall asleep on the couch. It's not even dark yet. I awaken to the deafening slam of the front door and the sound of whistling. I open my eyes and hear a bag hit the kitchen floor. My heart pounds as I remember. I'm not done. I didn't mean to fall asleep and I've left clues to my breakdown everywhere.

"Murray?" Grace walks into the living room, frowning. "Did you spill beer in here or something? It smells awful."

I sit up, rubbing my face and trying to think. A sharp pain divides my attention. My hand is hot and throbbing, and blood has seeped out from under the bandages.

"Yeah," I say. I can't even make eye contact with her. "I guess I didn't clean it well enough."

Grace doesn't say anything and after a few seconds I'm forced to look at her, to read her level of judgment. Her arms are crossed, but she doesn't seem mad. There's a little confusion there, but something else as well. Resignation, maybe. She might be about to intervention me.

"What about that?" she asks, indicating my hand. She sits in the chair across from me, right by the trash can I forgot to return to the kitchen.

I turn my hand over a few times. "I cut myself."

Her frown deepens. "Okay, so was—"

Grace is interrupted by a strong knock on the door. She looks thoughtful for a moment, then rises to answer it.

She's talking to someone, and her voice is serious. The door is blocking my view, but a deep voice from the hallway says, "It'll just take a minute." Grace nods and steps to the side, allowing a tall middle-aged police officer to enter our apartment.

My stomach flips and my eyes drop to the floor. I need to get out, but they're both still blocking the door, talking. They're talking about Jemma.

"There've been some complaints about this girl over the past few months," the officer's saying, "and we've now got probable cause to search her place." He produces a piece of paper and shows Grace.

"Murray, you know anything about this?"

I shake my head, unable to look at them. Grace must be annoyed with me now, with my inability to help her out. She lets out a long, exasperated breath.

"You want to show me her room?" the officer asks.

At least Jemma's not home. As usual, I have no idea where she is. Or what condition she's in.

Grace leads him down the hall and I can't take it anymore. They turn the corner and I stumble to the bathroom and throw up. I wasn't ready for him—his stern, businesslike manner and familiar polished uniform. I can hear them talking. It's taking him a minute to open the lock. I rinse out my mouth and change the Band-Aids on my hand.

I make my way back to the living room and grab the trash can, returning it to the kitchen. I sink down onto the couch again. I hear the familiar pop of Jemma's lock, and Grace comes back down the hallway.

"What is going on with you?" she whispers, glancing back toward Jemma's room.

"Is she in there?"

"No. I don't think she's been here for a couple of days."

I look away but I can feel Grace still watching me.

"You're being weird about this guy."

I crack my knuckles. "I don't like him."

"He's not here for you."

She sits and we listen to him digging around the room. After a minute Grace gets up and grabs her bag from the kitchen, saying she has to study. She closes the partition to her nook and leaves me alone. I don't want to fall apart, so I think about everything else—about the trouble Jemma's in, and what Grace was going to say to me before the knock on the door, and Rahmi with his impossible kindness, all while this police officer's presence seeps into my thoughts and wrecks my focus.

After about ten minutes he comes out of Jemma's room with blue latex gloves on, but his hands are empty. His face is grim. I stay on the couch while he walks around the rest of the apartment, but I don't meet his eyes. When he comes into the living room, though, I can't avoid him.

"Mind if I check the couch?" he says, eyeing the cushions.

I stand and move out of his way, forcing my hands into my pockets. He pats the cushions down, lifts them up, then replaces them.

"You're the other roommate, right?" He straightens up and wipes his brow.

"That's right," I murmur. "Murray Henderson."

He comes closer to me and I can read his nameplate. *D. Grant*. His hair is short and silvery brown. He smells like Old Spice. He gets out a little pad and pen, glancing up at me for a moment before he starts writing. I take a step back because I can't be this close to him. I see the gun at his hip and vomit forces its way back up my throat. I close my eyes and try Lamar's breathing technique but I'm afraid it's too late. Officer Grant flips to the next page, then pauses. He looks up.

"You all right, son?" he asks, his voice a little softer.

I nod. "I just—I'm worried about Jemma." My hand is killing me, but I don't want him to notice, so I keep them both in my pockets. "Is she in trouble?"

"Not today," he says, scribbling a few more lines before closing his notebook. "Her room's clean. Looks like the rest of the place is, too."

I do my best to hide my astonishment, but Officer Grant is already looking at me skeptically.

"Do you have any information about illegal habits Ms. Nicholson might have?"

"Nicholson? That's her last name?"

He nods.

"No," I say, shaking my head, "I haven't seen anything like that."

"Okay," he replies, in a neutral way, but I'm reading messages into everything he says and does. I can tell he's hard, I'm guessing former military, like my dad was. He's got the buzz cut, the rough hands, the serious eyes. Maybe I'm being unfair.

"Well, I'm finished here," he says, with a trace of disappointment. "Thanks for your cooperation."

I nod and watch Officer Grant take one more sweeping glance around the apartment. I should say something. But the light glints off his badge and his polished black shoes squeak across the floor, and the words never come. My breath moves fast and I need him to leave.

He walks out the door and I close it behind him. I stand for a few moments before I move to a kitchen chair. I wish I could talk to Rahmi, but he's working and won't be home for another few hours. I still smell the Old Spice. I think about his cold eyes, his gruff voice, the nameplate

A. Henderson

and badge with the light glinting into my eyes. Nausea pumps in the pit of my stomach again, but I've got nothing left to throw up, so I just sit at the table, breathing until it subsides. Grace's partition creaks and she comes over and sits at the table with me.

"That was so weird," she says. She sounds like her old self again, and it kindles a little hope that she doesn't hate me. "He didn't find anything?"

"No. Maybe she knew. I don't know."

"Yeah. I wonder who tipped them off?"

I shrug. "Wasn't me."

She laughs, and I touch my bandages under the table.

Chapter 23
Day Off

On Wednesdays, when my eyes inevitably glaze over during dinner, Grace sometimes asks how I can be so tired when it's my half day at work. I'll say something dumb, like it's because I spent the afternoon going down on Greg—just something to make her laugh—but it makes me think about how much more energy I use during counseling than at work. A half hour with Lamar, a half hour with Roger. Sometimes more. I guess I should be grateful Roger doesn't try to stretch our time out for his own sadistic pleasure. The couple of times we've gone an hour it's seemed like he needed it. I'm not losing track, though; we have four weeks left, and if he hasn't gotten what he needs, he'll have to figure something else out.

This Wednesday, though, I hang around the apartment for an hour, waiting for him to call. I'm already upset because my session with Lamar didn't go well. He says I'm not trying hard enough, pushing myself enough, being honest enough. And now I'm frustrated because I'm supposed to meet Rahmi in Brooklyn at five-thirty—we're eating at Marlow & Sons before we catch a movie. He's been working even harder than I have, and I know he's looking forward to it. I won't let Roger fuck that up.

I grab the phone and open the glasses cabinet. The inside of the cabinet door is filled with notes and numbers we've all taped to it over time. I punch in Roger's number and wait for the ringing, my annoyance tempered by the sinking feeling that he could be lying unconscious in a Vicodin coma. Or in a bright, cold room surrounded by blood and shattered glass. I frown and shake my head, but I can still see it.

I try him twice, both times it goes to the answering machine. He's not in the office.

I go back to the cabinet for his home number. I haven't had to use it yet, and I don't like crossing this line with Roger. I don't want to be part of his personal life. But I look at my watch and it's after four o'clock. I won't leave the apartment feeling like I owe him something. I dial the number.

I'm about to give up by the fourth or fifth ring, but he picks up.

"Hello?" His voice is small, unprepared.

"Roger? What the hell's going on?"

He groans. "Murray?"

"Yeah, of course it's me. You were supposed to call over an hour ago."

There's a faint sigh on the other end. "Huh. I guess so."

"You guess so?" I rub my temple with one hand and grip the phone a little tighter with the other. "Seriously, what's going on?"

"Well, looks like you get a pass this week."

"Why?"

"Just not up to it, I guess."

"Were you going to tell me?"

He clears his throat and I hear him take a drink. "No."

"A free pass? I don't have to add another week onto the end?"

"That's right, Mur," he says. "Three left. Can I go back to bed now?"

I nearly snap at him for calling me Mur, but he sounds so awful I stop myself. It'd be easy to assume he's sick—I'm sure that's what he wants—but that's not the problem. He's forgetting I've been there, too, and he won't get anywhere by hiding. I remember all the times I couldn't bring myself to leave my bed, let alone the house, and my exasperation with Roger softens.

"Think you'll be back to it next week?" I ask, sinking into a kitchen chair.

He laughs. "That's a long time from now."

"Okay. How about I call you then?"

"Whatever you like, champ."

"Roger?" I hesitate a moment. "If you need something before, will you call me?"

"I can suck my own cock, but thanks."

He hangs up and I sit there for a minute, still holding the phone in my hand.

Chapter 24
For People Like You

It's after midnight and I'm awake, again. Rahmi's next to me, asleep, like he's been for the past hour, and I'm getting a little jealous. Even when things are hard, he sleeps well. He's told me that stress tires him out, but I can't wrap my mind around that. It's still a problem, but it's one I'd like to have about now.

I give it another twenty minutes, hoping my mind wears itself out, but I remember Mr. Anders gave me another project I didn't write down. I slide out of bed and sit at the desk where the lamp is always on. Rahmi says he doesn't mind, which is nice of him. I grab my notebook and scribble myself a reminder to arrange for a small business advice booth at Pro Bono Week. I slump a little. This event is going to kill me. It's still over a week away but my mind insists I've already fucked it up.

I flip through the previous pages of notes. Rahmi shifts in his sleep and I glance over, but he settles down again. I haven't told him much about all this—I don't want to add to the strain he's already under from work and school.

I close the notebook and replace it on the desk, knowing I've done all I can for tonight and hoping my brain will also get a sense of finality and let me rest. I walk back across the room to our bed, but stop when I hear a soft click. I stay still, listening. She's gotten good at covering it, but Jemma's home. I look over at Rahmi. My heart beats fast as another stream of thoughts bombards my mind, and I decide I should just go or I won't get any sleep at all. I slip into the hall, closing the door behind me.

"Jemma," I whisper, standing outside her door. Faint light filters underneath, probably from a desk lamp. I knock. "Jemma, I need to talk to you." I stand there a minute. "Jemma, come on." Two minutes. I get annoyed and turn the knob. She must have yanked from the other side at that moment, because the door flings open and I'm faced with a chaotic mess of a room and a rabid-looking Jemma.

"What the fuck?" she hisses, glaring at me with a level of hatred I wasn't ready for. Her eyes are lined in heavy black, and the snagged sweater dress she's wearing hangs off her thin body.

I try to remember what I'm doing, but I've never seen her room and I'm catching glimpses of bizarre shit everywhere.

"Can I come in?" I ask, glancing around her.

She's got a small statue of a peacock on her windowsill. And a copy of *The Satanic Verses* on the floor. Next to a dildo.

"Fuck no," she says, pushing hair out of her eyes.

"Fine." I take a breath, trying to keep my voice low. "The police were here."

"So?"

"The guy, he was looking for you. And whatever shit you keep here. He went through everything."

"Don't worry. They're idiots."

I run my hands through my hair. She's playing a defensive game, trying to protect herself, but my patience is low tonight. And it's her fault he was here. "You're not covering very well, you know?" I say, leaning closer to her. "You got lucky."

Jemma laughs. "I'm more careful than that."

I shake my head and her eyes harden again.

"Don't waste your time on it." She starts to close the door but I move my arm to block it.

"I don't want them back here, all right?"

I keep the door open, holding her gaze so she knows I'm not fucking around. Her burning glare fades after a few seconds, but she doesn't look away.

"What are you hiding, Denver?" she asks. "Coke? Speed? You're afraid of the cops and it seems like you're always awake."

"I'm not on anything." I rub my temple. "And my name's Murray. I'm from Cleveland. If you can read the goddamn *Satanic Verses*, you can get that straight."

Jemma's still watching me with that curious, calculating expression, and I feel like I'm on the losing end of this encounter and should just go back to bed.

"You know what?" I say, holding up my hands. "Just forget I was here."

"I know what you could use," she says, studying my face. "Just something easy to help you sleep. It'll kick the hell out of that anxiety, too."

"What are you talking about?"

"Morphine. Thirty milligrams to start. Six bucks each."

"Jesus." I laugh. "You're out of your mind."

"You won't find a better price."

"I don't want a better price." I wince at the loudness of my voice. "I don't want this at all. I want you to keep it out of here, okay?"

She crosses her arms. "You think he's happy with you like this?" she says, nodding toward Rahmi's door. "Yelling? Strung out? Breaking shit?"

My eyes snap into focus. "What?"

Jemma smiles. "You don't cover very well, either." She looks away for a moment. "This shit is made for people like you, and it could help. That's all I'm saying."

"Listen," I say, my voice lowered again, "you might think you know me, but you don't. I'm not like you. And this isn't for me."

"Okay."

"Okay?"

"Do whatever you want," she says, rolling her eyes. "You always do."

I don't sleep at all the rest of the night. I don't even get back into bed because Rahmi's smooth, peaceful breathing will drive me insane. Instead I bring my notebook to the kitchen table and switch on the faint light above the stove. I slide the chair out slowly, careful not to disturb Grace. I read through my notes. I have to make a few hundred copies tomorrow, confirm site visits, and find a new speaker for the voting rights seminar since ours bailed. I make a note to try Dr. Sheldon; she might help us out. I rub my eyes.

Down the hall, Jemma's mattress creaks as she gets into bed. She'll sleep fine tonight. I stare hard at the words in front of me, but they blur together as I run our conversation through my mind. I would have been okay if she hadn't mentioned Rahmi. But the idea that I'm so unstable even Jemma has concerns about my relationship doesn't sit well with me. I close my notebook and glance over to Grace's corner of the room. I picture the expression on her face when she came home—it was like she didn't even know me. Now I have to worry about both of them telling Rahmi about the glass before I do. If I do.

The next day I don't see Rahmi until after ten p.m. He had an early class, and I was gone by the time he got back. I'm confident in my progress at work today, and Mr. Anders wasn't quite as frantic when I left. I think we can pull this off.

I'm in our room reading when Rahmi comes home, so before I see him I can hear him rummaging around the kitchen. The clinking of bottles tells me he'll need some time to relax before he goes to bed.

"Hey," he says, smiling as he enters the room, two beers in his hand. "Haven't seen you in a while."

I close my book. "I know. Everything's been crazy." I watch him collapse into his desk chair and pop the cap off his first beer. "How was work?"

"Oh, not so good." He smiles a little. "I quit."

I sit up straight. "You quit?"

"Yeah." He takes another drink. "You want this one?" he asks, holding out his other beer.

"Rahmi, what do you mean you quit?"

He sets it back down and runs his finger around the rim of his bottle. "My parents won't help me pay for school anymore. They want me to work for them full time." His eyes harden. "This is all Seda," he says. "They want to keep me close because they believe what she told them. They think I'm a drug addict."

I walk over to his chair and take his hand. "I'm so sorry. What did they say?"

Rahmi takes a long guzzle of beer. "I don't think I can do this tonight." He looks up at me. "I'm sorry, it's just too hard. I'm too fucking mad at them."

I nod. "It's okay."

He holds my hand a little longer before standing. "I'm going to watch TV for a bit."

"Sure," I say. "I was just going to bed."

"Okay." He heads toward the door, but turns to me before he gets there. "Your crazy week getting any better?"

I smile. "It's getting there. Today was pretty good."

"Good." He walks back over to give me a hug and kiss before he leaves.

I let out a long breath, wishing I could tap into Rahmi's innate decency. Even with all the shit he has to deal with, he's the same kind, even-keeled guy he's always been. I can count on that—on him. What can he count on? I frown. I can't think too hard about it, not now. There are so many dangerous pathways my mind can take, and I'm afraid they all end with me alone.

The next night I wait up for Jemma. This time it's two a.m. when her door pops, but I'm ready. I've made the decision.

"Jemma," I whisper outside her door again. "Jemma, open up."

She lets me wait, again. It's a minute or two before I give it another try.

"I'm interested," I say, lowering my voice as much as I can, "in what we talked about before."

A few seconds later the door opens. "You'd better be serious."

I start to reply, but I look at her and something stops me. She's different tonight. She's not wearing me down with her glare—in fact, she's not even looking at me. She's glancing around, distracted. She's more disheveled than usual, her hair matted in its hasty ponytail, and she's wearing her usual dirty black jeans and a gray T-shirt. Her eyes dart up, to give me a quick scowl, I guess, and I see she has a cut under her left eye. The skin around it is discolored.

My stomach hits the floor. I see Dani, crying in our apartment while I throw up. I see my first girlfriend, Emma, flinching when I raise my voice. And I see myself, using my Superman T-shirt to stop the blood pouring out of my nose. My eyes sting and my instincts tell me to get the fuck out, that I don't want to be in the middle of this again, but I can't move.

"Dipshit, are you buying, or what?" Jemma crosses her arms, looking disgusted.

I nod, still studying her, still processing the images of my past I've tried to forget. "Yeah," I say, clearing my throat. "I'll take ten."

She sighs and closes the door, and I guess I'm supposed to wait here while she gets it. I rub my face with both hands, hoping to clear my mind a little before she comes back. I pull the three twenties from my pocket. I need to get the pills and leave.

Jemma opens the door again with an envelope in her hands. She opens it and shows me the small purple pills.

"Start with one," she says. "If it's not enough, you'll know pretty fast."

The envelope quivers as she holds it.

"Are you okay?" I ask as she stares down at the pills.

She closes the envelope. "Got the money?" She blinks a few times and still won't look at me.

"Yeah." I hand her the cash and she holds out the envelope. "What happened to your eye?"

She gives me a hard stare. "I walked into a door, asshole."

"Okay." I take the pills. "Can I still drink with these?"

"Not within two hours."

I nod.

"And no matter what," she says, her eyes burning into me again, "you never mention me. Got it?"

"Sure."

I hear the rustle of paper and realize the envelope is shaking in my hands now. I can try to forget, but it won't work. One glance at Jemma pounds me with memories of my suffering and my failures, and they're not going away. She's not going away. I take a breath and meet her eyes.

"Was it that guy?"

I brace for her to lash out, to tell me to mind my own fucking business, but she doesn't. She just looks tired.

"There are a lot of guys."

I frown and my heart thuds because I get what she's saying. It's nothing unusual. Nothing to get worked up about. "From the convenience store, I mean."

"What are you trying to do?" She sounds nervous now, and her anger is rising again. "This is how we know each other, okay?" she says, gesturing to the pills. "That's it."

I should leave it at that. I got what I needed and I haven't made her really mad yet, so I should go. But my feet won't move.

"Jemma," I say, fighting to keep the emotion out of my voice, "I've known guys like this." My face is heating up and I hope it's not noticeable. "They're sick, and they never change. I can get him to back off, I swear, just let me kn—"

"Take one tonight," she says, cutting me off. "They kick in fast."

"Okay, but—"

"Just take the pills," she says, her voice stern, resolute. "You'll feel better."

I start to reply, but Jemma turns away, closing the door behind her.

Chapter 25

Just Roommates

I hurry back to Bleecker Street from NYU the following Monday. It's only four-thirty, but they let me leave early so I can be back in an hour to help kick off Pro Bono Week at the library. Mr. Anders is a mess, and I'm glad to have an hour away from him.

I walk into the apartment, intending to eat a quick snack and watch some TV. Rahmi's standing at the kitchen counter, but he doesn't move when I come in.

"Hey," I say, rummaging through the refrigerator. "Did you finish the Chinese leftovers?"

"No."

The flat tone of his voice makes me look up. "Are you okay?" I close the refrigerator door.

He looks up at me and his eyes are wet and glazed. He shakes his head.

"Hey." I walk over and wrap my arms around him. "What's going on?"

"My dad called me, about an hour ago. My mom had a stroke."

"Oh, shit." I take a step back. "Is she going to be okay?"

"I don't know," he says. He's staring off past me, and I can see he's trying to keep it together. "It was me, though." His eyes come back to me. "I left the restaurant, and this happened. I hurt them, and I left them without enough help. This," he says, rubbing his face with his hands, "is what Seda was worried about."

"No." I squeeze his arm. "You didn't do anything wrong. There was an actual medical issue behind the stroke." I pause. "Are you going to see her?"

"I have to," he says, his voice strained. "I have to know she's okay." Rahmi looks at me with an uneasy expression—warm but guarded—and takes a deep breath. "Would you go with me?"

I look at the clock. I nod. "Of course."

He visibly relaxes, and smiles a little. "Thank you. I don't think I could do it without you." He looks toward the door. "Are you okay to go now? We'll have better luck getting a cab before evening rush."

"You go ahead," I say. "I just have to make a quick call, then I'll be down."

Any other night, he'd question me about it, but not now. He just rubs a weary eye, collects his things, and heads out the door.

I hold my breath and dial Mr. Anders. He picks up, already annoyed.

"I'm sorry," I begin, focused on keeping my voice steady, "something's come up, and I can't be there tonight. I'm really sorry."

"Murray," he says, "I—hold on." He's talking to someone else, directing the placement of sign-up sheets. "Murray," he repeats, "I'm not one for high-stakes pranks, and I've got a lot to do, so if you can just get back—"

"It's not a joke. There's been—"

"No. No, listen," he breaks in, "there is nothing that important tonight. Not a damn thing, okay?"

I hear the stress building in him and I need to change course before he delivers the speech I know is coming next. The speech that ends with my termination.

"My mom," I say, wincing as soon as the words come out. "She had a stroke."

There's a pause. "You don't have family here."

"She's visiting."

"Visiting?"

"Yeah." I tap my fingers against the phone, anxious to get downstairs to Rahmi. "I'm sorry, I have to go. I've got to get to the hospital."

There's a pause. "What hospital?"

"What hospital?" My face is on fire.

"Yeah, what hospital?"

"... Sinai."

"And this happened just now?"

"About an hour ago." I glance up at the clock. "The, uh, the store she was in called the ambulance."

Mr. Anders lets out a long breath. "Well, keep me posted."

"I will. And good luck tonight."

Rahmi doesn't say much on the way to the hospital. He cracks his knuckles and jitters his leg, and I'm sure he's alternately worried about his mom and the probability that his father and sister will blame him for everything.

We arrive at the emergency room at around five-thirty. It's packed, but Rahmi spots his father immediately.

"There he is," he says, nodding toward a man with dark skin and dense gray hair. He looks to be in his early seventies. "He always sits by vending machines." Rahmi looks at me. "Always."

"And you're sure you want me here?"

"Yes," he says, pulling his eyes away from his father and looking at me. "You're the only one I want here."

We walk over, but Rahmi's father is staring ahead, out the window, and doesn't notice us.

"Baba," Rahmi says, touching his shoulder. "I'm here."

Mr. Yilmaz stands and hugs his son, holding him longer than I would have thought. But I'm glad; from what Rahmi told me, I was expecting him to be angry. They talk for a moment in hushed Turkish, so I stay a few feet away, but it's not long before Rahmi motions me over.

"Murray," he says, blinking rapidly, "this is my dad, Emirhan. Baba, this is my roommate, Murray."

"It's nice to meet you," I say, shaking his hand. "I'm so sorry for the circumstances, though."

Mr. Yilmaz nods but glances at Rahmi, making me wonder how much English he understands.

Rahmi turns to me. "She's in the middle of a CT scan right now. Some kind of blood clot caused the stroke, they think. But they're optimistic because of how fast my dad got her in."

"That's great." I nearly put my arm around him, but stop myself.

Mr. Yilmaz smiles. "Seda will be here soon."

Rahmi's face falls and I shift my gaze, upset he has to deal with her on top of all this, and wondering how I can comfort him when I'm supposed to be just his roommate.

"Boys, sit," Mr. Yilmaz says, indicating the plastic seats behind us. We do, leaving him the chair closest to the vending machine. He stays standing and digs through his coat pocket until he comes up with some change. One by one, he pumps the coins into the slot and chooses three of the same candy bar. Classic Hershey's. He pulls them out and hands one to each of us. We thank him. Rahmi looks like he's about to cry.

"How long does the scan take?" I ask, directing my question to Rahmi's father, trying to give Rahmi a chance to compose himself.

"Soon, I think."

I nod. "You know, I've had one before. Back in high school." I'm not sure if this is better than silence, but I decide to go for it.

"Oh?" Mr. Yilmaz says. "You were sick?"

"No, I was in a car accident. I slammed against the door pretty hard and they needed to check for internal bleeding."

He frowns and Rahmi gives me a subtle headshake that tells me I should try silence for a while.

"Hey, Baba, how is she?"

I turn to my right and see a tall professional-looking woman with flowing black hair. She walks over to Mr. Yilmaz and leans down, taking his hand in hers. She's trailed by a man probably in his mid-forties, with a sympathetic smile and ice-blue eyes. Must be the disappointing Midwestern Catholic.

"She's okay," her father says with a smile. "Having the tests now."

She nods. She doesn't even look at us. Rahmi's eyes are on the floor. I take a breath.

"Seda?" I stand up. "Hi, I'm Rahmi's roommate, Murray. Would you like to sit?"

Her smile fades as she looks at me, then at Rahmi. She straightens up next to her new husband. "I'm fine," she says. "Thank you."

"Murray, you said?" her husband asks, moving toward me with a warm smile. "It's nice to meet you." He extends his hand and I shake it. "I'm Will." He turns to Rahmi. "And you must be Seda's brother."

Rahmi sits up but doesn't look any better. His eyes are red and heavy. "That's right." He glances at Seda. "I'm Rahmi."

"It's great to meet you."

They shake hands and Will sits in the chair next to Rahmi. He asks him about his classes and the books he's reading, but it's not long before the nurse comes out to tell us we can go back and see Mrs. Yilmaz.

We follow the nurse to a small exam room, Mr. Yilmaz and Seda leading the rest of us. There's not a lot of room, so Will and I hang back in the doorway.

Seda gets to her mother first, hugging her and kissing her forehead. She looks better than I expected, sitting up and smiling. The nurse tells us she's already been given an IV drug to break up the blood clot, and the doctor will explain what medications she'll need in the future. The nurse leaves, but Will and I still give them space. Rahmi is with her now; he's holding her hand and murmuring to her in Turkish. Whatever he said, she smiles and pats his hand. I'm sure he's apologizing for causing her stroke.

After a few minutes, Mrs. Yilmaz notices us in the doorway. She waves us over.

"Come, come. Who is this, Will? Your brother?"

I smile. "No, I'm Rahmi's roommate. My name's Murray. I'm glad you're feeling better."

She nods and Seda lets out an exasperated sigh.

"Rahmi," Seda says, "let's go outside for a minute." It's the first thing she's said to him.

I raise my eyebrows at Rahmi, a silent indication that I'll come along if he wants me to. He nods.

We step into the hallway and as soon as the door closes, Seda glares at her brother.

"Why did you bring him here?"

He shrugs. "Why did you bring Will?"

Her jaw stiffens. "He's part of our family now."

"And what about me?" Rahmi says, his voice rising. "I didn't even get to be at your wedding. Maybe you don't think I should be here either."

"I'm talking about him," Seda says, her eyes narrowing at me.

"Hey, I'm just here to support Rahmi," I reply. "It's the least I can do."

"So, you're going to tell them?" she demands, looking back at her brother. "Now? The same day you put Ana in the hospital?"

Rahmi's face reddens and his hands are shaking at his sides. I've experienced this kind of fury enough to predict what's coming next. I take his hand and murmur, "I'm right here," hoping that will help bring him back a little, but he shakes me off and turns to Seda.

"You don't know what you're fucking talking about." His voice is low. "I was there for them, every night at that goddamn restaurant. I only quit because you turned them against me." He runs his hands through his hair and laughs. "And you're such a hypocrite. I mean, Will? Seems like a great guy, but he's not Turkish. Or Muslim. Not even close. How is this carrying on our heritage? How is this the traditional life you lectured me about?"

"At least he's a man," she hisses.

"Yeah," Rahmi says. "I guess I never could get that part right." He wipes his nose with his sleeve. "But you know what? I'm happy." He turns to me. "I'm happy and that's because of Murray."

My eyes burn and I move a little closer to him.

"You realize you're making a choice right now," Seda says. "You're choosing this backward life over your family."

"So far you're the only one who disapproves," he says, glancing toward the exam room. "You don't speak for them."

"Ana and Baba?" She laughs. "They will never approve. Do you remember our cousin, Beyza?"

"No."

"That's because they refused to speak her name after she told the family about her . . . lifestyle. They acted like she was dead. You were only four or five, but I remember. It shattered them. Now imagine if their only son told them that."

Rahmi's eyes cloud up. "Is this really so horrible, the thought of us together?" he asks, gesturing to me. "Would it be better if I were dead?"

I don't like where this is going. I touch his back. "It isn't worth it," I murmur. "You don't have to listen to this."

He nods and wipes his eyes.

Seda leans forward, her voice cold. "I can't protect you anymore. What you're doing is wrong, and it's not who we are."

Rahmi clenches his fists and looks so furious I'm worried I'll need to intervene, but then he releases his grip and takes a deep breath. "You don't get to tell me who I am."

He takes my hand and we walk back down the hall toward the lobby. He turns around for a moment. "Tell Will I'm sorry. I would have liked to have him as a brother."

Chapter 26
What I Deserve

We don't talk much on the cab ride home. Rahmi spends most of it staring out the window, cracking his knuckles every so often. I've come to understand that's his angry habit, one that stabs me with guilt. It's such an innocent, nonviolent expression. We're nearly to King Street before I get up the nerve to break the silence.

"I'm sorry," I say.

He nods a little but doesn't turn away from the window.

I watch him, my eyes welling up again. The small threads of hope he was clinging to have been cut, and he's alone. I just want him to know I'm not going anywhere.

We turn onto our street and I dig my wallet out of my back pocket for the cab fare. It's starting to drizzle.

"I'm glad your mom's going to be okay," I say as we pull up in front of the building.

"Yeah." He slides out of the cab as I pay the driver.

We climb the stairs in silence and Rahmi walks into the apartment first. He tosses his coat on the counter and says he's going to take a shower. The place is cold, so Grace must be at Greg's tonight; she always turns the heat way down when she leaves.

The answering machine is blinking, so I hang my damp coat on the rack and push the play button.

"Hey, Murray, this is Alan."

My face heats up as I remember how I abandoned him.

"So, I need to tell you, I talked to your mom today. She's listed as one of your emergency contacts. She didn't seem to be recovering from a stroke."

Frothing stomach acid makes its way up into my throat.

"She didn't even know you're living in New York."

The lights in the room begin to swirl and darken and I'm afraid I'll pass out before I get to the end of his message. Maybe it would be better that way.

"Needless to say, you don't need to come in tomorrow. I've got students covering for the rest of the week, and we'll figure something else out after that. I'll have your final check mailed to you. Take care of yourself, Murray."

There's a pause before that last line, and it comes out loaded with disgust and disappointment.

Rahmi walks back into the kitchen from our room a few minutes later, his hair wet and his eyes sullen. "What's going on?"

I must look pretty bad for him to even notice in his state. "I've been fired from the library."

He stares at me. "You're kidding."

"No, this is pretty fucking serious."

"What happened?" He comes a little closer, frowning with confusion.

I take a step back in case he's thinking of offering a hug or some other consolation. For some reason I don't want him to touch me right now. "I called my boss before we left tonight," I tell him, trying to find an object to focus on while I talk. I decide on Grace's teakettle. "I couldn't get out of this thing at the library without a good excuse. So, I told him my mom was the one who had the stroke."

"Wait, what thing at the library?"

My eyes move to him, and harden. "Pro Bono Week."

"That starts tonight?" He rubs his face with both hands. "I thought it wasn't until next month."

I shake my head. "That's why I've been working so many late days." I shove my trembling hands in my pockets. "It's why I kept needing to use Grace's print account at the computer lab. It's why I couldn't go out with you guys last week." My voice is irritated and Rahmi looks surprised. He crosses his arms.

"Murray, I'm sorry I didn't remember the date, but I've had a few things going on. Are you really mad at me about this?"

"It's fine," I say, glaring at the teakettle again. "It just seems like I'm pretty far down on your list of priorities right now."

"You can't be serious." He opens his mouth to speak again, but only a sardonic laugh emerges.

"This was a pretty big deal."

"Then why didn't you just fucking remind me? You could have said, 'Hey, I've got this big thing tonight, it's kind of important to me.' But you kept it to yourself. What, to make me feel worse now?"

His rising voice is making my palms sweat, but my anger overrides my fear. "That's not fair," I say, my ears hot. "I wanted to be there for you. I thought if I told you, you'd try to make me go."

"What do you want from me? You made the choice. You decided for both of us. I mean, I'm glad you went with me, but you can't fucking blame me for it later."

"It's not about Pro Bono Week," I say, my own voice rising and my temples pounding. "I don't have a job anymore. Do you get that?"

"You're going to blame me for that, too?"

"Jesus, Rahmi, not everything is about you."

I storm off into the living room, my heart racing. My eyes can't focus I'm so mad. Rahmi follows, and when I turn around, I can see the fury on his face as well. The changes are subtle but dangerous: his hard eyes, clenched jaw, fast breathing I can see in the movement of his chest. It's a side I've not seen of him yet. And I'm now acutely aware of our size difference—Rahmi is two or three inches taller than I am, and about twenty pounds heavier. I note the empty beer bottle on the coffee table and the two others on the TV tray, an old habit of self-preservation I guess I still have.

"What, are you going to break something now?" Rahmi asks, a glint of amusement—maybe mockery—joining the anger in his eyes.

"What?"

"The bottles," he says, nodding to the table. "Just make sure you do a better job cleaning up this time."

My eyes throb and my ears are on fire. "What the fuck does that mean?"

"You know what I mean," he says in a cold voice, "and you still won't tell me the truth." He glares at the floor. "No. We're not getting away from this," he mutters. "I won't let you make me the bad guy here. You can't tell me a job you've had for six months is more important than what happened today."

"I'm not trying to compete," I yell at him, still dazed. "I just want you to acknowledge that it sucks."

"But right now?" Rahmi yells back. "You can't give me a minute to digest everything that's happened?" He cracks his knuckles. "Let me tell you what: I'll take the night to get over my mom almost dying and my sister cutting me out of her life forever, and I'll see what I have for you in the morning."

"You're an asshole," I mutter, shaking my head. "And I'd still have a job if I hadn't gone with you."

A stunned, hurt look crosses his face and I lower my eyes. I went too far. I'm squeezing my hands at my sides, hoping I don't throw up. I'm not sure what's going to happen, how this pressure is going to escape. I'm destroying everything we have, and in some backward way expecting relief from it. Like I'm back in high school, picking fights to get hit.

"You'd still have a job if you didn't keep every goddamn thing to yourself," he says, taking a step toward me. "I never asked you to make that choice."

I take his advance as an intimidation move, and new sweat springs from under my arms. "Hey, get away from me, will you?"

He looks confused, like I've changed the subject, but he's the one who raised the stakes. He's trying to scare me, and I'm not going to let him.

"Listen, I'm not going to leave," he says, taking another step toward me.

The rage and fear inside me pounds to the surface and I reach out to push him, to make him give me the space I need. My hands connect with his shoulders and he stumbles backward, but it's not enough. My arms are pulsing with adrenaline and my sick desire for destruction and relief demands more. I grab his shirt with my left hand and cock my right arm back. But Rahmi doesn't flinch. Fury forces me on, the weight of this miserable night steeling my knuckles and driving my fist toward him.

He looks a little surprised, but moves fast and deflects my punch with his arm. It was easy for him, like a ball player reacting to a bad throw. My blood is on fire now. I can't believe he can disregard me so calmly. I pull my arm back faster this time, but I already wish I'd turned this anger on myself instead. Rahmi catches my wrist.

"Don't," he says, looking into my eyes. "Don't do this."

I can't read his face, and I swallow hard because now he has the power. I let go of his shirt, but his right hand rises out of the corner of my eye. I wince and turn my head, trying to pull free of his grip on my wrist.

"Hey," he says, and I look up because his voice is softer now. "I'm not going to hit you."

He lets go of my wrist and I step back.

My arms are shaking, and my anger dissolves. I don't know how he's so calm after what I did. And after the things I said. A wave of self-hatred rises in me, and I wish he would slam me against the wall. Punch me. Do whatever brutal act must be in the back of his mind because that's what I deserve.

I open my mouth to apologize but my thoughts jumble together, and the emerging kindness in his eyes is unbearable. My stomach lurches and I need to run to make it to the bathroom in time to throw up.

Rahmi doesn't follow me. I'm grateful for the chance to fall apart, sitting on the bathroom floor, waiting for the heaving pain to subside and letting the tears brim over. I don't understand how I let this happen again. I close my eyes.

Again.

And again. Like I always do. I lean my back against the wall and take a slow breath, but the pain isn't going away. I pull myself back up to the toilet. Lamar's words—his gut-wrenching observations—echo in my head. I could have stopped myself if I wanted to. I just didn't want to.

I'm lightheaded when I come down, and I see a flash of light from the corner of my eye. I taste blood in my mouth, so I touch my finger to my lip to check if I bit it, but there's nothing there. I panic and haul myself to my feet so I can spit into the sink, but there's still no blood. The taste is so strong, though. My heart hammers in my ears and I'm back in that place I can never really escape. I open the medicine cabinet and pull out the small bottle of antidepressants I never did refill. The gunshot rings out and echoes in my head. There are five purple morphine pills left at the bottom. I haven't taken more than one at a time yet, but I hear my father sputtering out his final plea for help, so I empty the bottle into my mouth and swallow them dry. It doesn't work fast enough; I end up watching him die again anyway. I sink to the floor, my face buried in my hands, and I cry because I can't even make these pictures in my head leave me alone.

After a minute, a few minutes maybe, I need to get up. I need to go find Rahmi and make sure he's all right, but I can't. I try to stand but my legs buckle. My whole body trembles and my forehead gleams with sweat. I'm getting scared because I can't see straight and I feel like I'm separating from my body. Images of blood and glass and hospitals and funerals dance along the baseboards as I sit, frozen. I'm watching myself and all these nightmares, and everything happens in sickening slow motion. Hours pass between each breath I take. Maybe even that isn't long enough.

Chapter 27
ICU
Rahmi

They won't let Rahmi see him yet. He paces the hallway next to the waiting room, glancing at the vending machine and wondering what used to be in A6. The slot is vacant and he smiles because he doesn't see Rally bars—Murray's favorite—so he lets himself decide it was that, even though in the back of his mind he knows it's a long shot.

He keeps pacing and trying not to imagine what might be happening in the ICU. Murray was breathing when Rahmi got to him, but his pulse was slow—a laboring crawl like a windup toy about out of juice. He still doesn't know what Murray took. The empty bottle of antidepressants was next to him, but Rahmi knew he was out; Murray said he'd fill the prescription tomorrow. Rahmi looks up at the clock. Tomorrow. It's eleven now, and no one's told him anything since they got here an hour ago, so he walks up to the nurse's station.

"Hi," he says, trying to sound composed to compensate for his ragged appearance. "I'm just wondering if there's any word on Murray Henderson."

She looks at her clipboard. "Let's see," she murmurs, running her pen down the sheet.

"We came in about an hour ago and they took him to the ICU." Rahmi's aware that he's tapping into his nervous habit of offering too much information. "It was an overdose."

He winces at the words he hadn't meant to think, let alone speak aloud. He's let his mind go to a lot of dark places today, but he hasn't been able to ask the question he fears the most: did Murray do it on purpose?

Rahmi blinks away the pain in his eyes. He was there. He was part of each horrible thing that happened before Murray went into the bathroom, and knows he was coming apart.

"Nothing yet, but I'll let you know. What's your name?"

He looks at her for a moment, forgetting that he'd been talking to her at all.

"Rahmi Yilmaz. His roommate."

She nods and he walks back to the waiting room.

Roommate.

Guilt stings his eyes and stiffens his throat.

Rahmi slumps down into a blue plastic chair, the one closest to the vending machine. He hadn't realized he'd picked up his father's habit. Obsession. After years of accompanying him to places like the doctor's office and post office, Rahmi internalized the need to be within arm's reach of cheap junk food, just in case. He digs in his pocket but only comes up with thirty cents.

He's tried to call Grace a few times, but there's no answer at their apartment. She's probably staying over at Greg's tonight and he doesn't have the number. He's a little relieved, because he'd rather not break down in front of anyone else. Rahmi glances again toward the nurse's station. He lets his head bow forward, rubbing his temples. He pushed Murray too hard. He made him say too much and feel too much that he wasn't ready for, and ignored all the signs telling him to walk away for a while.

"Are you here for Murray Henderson?"

Rahmi looks up, surprised at the emergence of a new nurse in blue scrubs and a surgical mask. He nods and the nurse pulls his mask down, giving Rahmi a sympathetic smile.

"He's not awake yet, but you can come back. His tests look good."

"His tests look good?" Rahmi echoes, standing up and hoping he heard him right. "He's not going to die?"

"No." The nurse laughs. They must appreciate the times they can give good news. "He'll be asleep for a while, though. And drowsy when he wakes up."

They go through the doors, back to a small room in the ICU. Rahmi's prepared, reminding himself everyone looks frail and ghostly in a hospital bed, but his pulse still picks up when he sees Murray. He's paler than usual, which Rahmi didn't think was possible, and his blond hair sticks out in disarray. There are IVs and monitors stuck all over him, and Rahmi just wants his eyes to open so he can at least know his boyfriend is still here.

The nurse leaves for a minute, so Rahmi walks over to the side of the bed and sits down on the doctor's stool. He hesitates to take Murray's hand and interfere with his IV, but decides that's irrational and after everything that's happened, it's the least of their worries. He touches Murray's hand, then more firmly takes hold when he realizes it feels just like it always did.

"Hey, Murray," he says, leaning forward. "It's Rahmi. They said your tests are fine, so you can cut the shit and wake up, all right?"

He brushes the hair off Murray's forehead and smiles, imagining what his comeback would be. Murray will be able to tell him soon enough.

Rahmi goes home to sleep for a few hours. He barely remembers how he got there. He trudges through the shadowy, still apartment and collapses onto his bed. Their bed. He was sure his swirling thoughts and doubts and anxieties would keep him awake the rest of the night, but it turns out they'd all exhausted him and he sleeps, unmoving, for the next five hours.

The sound of the front door closing wakes him up. It's not loud, but the familiar click-clack seeps into his subconscious, jolting him upright, convincing him Murray's home.

"Hey!" Rahmi calls out, before he allows his mind to calibrate.

He hears shuffling down the hall and Grace appears in the doorway. "Hey, yourself," she says. Her eyes move down to his feet. "You slept in your shoes?"

He rubs his eyes. "Yeah."

"Where's Murray?" Grace moves into the room. Her eyes are serious and she's not even making a joke about his abysmal appearance.

"He's in the hospital," Rahmi says. "He took something, but he'll be okay. They said—"

"He took something?" Grace breaks in, her eyes turning hard. "Like drugs?"

He nods. "He's okay, though. He's going to be okay." Rahmi doesn't know if he keeps saying that for her or for himself.

"That fucking bitch," she says, clenching her fists. "Jemma got him on something, right?"

"I don't know." This is making Rahmi tired. He glances up at the clock. "I'm going back to see him."

"You've talked to him?"

"No, he's not awake yet."

"Then how do they know he'll be okay?" Her voice cracks a little and Rahmi catches a rare glimpse of fear in her eyes.

"They did tests. He just needs to sleep it off."

He stands up and heads toward the door, intending to wash his face and brush his teeth before he leaves. Grace catches his arm, looking up at him like she needs to say something. After a moment she shakes her head and hugs him. "I'm so sorry," she murmurs.

He nods.

"Can I come by later?" she asks, releasing him. "Today or tomorrow?"

"Sure." It's strange to gatekeep Murray's visitors, but he's glad she asked. "I'll let you know when he wakes up."

Chapter 28
Being There
Rahmi

"**G**et out! Just get the fuck away from me!"

Rahmi hears Murray all the way down the hall, so he starts running. There's a clatter of metal on linoleum and Rahmi arrives in the doorway to see him thrashing around, a tray of IV supplies on the floor. Two nurses—the man and woman who have been taking care of Murray—are struggling to hold him down and secure a new IV in his arm. He looks up and sees Rahmi, but for a second there's confusion in his eyes.

"Rahmi!" he yells, his attention turning back to the nurses as he tries again to shake them off. "Tell them to stop. They're trying to kill me with these fucking needles!" His eyes are wild and Rahmi doesn't understand what's causing this change in him.

"It's okay," Rahmi says, rushing to his bedside. "They're helping you."

"We explained it all to him," the first nurse, Michael, says. "It's fluid for dehydration. And a mild sedative."

"A sedative?" Rahmi frowns. "You said he'd be tired when he woke up."

"Don't talk about me like I'm not here," Murray says, elbowing Michael as he tries again to insert the drip. He stops. He looks up at Rahmi. "Wait, you did all this?"

"Did what?"

"You brought me here? Told them to do this to me?" He waves at the nurses, who are taking advantage of his divided attention. "You think I'm crazy?"

Rahmi shakes his head as he tries to see this through Murray's lens. He kneels down next to him and takes his hand. "Murray, you're in the hospital—the regular hospital—because of what you took."

He looks past Rahmi for a moment, like he's trying to put it together. Trying to decide if he should trust him.

"Do you remember what happened?" Rahmi asks.

"We had a fight," he says after a pause.

Rahmi nods.

Gloria, the second nurse, inserts the IV while Murray's watching him. She gives Michael a look, then nods to Rahmi to let him know they're done. They slip out of the room, but Rahmi still needs an answer.

"Hold on, just a sec," he tells Murray, squeezing his hand before he lets go and jogs out the door.

"Excuse me," Rahmi says, catching Gloria before she turns the corner after Michael. "You said you gave him a sedative?"

She nods. "Normally in the case of an overdose like this, we'd expect more fatigue for the next few days. But sometimes, if a patient wakes up confused, disoriented . . . adrenaline kicks in and it can go the other way."

"Okay." He glances back at the room. "So, what he's doing is normal?"

"I've seen it before."

Rahmi takes a breath. "What was it? Did the tests say what was in his system?"

"I'm sorry," she says, with a regretful smile. "For privacy reasons, I can't tell you."

"Oh, of course." He holds up a hand. "Thank you."

She walks away and he turns back to the room. Murray's staring at the needle in his arm but not making any move to rip it out. Rahmi pulls up the doctor's stool and sits next to him. Fatigue is setting in now, visible and heavy in Murray's eyes.

"I missed you," Rahmi says, resting his hand on his shoulder.

"How long was I gone?"

"Just last night. Felt a lot longer, though."

Murray nods. "I'm sorry about that." He looks down. "I'm sorry about everything. I—I don't know what happened."

"What do you mean?"

He snaps his head up. "Last night," he says. "I pushed you. I yelled. I was going to punch you, I tried to." His eyes dart around the room. "That all happened, right?"

Rahmi nods. "We both yelled."

"I'm the one who fucked up. I'm sorry." Murray lets out an unsteady breath. "And I understand if you've had enough."

"Had enough?"

"Yeah." He leans back, looking up at the ceiling. "If you want to leave, I understand. You've been more patient than I deserve."

Rahmi's brow furrows. "Is that what you thought, when I got here?"

"What?"

"When I came in, you saw me, and you looked confused. Almost like you were surprised."

He nods and gets a shameful, guilty look.

A knot grows in Rahmi's stomach. "Did you think I wouldn't come? That I was breaking up with you?"

Murray looks away. "No. It's just, when I woke up, for some reason I thought I was in Cleveland. It was only for a couple of minutes, but it was like the past few months were gone. I kept calling for John. Then when I saw you, my mind kind of caught up, but I didn't want to say anything. It made me seem even crazier."

"It's all right," Rahmi says, relaxing. "The nurse seemed to think everything you went through was pretty normal." He smiles. "And I don't want to leave. I know you think you've got to handle it all yourself, but you don't. I'm still here, and I still want to help you."

"I'm so sorry for what I did to you."

Rahmi nods. "I know." He pauses. "Can I ask you something?"

"Sure."

"Do you remember what happened after the fight? When you went into the bathroom?"

Murray's silent for several seconds. Rahmi knows it must be hell, trying to search for memories you'd rather not have lived in the first place. Just when it seems Murray's not going to come up with it, his hands shake. He closes his eyes tight, like he's trying to make something go away.

"Murray, what is it?" Rahmi reaches for his hand, alarmed, but Murray flinches and pulls away.

"It was the worst one," he says, opening his eyes. "Like I was there. I tasted blood."

"What are you talking about?"

"When I went to the bathroom. I saw it—I saw everything that happened, when I . . ." His voice breaks.

"With your dad?"

"Right." Murray sighs. "So, I grabbed the bottle from the cabinet. There were five left, but I took them all." He looks down. "I thought it would go away faster if I just took them all."

"What was it?" Rahmi reaches for his hand again and this time Murray lets him hold it. "What did you take?"

"Morphine. I got it from Jemma." Murray glances up, but Rahmi tries not to react. "I've had the pills less than a week; there were only ten total." Murray rubs his eyes with his free hand. "Everything was building up so fast, and I wanted something that would make it better."

Rahmi's eyes burn. Removing his glasses would give him away, so he does his best to blink it back. He's picturing it now—what it must have been like for Murray.

"You can tell me the truth," Murray says, and Rahmi realizes he hasn't said anything yet. "I know I'm a mess."

"No." Rahmi grips his hand a little tighter. "I wasn't thinking that at all. I was thinking you're probably the strongest person I know."

Murray laughs, and he sounds more like himself again. "Now I just feel bad for you."

They only talk for another ten minutes before Murray's eyelids droop and Rahmi knows he needs to catch up on sleep. He gets up to leave but Murray holds his arm.

"This is going to sound pathetic," he says, reddening a little, "but do you mind staying a little longer?"

Rahmi sees his leg shake and the tremor in his hands is back. He sits down. "You want me to stay until you fall asleep?"

Murray nods.

"Of course."

He squeezes his hands together. "Thanks, Rahmi."

Rahmi smiles, but there's a hard lump in his throat. He scours his mind for something light to talk about to help Murray nod off, and ends up telling him a Turkish story he'd heard many times growing up. Murray smiles a little at the funny parts and as his eyes close, Rahmi lowers his voice. He keeps talking even after he knows Murray's asleep, then stays sitting next to him another twenty minutes after that, just to be sure.

Chapter 29
Just an Accident
Rahmi

The next day, Rahmi walks by NYU on his way to the subway station. He's hoping to catch Lamar before he leaves the office.

Rahmi climbs the stairs to the third floor, and the receptionist tells him Lamar's finishing an appointment but then should have a few minutes. Rahmi sits on the loveseat facing his office so he'll be ready when Lamar opens the door. He's not sure what he should say, and Lamar can't share anything with him. Privacy always gets in the way.

Rahmi's so preoccupied he doesn't even notice when Lamar emerges from his office and walks over to him.

"Rahmi?" he says, smiling as Rahmi looks up. "You want to come on back for a minute?"

He nods and follows Lamar. Murray always said he was young, and kind of sounded annoyed about it, but to Rahmi, Lamar's confidence is making him seem older. He's wearing a suit, which strikes Rahmi as odd, but he might have something else to do today. Lamar leads him into the office with quick, efficient steps and offers him an armchair to sit in. Lamar walks around his desk and tosses a file on top before sitting down.

"So, what can I do for you today?"

"I need to talk to you about Murray." There. Direct. Easy enough.

Lamar frowns. "I'm afraid I can't talk about the clients I see here."

"I know," Rahmi says. "I know you can't, and that's all right. I mainly have to talk to you."

"Okay." Lamar grabs a pen.

He takes a breath. "I'm sure Murray's talked about me; I'm his boyfriend."

Lamar nods and Rahmi feels a rush of confidence having owned up to their relationship.

"Anyway, Murray is in the hospital."

"The hospital? Is he okay?"

Rahmi nods. "Two nights ago he overdosed on morphine and I brought him in. He woke up yesterday and told me he was trying to stop a flashback he was having, but he took too much."

"It wasn't a suicide attempt?" Lamar scribbles something on his paper.

Rahmi pauses. "I don't know."

Lamar looks up.

"There was a lot going on before this happened, and Murray was headed toward a breaking point. The way he explained it made it sound like an accident, but ..." He shakes his head. "I'm not sure."

"What was going on before?"

Rahmi looks down. "We had a big fight. It was ... it was just a lot of things. I'm sure he'll fill you in when he's better."

Lamar nods and seems to understand Rahmi's not ready for therapy right now. "How long will he be in the hospital?"

"I don't know. I'm heading back over there now," Rahmi says, looking over his shoulder. "He wasn't great when he woke up, though. Very disoriented."

"I'm really sorry to hear this, Rahmi," Lamar says, writing on a small piece of paper now. "Will you have him call me sometime today or tomorrow, if he can? This is my home number if I'm not in the office."

"Sure," he says, taking the paper. "Do you ..." Rahmi glances down for a moment. "Do you think it was an accident?"

Lamar offers a faint smile. "I'm a Freudian. For us, there are no accidents."

Murray's been moved to the fifth floor, so Rahmi takes the elevator from ICU. He rides up alone, wondering if he should just forget about it. Murray's all right, and that's what matters.

When he walks in, Murray's sitting up in bed, reading a book from the bag of stuff Rahmi brought him. It looks like he's showered; his hair isn't greasy or disheveled anymore, and he's got a different gown on. He smiles when he sees Rahmi, and his eyes are clear.

"Hey," he says, setting his book aside.

"Hey." Rahmi leans down and gives him a gentle hug and kiss, still unsure about his condition. "How're you feeling?"

"Better. I haven't been awake that long." Murray moves a little and offers him a seat on the bed. "Did you call Lamar?"

"I went to his office," Rahmi says, avoiding Murray's eyes. "It was on my way, so I figured that would be easier."

"What'd he say?"

Murray's winding and unwinding a piece of thread around his finger while he talks. This isn't as casual as he's making it sound.

Rahmi shrugs. "He didn't have much of a reaction; he just hopes you're better soon. And he gave me this." He pulls the paper from his pocket and hands it to Murray. "He wants you to call him today or tomorrow."

"Sure." He takes the paper. "Thanks for doing that."

"Of course." Rahmi pauses. "I did want to ask—"

He doesn't get to finish because Grace walks in. He forgot she told him she'd come by after class. She stops in the doorway and gives Murray a huge smile.

"Off you go, Rahmi," she says, walking over and gesturing him off the bed. "You guys can fuck later. I need to see this guy."

Rahmi slides down, moving to the chair by Murray's nightstand. Grace takes his place and envelops Murray in a long hug.

"Are you okay?" she asks, pulling away to study his face. "I mean, really?"

"Yeah," he says, smiling. Rahmi can tell he's embarrassed. "I'm fine."

"Good." She crosses her arms. "Then tell me what the fuck you were thinking. What did you take?"

He runs his hands down his face. "It was morphine. I was just trying to take the edge off."

"Jemma has to move out," she says. "I know she gave it to you, and it could have killed you."

"Grace," he says, giving Rahmi a quick glare, "I asked her for it. It wasn't her fault. But you don't have to worry; I'm not doing it again."

Grace turns to Rahmi. "You're all right with this?" she asks, gesturing to Murray. "You think Jemma can stay after this?"

"I think we don't have to decide anything right now."

"Have you guys seen Jemma around?" Murray asks, winding the thread again.

Grace and Rahmi both shake their heads, and he looks down.

"She's in some kind of trouble."

Grace snorts. "No shit, buddy."

"No, I mean, when I picked up the pills from her, she had this bruise and a cut under her eye. From a guy she's been seeing." Murray frowns but he still doesn't look at them. "She seemed different. She doesn't know how to handle it."

Rahmi watches Murray study his thread, clearly retreating to a dark place in his mind, and his own worry sets in. Murray thinks he knows how to handle it. Rahmi rests his face in his hand. He wants to rescue her.

"I'll try to talk to her the next time she's home," Rahmi says, getting Murray to make eye contact. He nods.

"I wouldn't worry too much," Grace says, leaning back in the bed. "Jemma can take care of herself."

Murray nods again, but Rahmi knows he doesn't agree. His mind's made up.

"Man, I could get used to this," she says, messing with a few buttons on the side of the bed. "How long do you have to stay?"

"They said two more days, for tests and observation."

She nods. "I'm glad you woke up."

Murray smiles. "Me, too."

Grace stays for another twenty minutes before she leaves to meet Greg. Somehow she's changed the atmosphere in the room, and when she leaves, it's like the aftermath of a tornado. Everything's quiet and Murray's face is drawn and his eyes are tired again.

"You want me to bring in something for dinner?" Rahmi asks. "Will they let me do that?"

"Sure, that'd be great. Thanks." Murray leans back.

Rahmi stands up and puts on his coat. "Indian?"

"Perfect."

"All right, I'll be back in a few."

"Wait." Murray sits up. "You were saying something before, when Grace came in. You wanted to ask me something."

"Oh, yeah?" Rahmi frowns like he's trying to remember, but in truth, he's just lost his momentum and his nerve and he can't go through with it now. "I don't know." He shakes his head. "I guess it wasn't that important."

Murray smiles and closes his eyes. "I guess not."

Chapter 30
Another Hospital
Rahmi

Rahmi's been without normalcy for so long he can't remember what it's like. He's finally free from the restaurant, but his homework has been piling up and he still needs to see his mom. His dad called this morning, hinting that Rahmi will look like a horrible son if he doesn't visit her every day. He sighs. Another hospital, another bad memory.

Rahmi's dad is outside the room when he arrives, crunching on a mini bag of Cheetos and staring at a bland landscape print hanging in the hallway. His posture is slumped and his clothes are wrinkled.

"Baba," Rahmi says in a soft voice, "how are you?"

His father turns and Rahmi sees his eyes are heavy. He smiles and walks toward Rahmi, then gives him a hug.

"Did you sleep here?" Rahmi asks, standing back to look at his father again.

He nods. "Should be one or two more."

"Nights?"

He nods again. "I don't sleep much," he says, rubbing his eyes. "I don't like hospitals, you know."

"I know." Rahmi crosses his arms, leaning against the wall. "Why are you in the hall?"

He looks toward the room. "The nurse is there. I like to let them work."

Rahmi smiles. His father is the most squeamish person he's met. He can't stand to observe any sort of medical procedure, even a blood pressure reading. As a kid it was at times embarrassing and annoying, but also gave Rahmi a resilience many of his friends lacked. He learned at an early age how to treat his own cuts and scrapes, since his dad would be gone at the first sight of blood. Rahmi used to think it was funny that Seda became a doctor after growing up with all his aversions, but now he thinks she had something to prove. She always has to come out on top.

Rahmi emerges from his thoughts to see his father watching him.

"Baba, is something wrong?"

He lets out a slow breath. "What happened with Seda?"

Rahmi shrugs. "Nothing. It had just gotten later than I thought, and I had to leave."

"Do you need help?"

He's peering into Rahmi's eyes and it's making him uncomfortable, but he remembers his dad is working off the story Seda told them years ago.

"I'm fine. I promise."

"Okay." He looks away and Rahmi knows he's just giving in to avoid a fight.

The nurse opens the door. She smiles at them and holds the door so they can go in. Rahmi's mom is sitting up, awake, and other than the pale blue hospital gown and lack of makeup, she looks like her old self.

"*Selam*, Ana," Rahmi says, smiling and walking over to her. He gives her a gentle hug and she pats his cheek. "Are you feeling better?"

She nods. "I should go home right now," she says, rolling her eyes toward the door where the nurse just left, "but they don't like the . . ." She frowns, searching for an English word out of her grasp. She touches her upper arm. "*Kan.*"

"Oh, blood pressure? They didn't like the reading?"

She nods. "We'll see."

Rahmi smiles. "I'm sure you'll be out of here soon."

"Where were you yesterday?" She adjusts the pillow behind her. "Seda was here a few hours."

"Her husband brought those," his dad remarks, pointing to a vase of flowers on the table.

"I'm sorry I didn't make it," Rahmi says, his face reddening. "I meant to, but . . . something kind of came up. You remember Murray, my roommate?"

His mom nods and Rahmi feels the familiar twinge of guilt.

"He's in the hospital now, too. New York Presbyterian."

"He is sick?"

"Sort of," Rahmi says, glancing over at his dad who's listening now, too. "He took a medication that . . . gave him a bad reaction. Now they have to keep him until it's all out of his system."

His parents nod and look serious and solemn, but talking about Murray's situation out loud just makes Rahmi wish he could tell them something true. He wishes he could show how miserable he feels, and how much more Murray means to him than just a roommate. Rahmi looks back at his mom and sees she's still watching him. She smiles. Part of him thinks he's let Seda filter his perception of them for too long—that they can handle a lot more than she says. Maybe this is one thing he doesn't have to carry around forever.

Chapter 31
Trying to Get Home
Rahmi

Rahmi's heart pounds. He's lived in New York his whole life but now he's lost. Another train whooshes by, rattling the platform. They're all the same. When the next train stops, he gets on, adjusting his messenger bag on his shoulder. It's the C train. He lets out a long breath. Good. He can work with that. He'll catch the F and be back on track. The train's nearly empty and he collapses into a seat, wondering how he can be so scattered. He checks his watch. He can still make it home by six. Murray will worry if he's late.

The doors open and Rahmi runs out, checking his watch again. He only has to wait a few seconds before the F pulls in, and he climbs on. He sits, but as the train starts moving, his heart stops. It's going the wrong way.

"Hey!" he yells, jumping up. "We need to stop!"

The few people near him don't even react. They continue reading, or talking, or staring ahead, but no one looks at Rahmi.

"Stop!" he yells again, and moves to pry open the doors.

An older woman comes up to him, and touches his arm. "You'll get in trouble," she says, shaking her head.

"I'm just trying to get home," Rahmi explains, his voice choked with fear.

She pushes a button on the back of her seat and the doors open.

Rahmi races out of the train and up the stairs, into the crowded streets. He can't trust the subway anymore.

He runs for ten blocks before he sees his street, his apartment. He doesn't bother with the elevator, and runs up the stairs, three at a time. He bursts into the apartment, but Murray's already waiting, like Rahmi knew he would be.

"The trains," Rahmi gasps. "They're completely fucked." He leans over, shaking as his body tries to recover, pulling air into his lungs. He coughs a few times, then straightens up. He checks his watch. "I'm sorry."

But Murray's eyes are cold. He doesn't say anything. He just shakes his head, his ears turning fiery red, and pulls back his fist.

Rahmi opens his eyes. His shirt is sticking to him with sweat. He glances around the room.

Murray's coming home today.

He rubs his eyes. He'd been excited. Last night he and Grace had talked about surprising him with a nice dinner. But now he can't deny the unsettling thoughts—the uncertainty—that have crept into his mind the last few days.

Rahmi feels for his glasses, gets out of bed, and changes into a dry shirt. He walks to the kitchen, hoping to find Grace to talk to, but he only finds a note saying she'd gone to help Greg study.

He puts on coffee and runs through everything he has to do before he picks up Murray at three. He's neglected his classes, which used to be his motivation for everything. It's just temporary, though. When things settle down, he'll be back to drowning himself in a thousand pages a week. He might even start writing again.

Rahmi rubs his eyes under his glasses. He forces himself to think about today. If nothing else, he has to finish his paper for Southern Lit, and he needs to see his mom. His dad continues to make that clear. Rahmi pours a cup but lets the coffee continue to brew, knowing he'll need another. He sits at the table and stares off, images of his dream still lingering. It was subconscious, but he still feels guilty. He shouldn't think of Murray like that. It's not fair. Murray goes through hell every time he loses control, and he just needs help.

A door slams down the hall and Rahmi jumps.

"Fuck, you scared me," he says when Jemma shuffles into the kitchen. "I didn't think you were here."

She doesn't say anything.

He studies her face as she roots through the junk drawer, and remembers his promise to Murray. Her lower jaw is discolored, black fading to green. He sees the cut Murray was talking about, under her eye, but he hadn't expected such a nasty bruise surrounding it. His stomach burns and he can understand Murray's impulse to act. But he doesn't want to fight anybody, and Jemma's friends are probably dangerous.

She pulls pliers out of the drawer, which raises other questions, but she's turning back toward her room and Rahmi knows he won't get another chance.

"Jemma, wait."

She stops.

"I need to tell you about Murray."

"Yeah?" She crosses her arms.

"He's in the hospital. He overdosed on morphine."

Jemma stands there, her expression of hardened apathy unwavering.

"I want to ask you," he says, trying to find a hint of humanity in her eyes, "please don't sell to him again, okay?"

"I don't know what you're fucking talking about."

"Come on, Jemma, I kn—"

"No," she interrupts, her eyes blazing. "It wasn't me."

Rahmi sighs. "Okay. Well, if you see him buying from anyone, you'll try to stop him, all right?"

She shrugs.

"Fine," he mutters, understanding that's the best he's going to get. He looks down and almost expects Jemma to be gone when he raises his head, like an apparition. But she's still there, glaring at him. "Are you okay?" he asks. "I mean, looks like you got hurt."

This brings her out of her trance, and she gives him a disgusted look. "I'm fine."

He takes a breath, his leg jittering. "Do you need some help, maybe ... getting out of a bad situation?"

She rolls her eyes. "Not you, too."

"I just wan—"

"You've got your own asshole to worry about," she says, then storms off to her room and locks the door.

Rahmi puts off visiting his mom until the last moment, but as he finishes the dishes—his last distraction before leaving—the phone rings. Relieved, he answers, but doesn't recognize the voice on the other end.

"This is Roger Maldonado," the voice says, sounding annoyed. "Get Murray, will you? I only have twenty minutes today."

"Murray's not here. He's in the hospital."

Roger pauses. "Oh yeah? What'd he get himself into this time?"

Rahmi frowns. "He didn't get himself into anything."

"Okay. So, when's he coming back?"

"I'm not sure." Rahmi cracks his knuckles. Roger hasn't even asked if Murray will be all right. "I mean, you'll give him a week off, right? It wasn't his fault."

"You know about our deal, then?"

"Yeah."

Roger laughs. "Well, this is interesting. I thought we were keeping everything between us but, you know, that's fine."

There's something bizarre about this guy, and Rahmi gets the feeling he isn't sober. But maybe that's just Roger.

"He doesn't tell me what you talk about."

"But I'm guessing you've heard about everything on his end, right?" Rahmi hears him tapping computer keys. "I mean, this kid's dealing with some next-level shit."

"I'm not going to talk about Murray with you."

"But you know, then. That's good. Always important for roommates to be on the same page."

"Listen," Rahmi says, "I'll tell Murray you called."

"Did he tell you about the glass?"

"Roger, I'm not going to do this with you."

"Come on, it's not a secret. I'm just curious."

Rahmi sighs. "Yes, he told me. He said it helped him."

"That's right," Roger replies. "I'm beginning to think he was the only one."

"Well, I'm sure you guys will have lots to talk about next week."

"Have you ever tried it?"

"What?"

"The glass. Have you ever tried it?"

"Why the hell would I?"

"Oh, I don't know," Roger says. "It was big for Murray. All those guys got pretty obsessed with it. I figured you'd want to see what it was like."

Rahmi frowns. "I don't know what you're doing, but your deal is with Murray. I'll tell him you called." Rahmi hangs up before Roger can reply.

Chapter 32
New Normal
Rahmi

I t's still dark when Rahmi opens his eyes. He checks the digital alarm clock on the nightstand. 5:44 a.m. He turns over and sees Murray, sleeping soundly. He smiles. It's good to have him home.

Last night was the first time Rahmi felt relaxed in weeks. Murray was home, joking with Grace like they always had, being attentive and affectionate toward him—it was like the fight and the pills had been a bad dream. Rahmi frowns, watching the dim rays of streetlight shine on Murray's hair. A dream. He closes his eyes. He shouldn't have been so cynical. Everyone goes through shit. Everyone comes back out.

Rahmi starts work today, waiting tables at a mediocre Italian place a few blocks away. He comes home before his shift, knowing he won't be able to focus until he can share his news with Murray. He jogs up the stairs, his messenger bag bouncing behind him, and flings open the apartment door.

"Hey." Murray looks up from the paper he's reading and smiles. "You forget something?"

Rahmi shakes his head and adjusts his glasses as he walks into the living room. He sits next to Murray on the couch.

"My professor wants me to present at the general research conference. She loved my paper about religion and formal realism."

Murray sets the paper aside. "Wow, that's great. Is this the ball-busting professor?"

"Yeah." Rahmi laughs. "I mean, it'll be a lot more research and analysis and all that, but ..." He shakes his head. "She said I could go far in the field."

"No kidding? That's amazing." Murray leans over and gives him a hug. "Well, you deserve it. You've been working so hard."

"Thanks." Rahmi smiles. "I was starting to think English wasn't my thing—that I didn't even have a thing, you know, something I was good at—but . . ." He pauses as he searches for the right words. "It just means a lot, having someone at the top think I've got something to offer."

Murray smiles back. "You've got a lot to offer."

"Thanks." Rahmi takes his hand and squeezes it, then leans against the back of the couch. He glances at the paper resting on the arm. "What were you reading?"

"Oh." Murray reaches over and folds the paper, then clears his throat. "Nothing, just seeing what's out there."

Rahmi nods, hit with a jolt of guilt. In the midst of everything, on the day he's starting a new job, he'd forgotten Murray doesn't have one. He also sees the note from Lamar, with his home number, sticking out from between the folds of the paper. "Did you call Lamar?"

"No, but I need to." Murray glances at the note. "I've got to at least tell him I can't see him anymore."

"What?"

"Yeah, I mean, I was only able to see him because I was working for the university. Even if I were still allowed to be his patient, I could never afford it."

Rahmi's breath comes faster. "Maybe you guys could make some kind of arrangement," he says, running a hand through his hair. "Lamar might cut you a deal. I'm sure he wants to see this through with you."

Murray studies him for a moment, his dark eyes searching for something in Rahmi's. He lowers his head. "I'm not giving up," he says. "I know I still need help. I need it now more than ever." He doesn't look up. "I wish I could continue with Lamar, and I'll ask him if he'll make an exception, if there's any way I can stay on with him. But if not, I will find someone else." Murray lifts his head and meets Rahmi's eyes, determination on his face. "I'm going to get better."

Rahmi nods, and smiles, but can't stop the image of his dream-self running panicked through the streets, checking his watch every few seconds. He takes Murray's hand.

"I know," he says. "I know you will."

Chapter 33
Good Friends Are Like That

I don't have to wait long before Lamar comes out to get me. The receptionist tells him I'm here and he practically sprints out of his office. He's smiling and dressed in his usual formal attire, something I'd imagine an investment banker would wear. My stomach twinges as I think about all the time he's spent on me. All the patience. And this is what he gets for it.

"Murray," he says, shaking my hand as I stand to greet him, "it's good to see you again."

"You, too."

Lamar motions me back.

"Thanks for seeing me so soon," I say, sitting in my regular chair.

"Of course." Lamar reaches for his notepad. "I'm glad you're feeling better."

"Did Rahmi say much?"

"No." He looks at my hands, and I now notice they're shaking. "I'm glad he came by, though," Lamar continues as I cross my arms. "And of course I couldn't share anything with him about our time together."

I nod. I'm not sure what Lamar could say that Rahmi doesn't know already, but for some reason this makes me feel better. "Before we start," I say, frowning as he uncaps a pen, "I need to ask you something."

"Sure."

"When I called, I told the receptionist this would have to be my last session. That I lost my job with the university."

Lamar turns to a blank sheet in his notepad. "Right."

I take a breath. I think about Rahmi, the look on his face when I told him I had to quit. I can't let him down again. "I'm wondering if there's any way I can keep on with you. I've got some savings, and maybe if we scaled back the sessions—"

"Murray," Lamar interrupts, "let me stop you there." He pauses, twirling his pen. "I'd long ago made up my mind to work with you as long as you were interested, regardless of your financial situation or status with NYU. That's how strongly I feel about your potential to improve." He gives me a serious look. "I don't think it's a good idea to scale back on sessions. I was going to suggest moving to a full hour each week."

"An hour?"

"Yes. If you're willing, I'd like to start that next week. Nothing else about our arrangement would change. Is that okay with you?"

I pause. "You'd do that? For free?"

"Yes." He watches me for a moment. "Murray, this isn't just a job for me. If there's a way I can help a patient, I'm not going to let bureaucracy stand in the way."

I sit back. "Thank you." I try to smile. "Sorry, I just, I didn't expect that."

"I'm glad you want to continue." Lamar sits up at his desk again. "So," he says, "can we talk about the morphine?"

My wrists jolt.

The morphine. Jemma. The hospital. Rahmi. The fight. The flashback.

I shake my head. "I can't."

"You can't?"

"I won't get through it. Not today." I run my hands through my hair. "It's all pretty bad."

Lamar leans forward. "It's okay if you don't get through it. It's not supposed to be easy." He smiles. "And if you're worried about me, you should know it takes a lot to surprise me."

I nod. I should know that. When I told him I'd killed my father in self-defense, he didn't blink. He was on my side, as I assumed he would be, but that was different. That happened ten years ago. I was a kid. Now here I am, continuing down the same path as an adult.

"Is next time okay?" I ask, still fighting to untangle the threads in my mind. "I thought I was coming here to say goodbye, so I'm not really ready for all this."

Lamar nods. "It's all right." He's tapping his blank notepad and I'm wondering if I should make a move to leave. I stand, but he looks up. "How's everybody in Cleveland?"

"About the same," I say, sitting back down. "They're coming out this weekend."

"John and Austin?"

"Yeah."

"To New York?"

I nod. "Rahmi called them the night . . . when I was in the hospital. They were pretty worried. I've tried to tell them I'm fine, but I guess they don't believe me."

Lamar smiles. "Good friends are like that."

"Yeah." I crack my knuckles and glance at the clock behind him. "I'm sorry," I say, "I won't be able to get into much today."

Lamar sets his pen down and rises to his feet. "It's okay. I know you weren't prepared. But you have my number if you need me before next week."

"Thanks." I shake his hand. "Really, I appreciate what you're doing for me."

"You're very welcome." He gives me a side-smile. "Don't forget, it's a full hour next time."

"Okay."

As I turn to leave his office, I understand he's telling me to be prepared to fill it. I guess there are some things I need to say to Rahmi first.

Chapter 34
Murray's Flash

When I get home, I find Grace and Rahmi both reading in the living room, though Grace looks a lot less happy about it.

"Good," she says, slamming her book closed when she sees me, "I could use a break."

"How were your errands?" Rahmi asks as I move to the living room.

"Good." I sit on the couch next to him. "Really good."

Rahmi smiles and Grace is looking at us, so I clear my throat and turn to her.

"When's the test?"

Grace glances up at the clock. "An hour." She sighs and collects her stack of books from the coffee table. "I can't do any more. I'm going to take a walk before class."

"You want me to quiz you one more time?" Rahmi asks.

"No, that's all right." She pulls on her backpack. "Thanks."

"Hey, good luck," I say as she opens the door.

"Fuck chemistry," she mutters without looking back.

As soon as the door closes, Rahmi turns to me, thumping my leg. His face is lit with such genuine optimism, it makes my stomach sink to know how much he has riding on my sessions with Lamar. On my mental stability.

"So," he says, "it went well with Lamar?"

I nod. "He says I can see him for longer sessions, and he still won't charge me at all."

"Really?"

"Yeah. He was amazing about the whole thing. He thinks I can improve."

Rahmi's face breaks out in a broad smile. "Of course you can."

My stomach churns again and I'm losing the glow of relief I'd had leaving Lamar's office. I'm slipping back to a dark place. Rahmi's saying all the right things and I'm still overcome with dread.

"Rahmi," I say, unable to look him in the eye, "I know I told you this in the hospital, but . . ." I force myself to meet his face. To see him. "I am so sorry."

Rahmi takes my hand. "It's okay. It's just something we have to move past."

His grip is strong and secure, and it reminds me of how powerful he is. If he'd wanted to, he could have demolished me that night. But that's the difference between us: he didn't want to.

"You don't want me to mention it anymore?"

He shrugs. "I just don't think it's necessary."

I nod. "Can I say one more thing about it?"

"Sure."

"You said you were okay, and I know you can handle a lot." I look away and he squeezes my hand. "Please tell me if that changes, okay? I'll understand."

Rahmi doesn't say anything. He takes off his glasses and rubs his eyes. I feel like he does this sometimes to buy time before he responds, so now I worry I'm too late. That things have already changed. He puts them back on and smiles. "I will," he says, but I know it's not that simple. I look down—Rahmi's let go of my hand.

"I should get to the pharmacy," I say, looking back up at the clock. "I never did refill my prescription."

Rahmi nods.

I guess that's it, so I stand, but he stops me.

"Wait," he says. "Just a second, okay?"

I sit back down, my throat tight. "What's up?"

"Can I ask you something?"

"Of course."

"After the fight, when you went into the bathroom . . ." He pauses, like he's trying to work out a delicate way to say it. "Did you take too much morphine on purpose?"

I frown. "Yeah, I hoped taking a lot would stop the flashback."

Rahmi studies me. "So, you weren't . . . you didn't try to kill yourself?"

My whole body jolts. Stomach acid burns my mouth. I cover my face with my hands, shielding my eyes from the flickering fluorescent lights of Austin's bathroom. Water drips from the sink's faucet, and the intercept message blares from the phone down the hall where I'd left it off the hook. And Austin, unshaven and glistening with sweat, is lying on the floor, laboring to breathe. I see myself, trying to count the remaining pills on the grimy laminate tile as my hands shake, yelling for his neighbors who never did hear me.

I raise my head, trying to see past the blinding light that envelops my vision, but before I can recover, Chase's voice pounds in my ears. It's pulling me out, back to the funeral. He's telling me how he'd found Mr. Everett. He spares me the details, but my mind puts the pieces together anyway, and never lets me forget. The blood and shattered glass still seep into my imagination sometimes, but now it's an assault. I see Mr. Everett, making the decision. And I see him doing it, the part I'd always managed to censor from my mind.

"Murray!"

Someone's shaking me. I blink a few times and the light fades. My distorted vision clears. Rahmi. He looks scared. I glance around. I'm on the floor and he's holding my arms and staring into my eyes.

"Murray," he says again, "what happened? Are you all right?"

"It was Cleveland," I say, still dazed. "Finding Austin, and Mr. Everett."

"Flashbacks?" He looks confused. "I thought that was just your dad."

"I guess not."

I make a move to stand and Rahmi helps me back onto the couch. My heart's still racing and I don't trust my surroundings yet. We sit in silence for a minute or two, but then Rahmi grabs my arm, a wild look in his eyes.

"Oh, Jesus," he says, "I did it. I made you flash back." He presses his hands to his temples. "I shouldn't have said that, about the pills. I'm so sorry."

"No, no," I say, shaking my head. "They happen sometimes. It's not your fault."

"Are you okay now?"

I nod, trying to ignore the last fleeting images. "And I do want you to know, it wasn't on purpose. Not like that."

"Okay." He looks a little more at ease.

I think for a second he's going to say something else, but he pulls me in for a long hug. When he releases me, there are tears in his eyes, but also a strange uneasiness, and as usual I can't tell what he's thinking.

Chapter 35
Noel

Rahmi and I decide to take a walk before we meet Grace for dinner. I haven't felt back to normal yet. I still have a fog surrounding me, but being out with him, talking about simple, boring, everyday shit, I almost feel like myself again.

We watch a cab unload a crowd of older tourists in front of Artichoke's, then walk past a row of brightly colored apartment buildings before we round the corner from MacDougal back onto Bleecker. As I catch sight of our building, I see Jemma. She's with him, the guy from the convenience store.

"Rahmi, look," I say in a hushed voice, slowing down. "That's the asshole, with Jemma."

We stop and I pull him closer to the store we're walking by, hoping to be less conspicuous. I peer down the street. I can't see the guy's face, but he's pointing up to the apartment with an animated gesture. Jemma has her arms crossed and looks pissed, like always. She shakes her head and the guy raises his voice, but I can't hear what he's saying.

"He's just getting started," I mutter. "We should go help her."

"No," Rahmi says.

I turn and he's frowning at them.

"You don't even have a plan."

"What plan do I need?" My voice is louder than I'd intended. "It's pretty straightforward."

But Rahmi shakes his head and continues to watch. I turn back to them and see Jemma laughing. But the hair on the back of my neck creeps up because something's not right. The guy's not laughing. His back is still to me, but his hands are at his sides, squeezing open and closed.

"This is bad," I say under my breath.

"What?"

I don't answer Rahmi. I'm fixed on this guy now. He's about my height, but not as muscular. Good. Jemma looks like she's telling him off about something, and I don't like how quiet he is. And still. She doesn't even notice his hands. She makes a move to leave. She waves at him, in a sarcastic, fuck-you kind of way, and turns away, but that breaks his trance. He grabs her arm and pulls her back toward the building. I wipe my hands on my jacket and walk toward them.

"Hey," Rahmi calls behind me.

I keep going, making my way through the throng of pedestrians.

The guy pushes her against the wall and holds her shoulder with one hand while he lectures her, waving the other around. I know what he's doing. He's just getting started. My blood pumps like crazy, thudding in my ears and setting my face on fire. I run.

But Rahmi grabs me from behind. "Hey," he says, leading me out of view, "what the hell are you doing?"

"What are *you* doing?" I exclaim, shaking him off. "Don't you get what's going on?"

"Yeah," he says, glancing up at Jemma. "But you're going to make it worse. You'll make things worse for her. Okay?"

"Worse than that?" I yell, pointing toward them.

Rahmi holds his hands up, shushing me. "I need you to calm down before we do anything."

My head is throbbing, and I'm trying to breathe, trying to hear him, trying to do the right thing. But Jesus-fucking-Christ, Rahmi doesn't get it.

"I'm not going to scare him if I'm calm," I say through gritted teeth.

My eyes dart over and the guy's yelling now. Jemma's face is blank. Rahmi's watching too and I know he's worried. We need to go.

"Let me try something," he says, and motions for me to follow him.

I can't imagine what he's planning to do, but I don't really give a shit because at least we're doing something.

"Hey!" Rahmi calls out as we get close. "Jemma! Are you ready or what?" Rahmi's voice is booming and the guy looks startled when he turns to see us behind him.

"Who the fuck are you?"

Rahmi ignores him and continues talking to Jemma. "Seriously, we're going to be late. Grace is already waiting."

I don't have this kind of finesse, so I stand next to Rahmi, trying to look intimidating.

"Come on, Jem, who are these guys?"

Jemma pulls out her cigarettes. "Roommates," she says. She clicks her lighter on and holds it to the end of one.

"You better be fucking kidding me."

"It's fine, Noel," Jemma says, rolling her eyes. "They're gays."

Noel gives us a long, disdainful glare. "Yeah?"

I return his glare. "You need us to make out?"

He seems to be thinking about it, but I can't stand here much longer and maintain composure.

"Jemma, really, let's go," I say, stepping forward. "Grace will have to give up our table."

She nods and looks at Noel, who still seems confused by the whole thing. He's also stealing uneasy glances at Rahmi.

"Yeah," she says, taking a cautious step toward me and Rahmi. "Okay."

I move between her and Noel, but I'm not convinced it's over.

He checks his watch, then turns to Jemma again. "Hey, what about our thing?"

"It's fine," she says. "We'll do it next time."

"All of it?" he asks, his voice hard.

She nods. "Fine."

"Good." He flicks away the cigarette he'd been holding. "See you around."

I expect him to get lost at this point, but he doesn't. He leans his back against the brick exterior of our building and folds his arms across his chest, frowning at us.

"Let's go," Jemma mutters. "Now."

We start walking, Jemma in between us. Her steps are quick and focused and she's not looking back, so I don't either.

"What the fuck was that?" I ask when we turn the corner onto Mercer.

She keeps her eyes down. "Nothing."

I glance over her head at Rahmi. He gives me a quick headshake.

We keep walking in silence until we get to the pizza place. Grace is there, and she waves to us in exasperation from the window. Rahmi holds the door open and I turn to Jemma.

"Will you come in with us? I don't think you should leave yet."

She gazes down the street, back the way we came. Weighing her options, I guess. Trying to decide if potential retribution from a violent douchebag is worse than an hour with us. She looks back at me, then at Rahmi. She nods and walks through the door. I give Rahmi a surprised look and follow her.

"What the hell, you guys?" Grace says, pointing to her watch as we come up to the booth. Rahmi sits next to Grace, and I hang back to let Jemma go in first on our side, but she shakes her head.

"I'll take the outside."

I shrug and slide in, ignoring the shocked expression on Grace's face.

"Be nice," Rahmi murmurs.

Jemma's eyes are glued to her menu as the rest of us trade intense looks—Rahmi and me pleading with Grace to be cool, and Grace indicating she has no intention of playing along.

"Okay, wait," she says, holding up her hands. "Jemma, you're eating with us?"

Jemma doesn't lift her eyes. "Looks that way."

"Listen," I say, running my hands over my eyes, "it was a good time for us to get off the street. And, you know, we live together. We can all go out."

Grace narrows her eyes and looks at Rahmi, like she's hoping he'll tell her the truth.

"It's fine," Jemma says, still scanning her menu. "You can say it."

I pause. "What?"

She closes the menu and looks up. "That my asshole boyfriend was making a big fucking scene and you guys gave me an excuse to leave."

"Yeah?" Grace says, leaning forward. "I bet Murray decked him, huh?"

"No," I say, my face heating up. "Rahmi had a better plan."

"I wouldn't try to fight him," Jemma says. Her tone is flat, almost bored. "He always has a knife on him, sometimes a gun."

My heart rate picks up and I nearly drop my water glass. Why didn't I think of that? I was so high on adrenaline, caught up in how satisfying it would be to take this guy out, that I never considered he might have a weapon. Of course he does. I look over at Rahmi. It wasn't just Jemma he was looking out for.

"So where is he now?" Grace asks. "Your boyfriend?"

Jemma shrugs.

"But, you're going to break up with him, right?" Grace frowns, like she might be missing something. "I mean, he sounds like a huge dick."

"Yeah, maybe." Jemma looks at me. "Can you front me the cash for this? I can pay you tomorrow."

"Don't worry. I got it."

"Thanks."

Jemma shifts in her seat. The waiter comes and takes our orders, but now she looks even more uncomfortable without the menu to focus on.

I tap my fingers together. "Grace, how'd you do on the chemistry test?"

"Ninety-four," she replies, still watching Jemma.

"Wow," Rahmi says. "And you thought you were fucked."

"Yeah." She laughs. "I guess Greg and I are a good team after all."

"And don't forget I quizzed you," Rahmi says.

"Yeah, that was probably the difference."

"And you've got two more tomorrow, right?" I ask.

Grace nods. "Biology and Latin. But those shouldn't be as bad, they're just—"

"I can't break up with him," Jemma interrupts, staring at her water glass. She clears her throat and looks up at us.

"Why not?" Rahmi asks, his voice low and gentle. He glances at Grace, then at me.

Jemma shakes her head and sits there for a minute, and it seems like she's changed her mind. I don't blame her. I don't expect her to trust us. Grace's patience is wearing thin, though, and I hope Jemma says something before she demands it.

Then Jemma laughs. It's like before, outside the apartment. There are glints of fear and shame in her eyes, and we're close to losing her.

"It's all right," I say, leaning in a little, but she turns away.

"No." Her eyes are red and watery. "Never mind."

"Why can't you?" Grace asks, but it's over. We need to stop.

I try to give Grace a look, to tell her to lay off, but she doesn't see me.

Jemma's frowning and shaking her head. "No," she keeps saying. "No." She looks toward the exit like she might need to escape. "I shouldn't have said anything. Just forget it, okay? It's fine."

"It'll only get worse," Grace says, her eyes fierce. "It always does."

"Grace," I hiss, giving her a hard look. "Cut it out."

"No," Jemma says, louder. "I said forget it."

She jumps up and pushes past a man walking by.

"Jemma, wait," I call after her, getting to my feet. But she races out the door and there's nothing I can do.

I watch her hurry down the sidewalk, back toward Bleecker, and my heart plummets. Rahmi was right; I made things worse.

Chapter 36
John Steps In
Rahmi

It's only been a couple of hours, but Rahmi's sure Austin doesn't like him. He sits stiffly on the couch, his thick silver hair hidden under a faded baseball cap, giving Rahmi stern sideways glances. His dirty jeans and sweatshirt seem to indicate a hard travel day, along with the fifth beer in his hand, but John's appearance offers a stark contradiction. His long-sleeved T-shirt and khakis are clean and unwrinkled, his long hair looks well kept, and his eyes are clear. Sitting next to each other, they look like a before-and-after makeover.

Rahmi knows this visit means a lot to Murray, but he needs a new approach. The few times Austin has addressed him, he's only spoken in gruff one- or two-word responses. He mostly talks to Murray, which is fine, and Rahmi does his best to maintain a kind, welcoming manner, but it makes him wonder. It could be that he's Turkish. Austin's older, working class, military . . . Maybe that's unfair, though. He seems charmed by Grace, who laughs whenever he says something funny—usually about Murray— and asks myriad questions about his life in Cleveland. It's hard not to like Grace, though.

Rahmi stretches his arms above his head, digging his back into the stiff kitchen chair. He and Murray brought two of them into the living room to use so John and Austin could have the couch. Grace lounges on the recliner in her sweats, as if their guests were just two more roommates she's known for months. Rahmi's shoulder pops as he brings his arms back down, and he resists the impulse to put an arm around Murray. He shifts in his seat and sees Austin watching him again. Rahmi smiles but Austin doesn't. It could be the relationship. Austin isn't at ease with Murray dating men—Murray told him this before. But he mentioned it in an offhand, almost amused way, like he thought it was endearing. Rahmi wipes his forehead.

Grace gets up and announces she's going to bed. Rahmi glances at the kitchen clock. It's after eleven. He looks at the others but they seem content to stay. Rahmi frowns, wondering how they'll pick up Grace's share of the conversation.

"So, Rahmi," John says, his eyes warm, "Murray tells me you're a writer, too."

Rahmi coughs a little, his face reddening as he shoots Murray a look. "That's a pretty generous way to put it," he says with a laugh. "He probably meant to say 'waiter.'"

"No, no," Murray says, giving Rahmi's shoulder a brief squeeze. "Rahmi's good. I've read some of his poetry. And this project he's working on for the research conference is going to be amazing."

"That's great," John says, leaning back against the couch. "I admire anybody who can get their mind around poetry. Is that your concentration?"

"Part of it. I wanted to focus on creative writing and world literature, so I'm doing both."

"Wow, good for you."

"Thanks. I hope I can use it in real life someday."

John nods and gives him a reassuring smile. "I tell you, it might have taken me a while to use it professionally, but getting that English degree was the best thing I ever did. I can see you have that kind of passion, too."

Rahmi nods and is about to reply when Austin jumps in.

"So, when do you graduate?" he asks in a hard voice.

Rahmi stops, his mind blanking for a moment. He rubs the back of his neck. "Well, that's a good question," he says, his smile fading along with the confidence he'd gained from talking with John. "I can't afford to take many classes at once, so unfortunately it's slow going, even at a community college." He pauses and Murray rests his hand on Rahmi's leg. It's a sweet gesture, but right now it sends his nerves through the roof. "I, well, I'm hoping I can do it in two more years."

Austin nods and takes a long drink of his beer. His eyes are glazed and Murray's watching him, too.

"You getting tired?" Murray asks. He looks to John. They trade glances that seem to signal it's time to go.

Austin shrugs, setting his bottle on the coffee table in line with the others.

John clears his throat. "We should call it a night," he says, nudging Austin a little. He looks up at Rahmi. "But I'd love to talk writing with you more tomorrow."

"That would be great."

John stands and helps Austin to his feet.

"Come as early as you like," Murray says, giving them each a hug. "We'll be here."

"Good to meet you," Rahmi says, shaking Austin's hand.

He nods in return.

"I'll walk you guys down." Murray grabs his coat off the hook. "I want to show you the map I was talking about." He follows Austin to the door, but John hangs back.

"You guys go ahead," he says. "I'm going to use the bathroom first."

Murray nods and closes the door behind him.

Rahmi moves out of the way to give John a clear path down the hallway, but he doesn't move. Rahmi's palms sweat because John's just standing there, frowning into space like he's about to break some horrible news. But then he meets Rahmi's eyes and smiles.

"I'm sorry," he says, cracking his knuckles. "I was hoping we could talk for a minute."

"Sure."

"I guess I wanted to ask you—is Murray okay? I know he says he is, but . . . he keeps a lot to himself."

Rahmi nods, his muscles relaxing a little. "Yeah, I think so."

He pauses a moment, trying to read John, to gauge his trustworthiness. His calm and affable manner set Rahmi at ease right away, but this isn't small talk anymore. He has to be careful. He looks past John, forced again to remember that night.

"I did ask him about the pills," Rahmi says. "I asked if he overdosed on purpose. He said he didn't, and I believe him."

John lets out a long breath. "Good."

"And he's committed to therapy," Rahmi continues, wondering how much is his to share. "The counselor he's seeing is great."

John nods. "And what about you?"

"Me?" Rahmi's heart beats a little faster.

"Are you okay?" His face is serious, almost stern.

"What do you mean?"

"Murray told me you guys had a fight." John crosses his arms. "He said it was his fault—that he really messed up. I think he was afraid to tell me any more than that."

Rahmi swallows hard. He is okay, mostly. On some level it feels silly and embarrassing for him not to be. And to divulge this to a stranger . . . his face heats up. John is Murray's father figure, not his.

John's frown deepens with Rahmi's silence. "Did he get violent?"

"There was a lot going on," Rahmi says. "He'd just lost his job, and we'd been at the hospital that evening for my mom. We were both exhausted and nobody was thinking straight."

"So, he hit you." John's voice is hard.

"No."

Rahmi wishes he could leave it at that, but it would only delay what's coming. John already knows there's more. "He pushed me. He tried to punch me, but I stopped him."

John shakes his head and begins pacing around the kitchen. His eyes are focused and severe, and for the first time, Rahmi can imagine him as a soldier. His frustration seems to grow as he paces, his breath coming hard and fast. Soon he looks so furious Rahmi worries he made things bad for Murray.

"He's trying to get better," Rahmi says, watching him cautiously. "He knows what he did was wrong."

"Then he needs to stop fucking doing it," John snaps.

"He's never worked on it before. Not like this. It's going to take time."

John comes around the counter to where Rahmi's standing and looks in his eyes. "Listen to me," he says, his voice softer but still serious. "I love Murray. He is a son to me and I would do anything for him." John runs a shaky hand over his eyes. "But he isn't safe. And you can't ignore what he's doing."

"I'm not trying to ignore it; I just want to help him. I want to be here for him."

"Then you're putting yourself at risk. This is his pattern, Rahmi."

Rahmi's eyes burn. "I can handle myself. I stopped him, remember?"

John looks down for a moment, his jaw tense. "I know. Murray's a big guy, but you're bigger. You think you could set him straight if you needed to, right?"

Rahmi doesn't say anything.

"It doesn't matter," John continues. "It'll get to you in other ways. Even if you block every punch he throws, it doesn't change the fact that he shouldn't be throwing them in the first place."

Rahmi blinks hard, determined to cover this rising wave of emotion. "It's not who he is. That was one time."

"With you." John narrows his eyes. "So far."

The room blurs and Rahmi's stomach turns. John isn't being fair. And for Murray's closest friend, he doesn't seem to think very much of him. He doesn't see this as the temporary issue it is. And he's not giving Murray the credit he deserves—the acknowledgment that he's come so far. Maybe John just doesn't trust Rahmi to be the person to see him through it.

John's regarding him now with a strange mix of sympathy and frustration, and he needs to say something, to let John know he's wrong. But as the familiar uneasiness comes seeping back into Rahmi's mind, he realizes he isn't sure. He can't predict Murray anymore. But that's no reason to desert him. Rahmi levels his gaze at John.

"He can't do it alone."

John shakes his head, his eyes hardening again. "He has to do it alone."

Chapter 37
Unsettled
Rahmi

It takes Murray a few minutes to come back up after John leaves. Rahmi supposes they're working on a plan for tomorrow. He moves the kitchen chairs back into place and sinks into one, resting his arms on the table. He tosses his glasses aside and bows his head, his heart beating fast. He tries to shut out John's words but they saturate his mind.

It'll get to you in other ways.

His chest is burning and he presses his fists into his eyes, praying the feeling subsides. He breathes.

He doesn't want to think about Murray like that. Like he's an enemy. But Rahmi can't deny his behavior around him has already changed. He lifts his head from the table, releasing the pressure from his eyes and blinking away dark spots that cloud his vision. Last week he'd told Murray the cashier at JW gave him the student discount, even though he'd forgotten to ask for it. It was a small thing, and Murray probably wouldn't care, but Rahmi wasn't sure. He's never sure anymore.

Rahmi frowns, picturing the concern in John's eyes. Now fragments of their life together come rushing in, filling out the picture. The other day, he flinched when Murray reached over him for a box of cereal on the high shelf. A few days later, he gave in during an argument about where to go over the weekend, fearing an outburst. And ever since his dream, Rahmi has been obsessed with time. If he thinks he'll be even a few minutes late, he'll find a phone and call Murray. Rahmi rubs his eyes, then puts his glasses back on. Now he's the one being unfair. Murray wasn't at fault for any of those things. He never intended to hit Rahmi when he reached over him. He wasn't unreasonable during their argument last week; he just wanted his own way. And it's Rahmi's own subconscious making him check in obsessively—Murray has never been mad at him for being late.

"Hey," Murray says, walking back into the apartment.

Rahmi starts a little, but Murray seems unaware. He closes the door and sits across from him at the table, smiling.

"Thanks for having John and Austin over. It's good to see them again."

"Of course. I'm glad to get to meet them."

Murray shifts a little in his seat. "What were you and John talking about?" he asks, and Rahmi can tell he's trying to sound casual. "I figured maybe you guys got into a writing discussion or something, but when he came down, he seemed mad. He kind of blew me off."

"Oh yeah?" Rahmi's pulse quickens.

"Yeah. He was upset about something."

"I think he was just worried. He wanted to make sure you're okay."

"About the pills?"

"Right."

"You told him I am, right?" Murray laughs a little, but his eyes are serious.

Rahmi nods. "Yeah. He seemed to understand, but ... it's probably just hard for him, you know? Being so far away."

Murray drums his fingers on the table. "Yeah, I guess you're right."

"I'm a little worried about Austin, though," Rahmi says with a smile. "He doesn't seem to like me."

"No, don't take it personally. He's slow to warm up." Murray's face is drawn, and Rahmi knows he's still focused on John.

"Seemed to like Grace, though."

"Yeah." His brow furrows. "He's also got kind of a protective streak with me, for some reason. John called him on it when he came down."

"Really?"

"Yeah, he told Austin you're a good guy and he should stop being a dick." Murray smiles. "Tomorrow should be better."

"So, it's not a race thing? Or a gay thing?"

"Oh, no." Murray sits up. "I'm sorry, I didn't know you were worrying about that. I guess I should have prepared you more for him."

Rahmi waves his hand. "It's okay." He looks past Murray, toward the door. "It's nice that he's looking out for you."

Murray nods and Rahmi continues to stare off. John's probably already told Austin everything. They could both show up tomorrow pissed at Murray and he'd be blindsided. He'd see it as his best friends turning against him when he needs them most. And he'd hate Rahmi for it.

"I have to go to bed," Murray says, like it just dawned on him. He rubs his face and stands up. "Oh, what do you think about the Statue of Liberty tomorrow? The guys seemed into it."

"Sure, that'd be fun." Rahmi tries to sound upbeat, but right now the thought of playing tour guide is unbearable.

"And Austin wants to get a bagel. That's all he said."

Rahmi laughs. "We can do that."

"Awesome. Thanks." Murray walks around the table and rubs Rahmi's shoulders. "You're amazing. I really appreciate this."

Rahmi nods. "Don't mention it."

Chapter 38
Tour Guide

As Austin squints across New York Harbor, shielding his eyes from the mid-morning sun, I take the opportunity to study his appearance. He looks better than I thought. He's skipped a few days of shaving, still has on the same ratty clothes he wears for construction jobs, but his eyes are clearer today. The way John had been talking, I feared he was heading back to his inaccessible days, clouded with rage, alcohol, and relentless depression. Like the day we met.

He points out something to John on the horizon. The light catches his silver hair and highlights the creases that surround his eyes. He'll always be rough, unkempt, a little abrasive, but I've seen him in dark times and this isn't the same. The fact that he made this trip at all says a lot. So many times in his life, several in the decade I've known him, Austin's depression wouldn't let him leave his apartment.

"How deep's the water?" he asks, turning to me.

I blink a few times, bringing my mind back to the present. "Twenty feet, maybe thirty?" I shrug.

Austin nods and turns back to face the harbor. I'm not sure why he'd want to know, but my answer seems to satisfy him. Rahmi, who had been walking the length of pavement in front of us, comes over and stands next to me.

"We got the best day for this," he says, gazing up at the clear blue sky.

I smile. After what I worried was a traumatic experience with Austin last night, he seems happy today. And I noticed the two of them talking earlier, Rahmi giving Austin reassuring nods and smiles, after which Austin clapped him warmly on the shoulder.

"Yeah, we did." I put my arm around Rahmi and gaze out toward the shimmering skyline. It feels like a moment I'll come back to down the line.

The weather's clear and warm, so we walk around the park for a while, through the sprawling green space and along the waterline. Austin and I end up walking behind Rahmi and John, and I realize I haven't really talked with Austin yet.

"So," I begin, slowing my pace a little to match his, "how's work?"

"Steady, for once," he says with a dry smile.

"Oh, yeah? That's great."

"It is." He pauses. "Sometimes I think it's more than I can handle."

I frown. "But you can turn down jobs, right?"

He nods. "I shouldn't, though." He fixes his eyes on the paved brick path and I decide not to push it.

"Well, thanks for taking time off to come out here."

"You bet." He clears his throat. "And listen, I'm sorry about being shitty to Rahmi last night. I apologized to him earlier but I figure I owe it to you, too."

I glance over, but Austin doesn't look up.

"I guess I just wanted to show him we still have your back."

I nod, offering a smile even though a hard knot has settled in my stomach. "I understand. Thanks."

He doesn't respond and we walk in silence for a minute, listening to the light bits of conversation and laughter from Rahmi and John up ahead. The knot in my stomach rises to my throat as I think about how fucked up it is for Austin to be worried about Rahmi's intentions. If only he knew how many times Rahmi saved our relationship, and how many times I set it on fire. He'd be telling Rahmi to run.

"So, you like it here?" Austin asks, turning to face me. His blue eyes are bright and piercing.

I nod. "Yeah, I like it here."

"Ever miss Cleveland?" He smirks a little, like he's making a joke.

"Well ... I miss you guys."

He laughs. "Okay." He scuffs his shoe a little on the pavement. "I get it."

"I mean, come on, would you miss it?"

Austin shakes his head. "This isn't about me," he says, the humor gone from his eyes. "But when things get tough, I like to be in a place I know."

"When things get tough?"

"Yeah." He looks up toward Rahmi and John. "I'd be fucked if I left Cleveland now."

I nod, but my heart's heavy. I get what he's trying to say. And I can no longer pretend they came to New York just to check on me.

Chapter 39

Try Again

That afternoon I return to our place alone. The apartment is quiet, and at first I think Jemma's not here, but as I scan the kitchen and hall I see her lighter on the counter and a plastic grocery bag leaning against the wall by her door. She probably thought we'd be gone all day. I glance up at the clock. Rahmi will be back from the store in the next fifteen minutes or so. I leave my shoes and coat by the door and take careful steps down the hall, hoping to hear some movement inside her room. But I've already decided to go through with this, even if it means waking her up and enduring her rage.

"Jemma?" I call out, my voice unsure. "Hey, open up."

I knock a few times, but there's no answer. I press my ear to the door and there's a gentle rustling, like she's getting out of bed.

"Jemma," I call louder, "it's Murray. I need to talk to you." I rest my forehead against her door, my stomach pitching as it anticipates my next move. "I'm out," I say, closing my eyes. "And I've got money now." After a moment, I lift my head and knock again.

More noise from behind the door, then the slow click and pop of her unlocking it.

"How many?" Jemma asks, opening the door just enough for me to see her face. No new bruises as far as I can tell. My muscles relax.

"Ten. Same as last time." I dig my wallet out of my back pocket and pull sixty dollars from between its folds. I pause before slipping in another twenty while she reaches down to adjust her sock. She opens the door wide now and crosses her arms. She's wearing a shabby Hard Rock Café T-shirt, a few sizes too big, and black leggings. She glares at me while I hold the money out to her.

"He told me not to sell to you," she says, nodding toward Rahmi's door. "I know what I'm doing now."

She looks at the money, then back up at me. "Hold on." She disappears into her room, letting the door creak nearly closed while I wait, my nerves braced for Rahmi's return.

Jemma reappears a minute later with an envelope like the one she gave me last time. She opens it for me to see. Ten purple pills. My mouth goes dry just looking at them, and I force my hands into my pockets to stop them from shaking. I take a step back but nod to her, swallowing the emerging fear as best I can.

"Okay," I say, once again holding out the cash.

She looks at it dancing in my trembling hand. "You're sure?"

"Yeah. Just one at a time, right?" I smile.

Her hard, searching eyes don't waver from mine. "Right." She hands me the envelope and takes the money. She doesn't count it.

I sense she's about to close the door on me, so I shove the envelope in my back pocket and take a step closer to her. "Can I ask you something?"

"Oh, Jesus," she mutters, resting a hand on the doorframe and letting out a heavy sigh.

"You said before that you couldn't break up with Noel," I say, trying to get through it before she shuts me out. "But maybe I can help."

"Help?" Jemma laughs. "Like you did before?"

My face burns and I clench my jaw. "We got you away from him, didn't we?"

"Don't be an idiot, Denver," she says, her glare piercing me again. "I still had to go back. After you guys put on your bullshit macho show, how do you think that went?"

My stomach sinks. I rub my forehead and take a few breaths, subduing the need to throw up, for a little while anyway. "I'm sorry," I say, shaking my head.

There's so much more I want to say, but it's nothing Jemma wants to hear. I lower my eyes. I want to tell her I know this asshole's path so well, I could have paved it myself. I want to tell her it won't be long before he blows up again, and Grace was right: it will only get worse. I want to tell her she doesn't have to do everything herself. But she doesn't trust me, and she shouldn't.

"It was a nice try, though," she says, and I look up because her voice is a little softer.

I realize I must have been standing there with a pained expression on my face for several seconds, and now she's watching me with pity-infused hatred.

"Get somebody, then," I say. I can't handle any more of her deflections, and Rahmi will be home soon. "It doesn't have to be me, but you'll need help. He's dangerous."

She looks away. "It's more complicated than that."

My ears heat up again as my patience erodes. "You're making it harder than it has to be. Just let somebody help you for once."

She doesn't say anything but I can tell my harsh tone erased our millimeter of progress. I run my hands through my hair, trying to breathe, but I can't diffuse my building anger. "If you won't take care of this, I'll get the police involved."

Jemma's eyes turn cold. "That's the dumbest fucking thing you've said yet." Her grip on the side of the doorframe tightens so forcefully I wouldn't be surprised if she ripped it off the wall. "Noel will kill you," she says, her expression fierce. "And if you call the police, I'm not going to fucking care if he does."

She slams the door and the lock pops closed.

I stand there a moment before walking back down the hallway to the kitchen. I rest my arms on the counter, drained. I failed again. I have no idea how to help her and my clumsy attempts only drive her away. I need to stop. I just wish she could see the whole picture—the damage that ignoring her own instincts will do.

I straighten up, remembering the morphine in my back pocket. I dig out the envelope and open it, letting the anxiety wash over me again. Jemma said these pills were made for people like me, but she was wrong. One hundred fifty milligrams couldn't even stop me from killing my dad. I don't know why I expected anything to. I crumple the envelope in my hand and walk over to the sink. I open the cabinet below and throw it in the trash can, then unroll six or seven paper towels and push them down on top.

Chapter 40
Rai Rai Ken

It's John and Austin's last night in town. Rahmi has to work, so John tells me to pick somewhere for dinner. He asks if I have a favorite place, but he'll insist on paying, so I tell him it's Rai Rai Ken, an inexpensive noodle shop a few blocks away.

"This is great," Austin says as we walk in, gazing around at the flashy red-and-gold décor. He turns to me and smiles. "Very New York."

The restaurant isn't crowded and we're directed to an empty booth right away. John hasn't said much, except to remark that it doesn't seem like a very popular spot.

"There's a late crowd," I say, sliding into my side of the booth. John and Austin sit together opposite me. "Don't worry, it's good."

John smiles but doesn't respond. He's been strange all day—distant and distracted, like there's something on his mind. I watch him jitter his thumb against the table. It's not just today. John has grown quieter, more anxious, more serious these past few years. I guess it makes sense; this decade has taken a toll on him, too.

I pick up my menu, but my eyes glaze as I read it over. John's usually direct with me, but I'm sure this distance is his way of saying he's disappointed. I didn't get the job I came here for, and I lost the entry-level position I did get within six months. In his eyes, this whole thing has been a failure. I look up to see him scanning his menu, frowning.

"You're sure this place is one of the best, Murray?" he asks, scraping a bit of dried egg off the plastic menu cover. "Nothing here's over ten dollars." He raises his eyebrows at me. "You know you don't have to pick the cheapest spot."

I smile. "I know. It is good, though. One of those hole-in-the-wall places real New Yorkers love."

"I'm just glad it has pictures," Austin says, still flipping through his menu. "I couldn't tell what the fuck any of this was otherwise."

John laughs and his face lightens a bit. "All right," he says, "I'll trust you."

After we order, the waiter comes around with our drinks—beer for me and John, vodka tonic for Austin—and we settle in a little more.

"How's Roger?" Austin asks, resting his stubbly chin in his hand. "Still an asshole?"

"Yeah, not much I can do about that." I take a drink, shuffling through our sessions in my mind. "I've only talked to him once since I got out of the hospital," I say. "He seemed … distracted. He might be getting tired of me."

"That'd be all right," Austin says with a hoarse laugh. "How many more do you have?"

"Just one. If he keeps his word."

"Can you tell what he's trying to get out of it?" John asks, his voice serious, like it's been so much of the weekend.

I shrug, glancing up at him. "It's the same old Roger. He's depressed. He's got his perfect millionaire life but he's still lost. He wants to feel better without thinking too hard about anything."

Austin nods and I run my finger around the edge of my glass. "How are you doing with it?" I ask him.

"His glass place?" Austin lets out a sigh. "Better. It's not going away, so I guess it'll just take time."

I nod and glance over at John. He squints one eye a little like he doesn't agree.

Austin cracks a few knuckles. "I keep telling myself Ash would want me to let it go. That helps, I guess."

John looks like he wants to say something, but the food comes, so he stays quiet. We spend a few minutes eating, engrossed in our own thoughts, until John breaks the silence.

"Okay, this is pretty good," he says when he's about halfway through his noodle bowl.

"See?" I say, pointing my fork at him. "What'd I tell you?"

Austin doesn't acknowledge us, he's so intent on eating. John has to give him a shove so he'll respond to my question about his pork. As I watch them, I realize that, despite the asynchronous feeling of the weekend, we're still the same. And I've missed them.

"So," John says as we near the end of our meal, "how's the job search going?"

My face warms. He's beginning the conversation I was afraid of. "It's okay," I say, picking at my noodles with my fork. "I've had one interview, for an assistant job, but I didn't get it." I flash a weak smile. "Overqualified."

John nods. "That's a tough break."

"Yeah." Out of the corner of my eye I see Austin take a long drink of his third vodka tonic. "But I'm still looking," I say. "Something'll come up."

John shifts in his seat and he gets that hard, agitated look telling me that isn't good enough. Austin must have kicked him under the table or something, because John darts a glance his way. Now they're trading looks, and my stomach tightens because this is something bigger than I expected.

"What?" I ask, struggling to stay calm. "What's with you guys?"

The last few looks seem to indicate John will talk first. He leans forward, resting his forearms on the table. I'm afraid to look into his eyes, and when I do, they're devoid of their usual warmth.

"We think you should come back to Cleveland."

I glance over at Austin, but he's studying his empty bowl. I lean back and release my breath. I figured as much. John's always been skeptical and it wouldn't take much to get Austin on board. But to hear him say it—to know he really believes I failed—hurts more than I thought.

"I know it looks bad now," I say, looking down at the table, "but I can get another job. Lamar said he'd put in a word for me around campus, and I'm going to apply more. It's just been a crazy few weeks—"

"Murray," John interrupts, "this isn't about your job."

I stare at him, uncomprehending.

"There's more pressure on you here," he says. "It's just . . . it's not good for you."

I frown, still unable to see what this is all about. My hands clench open and closed, and I notice my left leg shaking.

Austin's watching me now. He nods. "I been there, too, Mur," he says. "You're getting in over your head. You've got us to help you out back home."

"I've got Rahmi here, and Lamar," I say, straining against my tightening throat. "You think I could just leave Rahmi? Where's this coming from?"

"This is coming from Rahmi," John says. "I talked to him about what happened. You are losing control, and your old patterns are coming back."

My face and eyes are burning now and my heart's thudding in my ears so loudly I can't focus. "Rahmi talked to you about the fight? He never told me that." I close my eyes for a moment. I'm glad he's not here now. "He never fucking told me that."

"Can you blame him?" John shoots back. "The way you're acting, he's never sure which Murray he's going to get."

"He said that?"

"He doesn't have to. He said enough."

I glower at him. "Hey, I was wrong, and I apologized for it. But he said some shit, too."

John shakes his head. "You can't put this on Rahmi. You took it to the next level; you started throwing punches."

I scoff and rub my forehead. "It's not like I can scare him, come on."

This time it's Austin who shakes his head. "You're not the skinny kid you used to be. When you get worked up, I bet you do scare him."

"And it doesn't even matter," John says, his words laced with irritation. "When you lose control, it's not any different than it was with Dani or Emma."

I wince when John says their names. My breath rattles as it escapes my lungs. I can't handle this, hearing them build each other's cases against me. They're supposed to be my friends.

"I know you don't want to hear this," Austin says, fidgeting with the brim of his baseball cap, "but you're doing the same thing I always did—letting that rage take over your whole goddamn life." He pauses. "And I always said I'd be there for you. We both did. Just looks like you could use some help."

"This is fucked up, the way you guys are ganging up on me," I mutter. "I'm trying, all right? I'm trying to get better."

"Then you need to be honest about what that's going to take," John says. "I think you need to get some things off your plate before you can focus."

I glare across the table at him. "Like Rahmi."

John shrugs and Austin downs the rest of his drink.

"So, what, I just leave him? Ditch everything and go back to Cleveland where I was miserable?"

John's expression softens for the first time. "It's not easy," he says. "None of this is. But you need to think about why you're here, and how much you really care about Rahmi."

I shake my head as it pounds with the harsh words I long to say. They haven't been here, and they don't understand. I'd do anything for Rahmi. I've had setbacks—horrible, indulgent fits of violence that haunt me—but that doesn't mean I give up. I want to get better because of Rahmi, and with Rahmi. If he were gone, I'd be lost. I wouldn't make it. And it's only darkness and despair that call me back to Ohio.

Chapter 41
Fathers and Sons

I trudge back into the apartment and set my keys and leftovers on the table. John and Austin follow me, but I wish they would leave. I don't have much civility left, and one false move could expose my resentment smoldering underneath.

John rubs his face with his hands. His eyes are red and weary. I guess he's past the point of sly signals, because he just tells Austin he needs to talk to me alone for a minute.

Austin nods. "I'll be downstairs." He looks like he wants to say something, but instead he squeezes my shoulder before turning and heading out the door.

I cross my arms as I stand next to the kitchen table, too on edge to sit. John leans against the counter, looking past me. He likes to get words just right before he says them, but the longer he stands there, the worse I feel.

"What? You didn't cover everything at dinner?" I say, my voice irritated. "It didn't seem like you were holding back."

"I can get you a ticket as soon as next week," John says, like he didn't hear me. "But I understand if you want more time to get things together. Do you still have Glen's number? At your old law firm?"

I stare at him, heat creeping up my neck. "I'm not going back."

"What?" His hard eyes meet mine.

"I'm not going," I repeat. "I thought you understood that."

"I understood you were upset," John says, "but I still trust you to make the right decision."

The right decision. My blood flows fast and hot now. I dig my fingernails into my palms and try to recognize what's happening. My breathing, my head, my chest. But John's the one being an asshole. He's trying to control me and I can't let him. I can't let him tell me what the right decision is.

"No. I'm not giving up."

"This isn't giving up," John says with a sigh. "It's recognizing you need help. You need more support than you have here." He looks down for a moment. "And yes, I think you and Rahmi should be apart, for a while at least. You're too volatile for a relationship right now."

I glance down at my hands and see little pink crescents where my fingernails nearly broke the skin. It's so easy for him, spending two days in New York, then telling me how it's going to be. He still thinks of me as a teenager—the weak kid with the black eye he met at Mr. Everett's funeral. I guess I still thought of him as the father I wish I'd had, but now I see we were both wrong.

"You should go," I mutter, unable to look at him.

"Are you going to consider what I said?"

"No." I rub my forehead. "You don't get it. You don't know what it took for me to get out of Cleveland."

John's face is neutral, which only makes this worse.

"If I went back ..." I shake my head. "I can't go near Cleveland Heights without thinking of my dad. Anywhere around the university is shot, because of Emma." I wipe my eyes with the back of my hand. "And now my apartment, my street ... it's all Dani." I look up at John. "Even Chase's place," I say, "even the one spot where I could forget those things is still above Mr. Everett's apartment."

He doesn't say anything and my blood pressure rises again.

"Do you even get that?" I yell. "Do you not care how hard it would be?"

"I know it's hard," John says, in that calm, easy manner that makes me crazy. "But what's harder is hurting someone you care about. Again."

I blink, trying to clear away the haze of rage clouding my mind. I lasted longer than I expected, but this is over. I need it to be over.

"Austin's waiting," I say, glancing at the door. I take a few deep breaths.

"He can wait." John's eyes don't move from mine.

My deep breaths turn quick and shallow. "I'm not going to change my mind."

"Then you're more selfish than I thought."

I swallow against the hot, acidic bile my stomach just forced into my mouth, and squeeze my fists as hard as I can. I don't care if my nails go all the way through. I open my right hand and slam it down on the table, causing John to jump. The cup that was sitting on the edge of the table crashes to the floor. It shatters and shards shoot across the linoleum. I glance down. It was Grace's coffee mug.

My head is clearing now, and my stomach is settling. I don't want to lose this feeling. John's watching me with disappointment, maybe fatigue.

But I'm not the bad guy this time. He tried to take over and I showed him that kind of thing doesn't work on me anymore. I stand taller, taking even breaths. My hand twitches. I shift my focus to the shattered mug, counting the pieces as I try to clear the thoughts that threaten to get me in trouble.

"Murray," John says, breaking my focus, "I need you to listen." He's frowning. "You are out of control. If you do this—if you stay in New York and continue down this path, that's your choice." He takes a breath. "But you're on your own. I'm not going to be a part of this anymore."

"Yeah? That's fine." I brush the hair off my forehead. "I don't need a babysitter."

John nods, like he's already checked out of the conversation. His eyes are on the floor where the remains of Grace's mug lie, inanimate now. "It's late," he says, running his sleeve across his eyes. "I'll let you go."

He holds out his hand for me to shake, and the vague remains of my temporary high disappear. It's so formal a gesture for him that it's jarring. John shakes hands with colleagues, acquaintances. Strangers. But that's what I am now. I force my hand to steady as I extend it to his.

I nod. "All right."

"Take care of yourself."

John releases my hand sooner than I expected and gives me a weak smile before he turns and walks out.

I stare at the door for another minute after he closes it. Maybe Austin will tell him he was too hard on me and they'll both come back up. I don't know. I don't even want them to.

My face is hot. I can't stand in the kitchen any longer, and I turn to go down the hall to the bathroom. I forgot about the mug, though, and after a few steps a sharp edge digs into my foot.

"Fuck," I mutter, as I lean over and pull the shard out of my sock. I grab the broom and sweep up as much as I can, dumping the pieces into the trash, but before I can go back for a second scouring my nausea forces me down the hall. I throw up in the toilet and, for the first time, wonder if Jemma's home. She always seems to know what's going on, and I can picture her shaking her head, making judgmental notes as she listens to me hurl. She probably thinks I took too much morphine again.

The morphine.

I wash my face in the sink, imagining the little envelope shoved under paper towels, banana peels, takeout containers, and now covered with shattered porcelain. I dry myself off with the hand towel and cringe at my reflection. I already look like I've overdosed. But my hands quiver and my eyes sting because it wasn't even up to me. I wouldn't be thinking about the pills if John hadn't tried to force my hand. I wouldn't have shattered the mug or yelled or thrown up if he had just understood that I won't start my life over again on his command. I shake my head. He's never understood. Not like Mr. Everett.

My chest tightens. I close my eyes, trying to picture Mr. Everett in his office, trying to hear what he'd say to get me through this. But all I can see is John, telling me I'm an abusive fuckup with no hope of surviving on my own. I open my eyes, and I'm back in that place where all I want is relief. My reflection glares back at me, and for a moment I freeze.

Oh, shit.

This is what I've been running from. This is the moment I've hidden from, denied, retaliated against. It's the shadow I can never shake.

I touch my face, turning slightly, but it's undeniable now: I've never looked more like my father. His voice is in my head. His rough tone, like a low warning, still sends my body into self-defense, but this time they're my words he's saying.

I never hurt Rahmi. He can take it, right? If everyone would stop treating me like a goddamn kid . . .

I shake my head and lean forward, gripping my hair with both hands, willing his voice to stop. But I already know the truth. If my dad were here right now, he'd have my back. He'd say John and Lamar and all the others are full of shit, and Rahmi's being weak. He'd say I'm just standing up for myself, and solving problems the way he'd taught me to. He'd grip my shoulder like he would the guys on the force. He'd be proud.

I'm breathing fast now, and my head is light. I stare into the mirror again, but the resemblance is somehow stronger and my stomach lurches. It's him. The dark, sullen eyes, hard jaw, and dangerous expression. If I had a military crew cut and a belt in my hand, we'd be identical.

I close my eyes again, forcing away that haunting, mocking image, and when I open them, lacey cracks cover the mirror in front of me. I look at my hand. It's bleeding but I can't feel it. I can't feel anything.

You're really growing up, Mur. Only took you thirty years.

I shake my head and cry out, then pound my bleeding fist into the center of the glass. And I do it again, just to hear that satisfying crystalline crunch. I look back at the mirror, at my hollow eyes, my ragged hair and pale skin. I have nothing left. I'm finally alone. Somehow John got what he wanted after all.

Chapter 42
Something True
Rahmi

Rahmi gets home a little after midnight. Closing the restaurant is one of his least favorite jobs because at that point, everyone is drunk, and it takes about an hour longer than it should. He eases the door to the apartment closed behind him, and sheds his jacket, shoes, and bag before moving to the kitchen. He glances toward Grace's nook, but the partition is open and the bed's empty, so she must be over at Greg's again. The soft light of the microwave's clock guides Rahmi to the refrigerator, but before he can open it, he kicks something that rattles into the baseboard. He switches on the light. Squinting as he adjusts to the harsh fluorescence, he squats down and pulls a broken piece of a mug from under a cabinet. He glances around and sees another next to the oven. He shakes his head, recognizing the yellow-and-blue floral design. It doesn't look like Grace tried very hard to clean it up. He grabs the pieces he can see—five more scattered across the floor—and tosses them into the trash can.

It's late, but he worked through dinner, so Rahmi once again goes to the fridge and is thrilled to find leftovers from Rai Rai Ken. As he settles in at the table with the Styrofoam container, Rahmi's thoughts turn to Murray's evening. It must have been hard, saying goodbye to his friends again. Rahmi frowns, pushing the cold shoyu chicken and noodles around with his fork. He's sorry he missed their last night. Even with Austin's early antagonism and John's unsettling warning, it had been nice getting to know them. After a few bites, Rahmi returns the leftovers to the fridge and fills a glass at the sink. He drinks the water in one breath. 12:25. He needs to get some sleep.

With a yawn, he drags his feet down the hallway to the bathroom, rethinking his earlier plan to take a shower. He barely has the energy to brush his teeth. Rahmi flips the light switch on, and freezes.

"Oh, shit," he murmurs.

His left hand quivers and he wants to run, yell, do something, but is paralyzed by the shattered mirror in front of him.

John was right.

The spiderweb cracks running out from three separate centers amplify the nightmarish feeling of the moment, jaggedly reflecting Rahmi's panic-stricken expression. Below, resting on the sink, is a note scrawled out in Murray's handwriting: *Sorry, I'll get it replaced.*

Rahmi's heart takes off, pumping wildly, while his eyes, heavy with exhaustion only a moment ago, are now alert and discerning. *He knows.* Rahmi wipes his forehead. *He found out I talked to John.*

There's only silence in the apartment, but Rahmi senses even that is a warning. He looks to their bedroom door, new perspiration forming on his brow. He can't. He can't go in without knowing who's waiting for him.

Rahmi forces his feet to move. He leaves the bathroom and walks to the front of the apartment, pulling on his shoes and jacket. He grabs his bag and slips out the door, careful to close it without a sound.

"Rahmi? *Sen olduğunu?*"

Rahmi opens his eyes. It takes a moment for him to place his surroundings. He rubs his face with his hands.

"Yes. It's me, Ana."

He sits up on his parents' faded green couch, still in the clothes he was wearing last night. Early morning light filters into their small apartment through chintz curtains, and for a few seconds, Rahmi is able to pretend he still lives there—that his adult life was just an unsettling dream. His mother comes over, shuffling to the couch in her white bathrobe, concern emanating from her dark eyes.

"What trouble are you in?" She sits next to him, studying his face.

Rahmi smiles, but his eyes well with tears. He doesn't know where to begin, there's so much he's kept to himself. The place is quiet, except for the dull grating sound of Rahmi scratching at his fingernails. He hadn't realized he'd been doing it.

His mother takes a breath. "You need to stop these drugs," she says. "I see the young men on the streets ... they have nothing."

Rahmi's head pounds. "I'm not on drugs," he says. "I've never been on drugs."

"But Seda has always said—"

"Seda told you that because ..." He pauses, wiping his palms on his pants. "Well, because she thought it was better than the truth."

"What truth?"

Rahmi sinks into the back of the couch. His body aches and his chest burns, but it has little to do with the current conversation. Coming out to his traditional parents is so far down on his list of worries, it's laughable.

He sits up again. "Ana, the truth is, I'm gay."

His mother nods. "Yes."

"Yes? Do you know what that means?"

She gives him a look. "I know things, Rahmi. I have seen that woman they all talk about, with the show ..."

"Ellen?"

She smiles. "Yes. Ellen."

"Okay." He runs his hands through his hair. "You mean you already knew?"

She nods.

"Why didn't you say something? I spent my whole life thinking you'd hate me for this. You could have at least—"

"It is not something to talk about," his mother snaps. "You are too American in that way."

"But Seda said this would crush you. She said we had a cousin, Beyza—"

"Beyza," she says, holding up her hand, "was a long time ago."

"So, what happened?"

She shrugs. "We know more now."

Rahmi furrows his brow. "What does that mean?"

She sighs. "After coming to New York," she says, "it was very hard. People told us to leave. They made horrible markings on our restaurant. They didn't even know us."

"What does this have to do with her?"

His mother shoots him a glare. "You don't listen." She shakes her head. "After some time—too much time—we understood. Back home, we were no better. We were wrong about Beyza."

Rahmi's throat is so tight he can't swallow. "Baba, too?"

She nods.

The air in the room is thick and suffocating. Rahmi's hands tremble as he brings them to his temples. It's too much. He closes his eyes and he still sees the broken glass. He wishes he could be with his mother, embrace the relief that he's shared something real, but he can't escape the fear pounding his brain.

"Oh, Rahmi. *Ağlama.*"

She puts her hand on his leg and he looks up.

He hadn't realized he was crying, but at his mother's words he touches his face, then hastily wipes away the tears. But the look in her eyes—the simple compassion he'd missed so much—causes the emotion to swell in his chest and he can't keep it inside any longer.

"I don't know what to do," he says, leaning forward.

She peers at him. "This is not drugs?"

"No. I promise it's not." Rahmi rubs his eyes with his sleeve. "It's the . . . well, the person I'm seeing. We're having trouble, I guess."

"The boy from the hospital."

He looks up. "Ana, I really wish you'd told me you knew. It would have—"

"Who is this boy?" she interrupts, her face serious. "What is wrong that makes you come here in the middle of the night?"

"He's not a bad guy," Rahmi says, his stomach already in knots from doing this again. Talking about Murray when he's not here to defend himself. Telling everyone but him about their problems.

His mother is looking at him with growing suspicion.

"I mean it," he says. "Murray's amazing. It's just, he has some problems."

"What problems?"

Rahmi scratches his head. "He has trouble controlling his anger sometimes," he says. "I'm not sure how to help him anymore. Sometimes I think I make things worse."

"So, you must run from him?"

"No, it wasn't like that. I didn't even see him last night. He was asleep. But when I got home from work, I saw that he'd broken a mirror, and I wasn't sure what had set him off." He pauses. "I guess I didn't want to find out."

She nods but doesn't reply. For a few minutes they sit in silence, Rahmi leaning forward with his elbows resting on his knees, his mother sitting stiffly, frowning off into space.

Rahmi had hoped speaking aloud would lessen his burden, but instead it's given it new life, and a broader space to dominate. His parents can judge him now, like John and Austin. Like Jemma. His failure and weakness will define him in their eyes, as well as his own.

"I have to go," Rahmi says, unable to endure the silence any longer. "I should get ready for class."

"Wait." His mother touches his arm before he can stand. "This I feel is for Baba to tell you, but . . ." She looks toward their bedroom, like she wishes he would emerge. "You cannot help this boy."

"What? Why?"

"You are not hard like that. You are kind—maybe even too kind. You cannot help him, and it will only hurt you to try."

"No," Rahmi says, "he's not like that. He wants to get better, he just needs some help."

"He makes you like this," she says, indicating Rahmi's miserable expression. "I don't like him."

Any words Rahmi thought he could say catch in his throat. His mind is a nauseating mix of relief and dejection, and it won't let him think. He needs to get out.

He nods. "Okay," he says, managing a weak smile. "I understand."

Rahmi hugs her and she kisses his cheek. He stands, still shaky and exhausted, but needing to be in the open air on familiar crowded streets, surrounded by strangers.

Chapter 43
Glass
Rahmi

Rahmi walks back to the apartment in the gray haze of early morning. He holds his key ready as he comes up to the door, but finds the knob turns easily. Panic jolts through his chest—he was the last one out last night. He didn't lock the door when he left. Rahmi walks in and his eyes dart around the room. There isn't much to take, and the place appears untouched. Grace's books on the coffee table. Murray's winter coat. The VCR, the television. Everything looks normal. He releases the tension in his shoulders, but the uneasiness remains in the pit of his stomach.

"Rahmi?"

At the sound of Murray's voice, Rahmi's heart skips. For a moment he'd forgotten, but now he hears the sound of glass clinking, their fragments rattling together, and it drags him back.

"Yeah, hey."

Rahmi follows the sound of Murray's voice down the hall. He finds him in the bathroom on his knees, tossing pieces of the broken mirror into a plastic bag. The medicine cabinet itself rests on the floor, leaning against the wall, its shattered side turned away. Rahmi's relieved he doesn't have to see it again.

"I'm so sorry about this," Murray says, pulling himself to his feet. "I know it looks bad."

Murray's gaze is still lowered, but Rahmi can tell he's been crying. His face is puffy and his left hand shakes. Smears of blood, dried in brown chaotic streaks, cover the right leg of his pants.

"Are you okay?" Rahmi glances at the red blotches that have soaked through the bandage around Murray's knuckles. He pictures the fury on his face last night as he let go, as he punched the mirror at least three times. He thinks about how hard he must have hit it to make those kinds of marks.

"It's fine," Murray says, turning and flexing his hand. He looks up at Rahmi. "I shouldn't have let this happen again."

"You must have been pretty mad."

"Yeah." He runs a hand over his eyes. "I don't know what my problem is." Murray sighs and stoops to pick up another shard of glass lying between them. He puts it in the plastic bag. "I took another morphine last night," he says as he straightens up.

Rahmi's heart thuds and he's sure he didn't hear him right. Not morphine. Murray isn't going down that road. He isn't messing around with the same shit that almost got him killed. He isn't that far gone.

"What?" Rahmi demands, in a harsher tone than he'd intended.

"I'm trying to be honest with you," Murray says, a defensive edge cutting his own words. "I only took one. I flushed the rest after." He glances away. "Last night was rough. But it's over now. I promise."

Rahmi shakes his head, ready to kill Jemma for selling to him again. "Murray, after everything that's happened ..."

"Hey, it's not like I took five. It was one. People take that much all the time."

Rahmi's cheeks flare. Murray doesn't regret it. He's trying to fix things but he still doesn't think he was wrong. Rahmi rubs the side of his face. "I just don't want this to be the thing you go to when things get hard. That's what I'm here for."

"Oh, yeah?" Murray's voice wavers. "Where were you last night?"

Rahmi pauses, running through the story he'd prepared about a burst water pipe at the restaurant. But he can't say it. Murray's face, tired and miserable, tells him that his night must have been just as bad as his own. He knows what they're doing—the lying, the hiding, the constant covering—is bad for both of them. He can't keep telling Murray the opposite of what he's feeling. And he can't pretend they're okay anymore.

Rahmi turns away, squeezing his sore eyes shut in an attempt to stall the tears, but they come anyway. He takes off his glasses and clenches them in his hand. His nerves are shot and he's too tired to be strong. He stands with his back to Murray, letting the misery flow through his body. He bows his head and for some reason recalls the beginning—their beginning: running out of the building to meet a guy about the apartment. Rahmi had seen the serious young man with disheveled blond hair and deep, brown eyes and knew it would be more involved than that. He wishes they could go back to when things were easy. It's as hazy as a dream now.

"Hey."

Rahmi feels a gentle hand on his back and turns around. Murray's eyes are red and brimming with tears as well. He searches Rahmi's face for a moment, then pulls him into a hug.

"I'm sorry," Murray says, his grip strong and comforting. "I never meant for this to happen."

Rahmi breathes in, wanting so much to be soothed by this moment, but his muscles are unable to relax.

"I don't want to be this person," Murray continues. "And I hate what I'm doing to you. I'm sorry."

Rahmi nods but his pulse won't even out. He pulls away and looks at Murray. "I was here, last night. But after I saw the mirror, I left."

"You left?"

"Yeah."

"It must have been after midnight." Murray rubs the back of his head. "Where did you go?"

"My parents' apartment."

He frowns. "Why?"

Rahmi studies Murray's face for signs of frustration, but it seems he's genuinely trying to understand a scenario that should be obvious. "I thought it must have been me you were mad at."

"Jesus," he murmurs.

He turns away and Rahmi worries he's ramping up again. He's still for several seconds, with his back turned to Rahmi and his hands on his head, but when he turns back around, he's crying.

"No, it wasn't you," Murray says. He wipes his eyes. "I wasn't mad at you at all. It doesn't even matter, but it was John."

"John?"

"Yeah. I've never seen him be such a dick." He shakes his head. "But that's all it was. It was him. I was never going to let it get to us."

Rahmi frowns. "But you see what I mean, right? Things are always building up, and I'm just waiting for some kind of ... explosion." He glances again at the mirror.

"I'm trying," Murray says. He rubs a sleeve over his forehead. "I just can't keep up with everything sometimes, you know? Sometimes I feel like if I don't let the pressure out, it's going to kill me." He looks at the empty space on the wall. "But, I mean, you're right. Of course you're right. Things keep building up, and I have to learn how to keep my shit when they do."

Rahmi nods, but the familiar tightening of his chest steals his focus. Murray's saying all the right things, but there's something unsettling about it. It's like he's playing a part, reciting the phrases Rahmi wants to hear, but only half listening while he runs his next lines through his head. "So, you understand why I couldn't be here last night?"

"Yeah." Murray blinks a few times. "I understand. And I'm not going to let it happen again. I promise." He takes Rahmi's hand. "I'm sorry."

Rahmi smiles but his stomach turns every time Murray talks about promises. He doesn't want to do this anymore. He doesn't want to talk about them—about how everything's different now and it won't happen again. There's an underlying tension that fills the room. He can't breathe.

"What happened with John?"

"Oh." Murray's brow furrows. "He wants me to go back to Cleveland."

"What?"

"He says I'm failing on my own. He doesn't think I can do anything without him." Murray's face darkens. "He's never trusted me."

Rahmi gently pulls his hand back. Murray's eyes are colder now. It's occurred to him before, that Murray might go back to Cleveland. Sometimes he wishes it would happen, but sometimes he thinks it would destroy them both.

"Trusted you to do what?"

Murray blinks a few more times, like he needs to reset his mind. "He said you're not safe with me." His gaze scans the room, then rests on Rahmi. "He said you don't feel safe with me."

Rahmi's stomach sinks because he's back in that place where he needs to pretend. He needs to hide, to protect himself. He doesn't feel safe anymore, but he's not sure it's all Murray's fault. And to admit it would be devastating to him. Maybe even dangerous. Rahmi clears his throat. The few seconds of silence appear to agitate Murray.

"Did you tell him that?"

Rahmi shakes his head. "I told John I could handle myself. He didn't seem to believe me."

Murray scowls. "You see? That's what he's always doing. He gets in everybody's business and ends up fucking things up." He rubs his face with his hands. "Well, I told him I'm not going back to Ohio. He can't make that call."

"What did he say?"

"Nothing."

Rahmi senses there's more to it, but he won't push Murray. Not while his eyes are so distant and hard, or while his hands keep squeezing into fists. Not while he's surrounded by shattered glass. "I have to go," Rahmi says, trying to sound regretful. "I've got class."

Murray nods. "Okay." He sighs, looking miserable again. "I really am sorry," he says, glancing down at the plastic bag in his hand.

Rahmi looks at the floor. He isn't sure what to say.

"But I'm seeing Lamar on Wednesday, and I promise I'm not going to quit until I figure it out."

"Okay." Rahmi gives him a weak smile.

Murray leans forward and kisses him, the glass jingling as the bag moves in his hand. But the air is closing in and Rahmi can't be there anymore. He squeezes Murray's arm, getting him to step back.

"We'll have dinner tonight?"

Murray nods. "You need to change before you go?" he asks.

"Oh." Rahmi looks down at his rumpled, dirty clothes. "Yeah."

He steals one last look at the bathroom, somehow transformed by the empty space above the sink, before moving into their bedroom. He pulls on a new long-sleeved shirt and jeans and runs a brush through his chaotic hair. His hands are stiff, like he's not even controlling their movements. It all feels like sleepwalking. Rahmi sits on the bed for a moment, his head in his hands, contemplating his next move. He wanted this to go better but isn't sure why it didn't. Sometimes he feels like he's the problem—that he makes too much of everything and can't just move on. Rahmi checks his watch. He has to go.

He leaves their room and sees Murray collecting the last few pieces of glass in the bathroom. Murray stands and smiles when Rahmi comes out.

"I'll walk you out."

Rahmi nods and leads the way to the kitchen. He grabs his backpack off the chair and slings it over his shoulder. Another sliver of Grace's mug catches his eye. "Careful," he says, pointing to the broken porcelain in Murray's path. "Grace broke her mug."

"Oh, man." Murray pauses a moment, then picks it up and tosses it in the trash. "Thanks for the warning." He pushes the bag of glass down on top.

Rahmi smiles. "I guess it was a bad day for breaking shit."

"Yeah." Murray smiles back, but his eyes are on the floor now, searching. "We can't keep anything nice around here."

Chapter 44
No Reason

Lamar's office is hotter than it used to be. He cracks the window after I complain long enough, but it doesn't stop my shirt from dampening with perspiration. He has rearranged the furniture, too. Now I sit across from him with only a small coffee table between us, and his desk is pushed to the corner of the room. He's got soft music playing from a little radio that sits on top; he says it helps people get comfortable. He has other patients and it's self-absorbed for me to assume this is about me, but it's like he's been preparing for my return. Like he wants to change his approach. Maybe he feels like he's running out of time.

"So," Lamar says, glancing over his notes from the past half hour, "it sounds like you've had three outbursts since we last met for counseling."

I frown. "I think it's just two."

"Rahmi and John?"

"Yeah."

"We should also count the episode with Noel. You didn't end up fighting him, but that's only because Rahmi stopped you. You weren't able to stop yourself. That's an important distinction."

"No, that was different," I say. "I didn't lose control. I knew what I was doing—what I wanted to do, anyway."

"You're saying you made a choice with Noel?"

"Yes."

"Okay, but that's the point: you always have a choice. Every reaction is a choice, and they're all under your control."

I give him a look. "You know what I mean. It was more deliberate this time."

Lamar doesn't reply but his face is irritated, and I sense that's not what he was hoping to hear.

I grip the front of my T-shirt and billow it, fanning cool air across my body. He's still silent. "What?" I ask.

Lamar sets his notebook on the table between us. When he looks back up at me, his eyes are serious. "We have a lot more work to do."

I let go of my shirt. "Am I getting worse?"

Lamar sighs. "Murray, you're doing it again. You're acting like an outsider in your own life. You can't just do your time in therapy, take your meds, and hope it gets better. You need to work really, really hard." He narrows his eyes at me. "I'm not sure you understand that."

"I do," I say, my head starting to ache. "Of course I do. But these things keep coming up, and I have to do something. I mean, you want me to let Jemma get the shit beaten out of her?"

"No. But if you'd gone ahead and attacked the boyfriend like you wanted to, all of you could have gotten seriously hurt. It was Rahmi's nonviolence that helped her."

I shake my head. "She told me it made things worse. I guess he was pretty worked up when she went back to him later."

"But fighting him would have been better?"

"Yeah," I say, crossing my arms. "If Rahmi had backed me up, we could have made him scared to hurt her again."

"Murray," Lamar says, reaching for his notepad again, "it sounds like you're standing by the choice to use violence."

I shrug. "With that guy? Yeah."

He scribbles a few lines. "Okay, but what about with John? The way you were talking about what a jerk he was, it sounds like you'd justify your actions there, too."

I lean forward a little, trying to see Lamar's notes. "I never got violent with John."

"You broke the mug."

"No," I reply, sitting up straight, "that was an accident. I hit the table a little too hard and the mug fell."

"Your actions broke the mug." Lamar taps his pencil on the table to emphasize his words. "Don't try to dodge responsibility."

"Hey, I lost my temper. I wasn't trying to hurt him."

"What were you trying to do?"

I try to think, but the big band music is crowding out my thoughts. "I don't know."

He looks up. The hardness in my voice is starting to betray my frustration.

I take a slow breath. "Let some pressure out. And get him to stop talking, I guess. He said some pretty horrible things."

Lamar nods. "And what about the mirror?"

"It's the same thing," I say, pulling at my sticky shirt again. "There was just too much tension. And I didn't hurt anybody."

"You made Rahmi think he was next."

My eyes sting and the sweat on my brow turns cold. "Well, he wasn't."

I crack my knuckles and glare at Lamar, but in my mind I can still see the way Rahmi edged away from me in the bathroom, stealing glances at the medicine cabinet on the floor. I see how he's changed. He used to be so laid back, so strong and reassuring. His smile was easy in the beginning, and he could always make me laugh. But now he rarely shows a genuine smile. He's always on edge, always worried. I told myself it was his schedule; he's working all the time, spreading himself too thin between school and the restaurant and his family, but now I think he threw himself into those things as an escape. He doesn't feel safe with me. He's not safe with me.

Lamar has finished writing and is watching me. "Can I assume this is another outburst you're standing behind?"

I shake my head and blink hard. "No."

Lamar taps his pen against the arm of his chair for a moment, then rips a sheet of paper from his notepad. He sets it on the table between us and begins drawing a diagram.

"I've counseled a few abusers as well as several victims of domestic violence," he murmurs, the phrase causing me to wince, "and this is the cycle they follow, without fail." He turns the paper around so I can see. "It seems these episodes always take you by surprise, so understanding the cycle could—"

"I know what this is," I break in. I push the diagram back toward Lamar. "After my dad died, I got sent to counseling, remember?"

"They talked about this?"

I nod. "I was hung up on the fact that he wasn't a bad guy all the time. My therapist said his good behavior was part of the cycle. She was trying to tell me it wasn't my fault, I guess."

Lamar sits back in his chair. He picks up his diagram again. "You're familiar with the cycle of abuse, as it applied to your father," he says, tucking the paper back into his notepad. "But it also applies to you now." Lamar looks up at me. "Do you understand?"

My muscles tense. "You know, my dad never went to counseling on his own," I say, bitterness straining my words. "He was ordered to. He never thought he was wrong, about any of it."

"I don't mean to equate you with him."

"But that's what you're doing," I say, my voice rising. "You're saying I'm taking his place—picking up where he left off."

"Your cycle is not the same. I just want you to recognize what's happening."

"That I'm never getting better, because that's also part of the goddamn cycle?"

Lamar shakes his head. "You can sit here and feel sorry for yourself, but you're missing the point. You're smart enough to understand a cycle can be broken. That's why you're here."

"Then what am I doing wrong?" I yell, springing from my chair and pacing the floor next to Lamar. "Why do I keep fucking up?"

"You know the answer."

"No. Stop using these bullshit shrink tricks and tell me why."

"Honestly?" He folds his hands together. "Because you want to."

I turn away, walking toward the opposite wall. "Fuck you," I mutter under my breath. I clench my hands, blood pounding through my veins.

"You've told me as much in our sessions," Lamar says, watching me like he might watch a glass placed too close to the edge of a counter.

I glower, distracted by the throbbing in my head. I want to tell him it's bullshit, but of course I already know he's right. I let my anger build because I want the relief that comes when I explode. I've been over it in my head a million times, but when I'm in the moment and the time comes to choose another response, I can never deny myself that satisfaction.

I slump back into my chair. I bow my head and massage my temples.

"It's nothing new, Murray," Lamar says after a minute.

I nod, still bent over with my elbows on my knees.

"You always have a choice. Even if it feels like you don't."

"I just don't want to lose Rahmi."

"Why?"

My head jolts up. "What do you mean, why? I love him."

Lamar studies me. "You do?"

"Of course." I'm not sure why I'm so defensive. I've never said this to Rahmi or anyone else, but saying it now, I know it's how I feel.

Lamar looks down at his notepad, like he has a lot to put down but isn't sure where to begin. "Murray, I want to say something, and I want you to try to hear me."

I frown and my leg jitters. "All right."

"I agree with John."

"What?" I nearly shout.

"Let me expl—"

"You want me to go back? I mean, we've talked about Cleveland; I told you what it was like for me there." I wipe my forehead. "Jesus, how can you side with John on this?"

"I'm not talking about Cleveland."

"What?" The heat is too much and I can't even follow him anymore.

"I'm talking about Rahmi. I think you need time on your own to work through this."

"So, you want me to get rid of the one good thing in my life? He likes me, too, you know."

"But can you honestly say that being with you, right now, is good for Rahmi?"

"Why don't you ask him?" I grumble.

"Because he wouldn't tell me the truth," Lamar answers. "He would say you're trying your best to control your anger, and he just needs to do a better job of staying out of your way."

"Hey," I snap, my face burning. "Stop making me sound like that."

"Like what?"

"Like I'm some kind of monster."

"Is that what I said?"

"That's what you meant. You know that's how I thought about my dad—that I'd be all right if I could stay out of his way."

"I want you to remember what it's like to be in Rahmi's position. I'm not saying the situations are the same, but the feelings are."

My whole body's on fire now and I can't breathe in this room. Lamar is still using tricks. He's using my feelings about my father against me, trying to say I'm no better. But that's not fair. To claim I've willfully modeled myself after a horror show like Adam Henderson is wrong, and it minimizes the hell I lived through. It makes us sound like a team. "This is absolute bullshit," I mutter.

"What?"

"It's bullshit," I say, louder. "I am not my dad."

"Murray," Lamar says, leaning back in his chair, "I never said you were. In fact, you are the only one who has brought up your father today. Why has he been on your mind more?"

"He hasn't," I yell, my heart slamming in my chest. "You're doing it— you're saying I'm repeating his cycle. And I'm a selfish, dangerous asshole, just like him." I jump to my feet. "This isn't a fucking game to me, all right?" I run my hand through my sweaty hair. "You know what, I'm done. You're just a fucking kid who thinks he has all the answers, and I don't need your help. I don't need this."

Lamar moves to get up, but I push past him and out the door before he can reply.

I rush down the stairs and don't stop until I'm outside the building. My eyes burn and I squint in the sunlight. I move to the side of the building and lean forward, sucking in shallow breaths while my legs quiver. My shirt is soaked. And I don't even have time to run to the corner trash can before I throw up.

Chapter 45
Roger Calls
Rahmi

"**D**amn it," Rahmi mutters, rubbing his forehead. He leans back in his chair and tosses his pencil back on his desk. The research conference is next week and he's nowhere near ready to present. Shot nerves break his focus and worries about Murray derail every productive thought he has. Rahmi looks at the clock. He hopes the session with Lamar is going well.

"Hey, Rahmi," Grace calls from down the hall, "I'm going to JW. You need anything?"

He closes his eyes. "Yeah, just a pack of Lucky Strikes." A few seconds pass in silence. Rahmi opens his eyes. "Grace?"

"I didn't know you were smoking again," she says, standing in his doorway.

He swivels his chair around. "Yeah, just the last couple of days, I guess." She frowns. "You doing all right?"

He nods but doesn't meet her eyes. "There's a lot happening at school, and a cigarette now and then helps me relax."

Rahmi grabs his wallet off the desk and pulls out a few dollars. He walks over to Grace and holds the money out to her. "Thanks."

"Sure." She takes it. "Does Murray know?"

"No. I mean, he probably wouldn't care, but he doesn't know I ever smoked." Rahmi sighs. "It's stupid."

Grace squeezes his arm. "It's all right. I got your back."

Rahmi nods and turns back to his desk but can feel her watching him for a few more seconds. After she leaves, he lets out a deep breath and picks up his pencil again.

But after ten more minutes, his jumbled thoughts still won't cooperate. His words won't flow in a straight line, and Rahmi's left with a paragraph he'd be embarrassed to turn in to a middle school teacher. He rests his arms on the desk and leans forward, rubbing the back of his neck. The phone rings.

Rahmi considers ignoring it, but decides he'd rather have the distraction. He gets up and jogs to the kitchen, catching the phone on the fourth ring.

"Hello?"

"Yeah, I'm calling for Murray."

Rahmi shakes his head as he recognizes the apathetic voice on the other end.

"He's not here." Rahmi glances at the clock. "He's busy till three now on Wednesdays."

"Three?" Roger lets out an irritated sigh. "Shit, I've got appointments to keep, you know. And this was supposed to be our last one." Computer keys tap in the background. "We could have finished today."

"Then call it even," Rahmi says. "You're the one making him do it. If you want it to be over, just say so."

"Yeah, he'd like that," Roger mutters, still typing.

"So, it is a game. You're having some fun at Murray's expense."

"Not much." Roger pauses for a few seconds. "Don't you ever have class?"

"What?"

"Seems like you're always the one answering the phone."

"What does it matter?"

"I just thought—well, I just thought you were the responsible one."

"What are you talking about?" Rahmi flops into a chair. "You don't know anything about me. You don't even know my name."

Roger laughs. "Rahmi Yilmaz. You're from Uşak, Turkey. You're thirty-three, but you've got a birthday coming up in a few w—"

"What the hell is this?" Rahmi's breath is coming fast. "Murray told you all that?"

"Hey, relax. It's public information."

"Yeah? What exactly do you guys talk about?"

"Mostly sports."

Rahmi's hand tightens around the phone and he wishes Grace would get back with those cigarettes. "This is not a joke, Roger."

"Oh, I know it's not," he answers. "But if you're worried about what Murray says, you shouldn't be. It's always like pulling teeth with him. He didn't tell me you guys were fucking either, but that's pretty obvious."

Rahmi's face burns, and he's starting to understand why Murray could never keep his head around this guy.

"Then how did you know that stuff about me?"

"I do my own research."

"That's sick."

"Don't feel special," Roger says with a laugh, "I do it with everybody. I never like to be surprised."

"None of that came from Murray?"

"No, he didn't even mention you until I asked if there were still times when he thought about the museum—about what it'd be like to go back. I got him to admit it's been on his mind. He thinks he may need an outlet, because he doesn't want to keep taking things out on his roommate."

Rahmi leans back and takes off his glasses, resting his hand over his eyes. This is getting too hard. If Murray's thinking about trying the glass again, the small semblance of control Rahmi has over their circumstances will be lost. Murray's told him what it was like there. Sure, he got relief over time, but it came at a price. He had to let himself go, and to Rahmi, it's not a safe bet.

"That's when I figured you guys were together," Roger continues after it becomes clear Rahmi isn't talking.

"Roger, I'm not sure what you're getting at," Rahmi says, replacing his glasses, "but you need to stop jerking Murray around, all right? Just end the deal."

"Hey, it's not like he's some innocent angel," Roger says. "My questions aren't going to fuck him up any more than he already is." He pauses. "You know he killed his dad, right?"

Rahmi's heart races again. "Yeah, he told me, but this would have been a really great way to find out if he hadn't."

Roger laughs. "You're funnier than he is, you know."

"I have to go."

"Yeah, all right."

"So, what should I tell Murray?" Rahmi hears the computer keys again.

"Tell him it's done."

Rahmi frowns. "Really?"

"Yeah, it's fine." Roger sounds distracted. "You said he's busy till three now?"

"Yeah, but why would it matter if he's done?"

"It doesn't," Roger replies, and Rahmi can tell he's smiling. "Just more research, I guess."

Chapter 46

It's Over

I stop at the gas station bathroom on my way home. I look like hell and I can't let Rahmi know how badly the session went. I wash my face in the sink with slow, deliberate movements, trying to even out my speeding pulse. I wash the sweat off the back of my neck and smooth down my wild hair. I take off my shirt and hold it under the air dryer for a minute.

The irony is, when I calm down, when I catch my breath and regain my composure, I'm left with something much worse than the chaos I felt leaving Lamar's. The reality of what happened, of what has been happening, settles into my brain, and I can no longer ignore it.

I'm not the victim I thought I was.

I drag my feet down Third Street, thinking back to the night I broke the mirror. It was never about John. I couldn't handle what I saw. I couldn't handle facing what I've known all along.

Grace is at the kitchen table doing homework when I walk in.

"Hey." I toss my bag on the floor.

"Hey." She looks up. "Damn, what happened to you?"

My stomach sinks. "I look that bad?"

She nods. "Did you get mugged or something?"

"No, I just walked the long way home. It's hot out."

Grace looks doubtful but nods. "Hey, thanks for the new mug. Took me a while to figure out the unicorns glow in the dark."

I smile. "I thought you'd like that." I glance down the hall. "Is Rahmi home?"

"Yeah." Grace motions for me to come closer. "He's really stressed about this conference. Go easy, all right?"

I nod and head toward our room, my breath ragged against the knot in my throat. I need to be told to be nice to my boyfriend. I'm a cause of stress in his life when I should be the one easing it.

187

I slip into the bathroom to check my appearance before going in to Rahmi, but I'm faced with the faded off-white rectangle of wall where the mirror used to be. My shoulders slump in disgust. I promise myself I'll replace it by this weekend.

I open the bedroom door and see Rahmi hunched over his desk, writing. I practice smiling. Practice impersonating a human.

"Hi," I say, walking over to him. "How's the presentation coming?"

Rahmi turns and smiles but looks sick to his stomach. "It's absolute shit," he says with a laugh.

"Anything I can help with?"

"I'm hoping to have a good draft by this weekend. Then I'd love your opinion on it. Thanks."

"Sure." I move to the bed and sit heavily.

Rahmi's still watching me. "How was Lamar?"

"Good," I say. "He had a lot of ideas for me."

Rahmi smiles. "That's great." He takes a breath and his smile fades. "Roger called while you were gone."

"Oh, shit." I close my eyes for a moment. "I forgot all about him. Fuck." I shake my head. "What did he say?"

"Well, he said you guys are done."

"What?" I narrow my eyes. My mind senses a trap and races to figure out Roger's angle. "We're done?"

Rahmi shrugs. "That's what he says. It sounded like he didn't need the last one anyway."

"Huh." I sit there for a minute, running our past conversations through my head. Rahmi shifts in his chair, and I wonder if he wants to get back to his writing. "Did he say anything else?"

Rahmi shakes his head and my frown deepens. After all that bullshit and drama, he's done. I'll probably never talk to him again.

I didn't expect it to feel this way. I should be ecstatic to be rid of Roger, but now it feels like part of a pattern. Another severed relationship. Another image torn out of the photo album.

"Well, that's a relief," I say when I realize I've been quiet for several seconds.

"Yeah?" Rahmi tilts his head a little. "I thought you'd be happier."

I rub my forehead. "He didn't say anything else? I mean, it's Roger; there has to be something in it for him."

Rahmi's leg vibrates and his fingers keep tapping the pencil against the desk. I'm keeping him from his work.

"I'm sorry," I say before he can respond, "you've got a lot to do."

"No, it's all right." Rahmi gets up and comes over to the bed. He hesitates a moment, then sits next to me. "It didn't seem like Roger had an angle this time. I think whatever it is isn't working for him, and he just wants to be done."

I nod. "I guess you're right."

Rahmi takes a breath. His leg hasn't stopped jittering. He turns to me with a faint smile, but maintains some space between us.

"He did say one thing," Rahmi says, looking down at his hands.

"Oh, yeah?" I try to sound casual, but Rahmi's guarded manner tells me I won't like it.

"He said you were thinking about trying the glass again."

"What?" My harsh voice jars the quiet room. "Why did he tell you that?"

"I don't know," Rahmi says, subtly edging away. "I really don't know."

"But that's all he said? Out of nowhere?"

"Yeah." Rahmi's face reddens. "You know him; he'll say anything if he thinks he can get a rise out of somebody."

"Well, I'm not doing it again," I say. "I just said I thought about it sometimes." I shake my head. "Roger is such a fucking piece of work. I bet he was trying to start shit between us."

"Yeah." Rahmi's watching my hands. I look down and see they're clenched. "I bet you're right."

I nod and cover my mouth, taking controlled breaths and remembering Grace's instruction to go easy. Remembering Lamar's remark about Rahmi feeling like he needs to stay out of my way. Remembering my own ragged reflection in the bathroom mirror.

I allow my muscles to relax. "Don't worry," I say, giving Rahmi a slight smile. "I won't let him. I'm done giving Roger that kind of control."

"I'm glad it's over." Rahmi clears his throat. "For you, I mean. I'm sure it'll be a weight off."

A weight off. He says it with hope, like now that Roger's gone I'll get my shit together and start treating him better. Maybe this was the last storm he needed to wait out. I smile again but my chest is hollow. I form the shallow, empty words I want to say, but my mouth won't force them out. It won't let me make another promise I can't keep.

Chapter 47

Stranger

Rahmi

Rahmi had said he didn't want anybody at the conference—it would just make him more nervous—but he's secretly happy when Murray shows up. He sits at the back and slumps a little in his seat, so Rahmi can tell he's trying to keep a low profile. It's a nice gesture and gives Rahmi a boost of confidence as he waits to present.

After it's over, Murray stays at the back of the room, which allows Rahmi the chance to shake hands with professors and congratulate other presenters. It's a better feeling than he can remember, finishing the nerve-racking task only one of his professors thought he could manage in the first place. By the time he makes his way back to Murray, Rahmi has shed some of the anxiety he began the day with.

"You're here," Rahmi says with a smile, gripping him in a strong hug. "Thank you."

"You sure it's okay? I know you said not to, but you've been working so hard on this, and I—"

"It means a lot," Rahmi interrupts, taking his hand. "Really."

Murray smiles. "Well, you were great. Yours was the best one. No contest."

Rahmi laughs. "Thanks." He looks around the room. "Ready to go?"

"You sure you're all right?" Murray asks when they're back at the apartment, having a beer at the kitchen table. "You've been pretty quiet."

"Oh." Rahmi shakes his head. "Sorry, I didn't mean to shut down like that. I guess there's been a lot on my mind."

"Yeah?" Murray leans in a little. "Not just the conference?"

Rahmi's chest tenses. He can't back out now. He'd made the decision, and now he's in the middle of it.

"Right." He swallows and forces himself to look at Murray. He tries to freeze this image of him in his mind—the concern in his eyes, the warm hint of a smile on his lips—before it all turns to anger. "There's something I wanted to talk to you about."

"Sure." Murray sits back and takes a drink of beer, but his eyes are already serious.

Rahmi frowns, steeling his nerves. "I think you should consider what John said. You know, about going back to Cleveland for a while."

Murray's face is blank.

Rahmi takes a fast gulp of beer and immediately feels sorry. He shouldn't have sounded so serious, and he shouldn't have mentioned John. Maybe he could take it back. But Murray's expression is grim. It's too late.

"Are you breaking up with me?" Murray asks, leaning forward again. His voice is low.

"No," Rahmi says, shaking his head. "No, I don't want that at all. It just might help to have some time away." He squeezes his hands in his lap to make them stop shaking.

"Like, how much time?" Murray's voice is still monotone. It's almost worse than yelling.

"I, well, I'm not sure," Rahmi says, glancing away from Murray's rigid gaze. "I guess that'd be up to you."

Murray makes a small sound in his throat, like he just confirmed something he'd known all along. "And that assumes I'm going to agree with John," he says. "That whatever bullshit he and Austin have up their sleeves will even help. And it assumes I'll want to go back to a place where I was miserable. To the same shithole that got me in this mess."

Rahmi opens his mouth to speak, but his jumbled mind can't form a diplomatic response.

"That is what you're telling me, right?" Murray demands, his voice getting louder. "You're saying you're done trying to handle me, and you want John and Austin to give it a shot?"

"No, Murray," Rahmi says, his face burning. "It's not like that. I'm not done with anything." He tries to stay steady but his voice wavers. He doesn't want to break up with Murray, but everything he says is coming out wrong. This is getting away from him.

Murray sits in silence for a moment, then scoots away from the table and springs from his chair so suddenly it makes Rahmi jump.

"This is bullshit," Murray says, pacing in front of the table. "You don't have the guts to tell me it's over, so you drag it out. You tell me to go to Cleveland so I can get my mind right. Then you'll tell me it's not a good time to come back because things are crazy here." Murray stops and runs his hands through his hair. He locks eyes with Rahmi. "Then you'll say you met somebody else. It would be awkward if I came back to the apartment. I should just make things work in the city I already know, with people who understand what they're up against." Murray's eyes narrow. "Say what you mean, for once."

"Hey," Rahmi says, jumping to his feet as well, "don't tell me what I mean. That's not what I'm saying at all. I'm trying to make this work, okay?"

"Yeah, with me on the next plane out of town," Murray yells, gesturing toward the door. "I can't believe you let John get into your head like that."

"What are you talking about?" Rahmi's head is throbbing with adrenaline and he catches himself trying to match Murray's anger.

"Oh, come on, don't act so fucking innocent." Murray's ears are bright red and his right hand is already a fist, lying in wait. "You put him up to it."

"Put him up to it?" Rahmi pulls off his glasses to rub his eyes, then tosses them on the table. "I told him you were trying. I told him you needed my help. I defended you."

"Stop lying!" Murray shouts, sending Rahmi back to uneasy self-defense. He shouldn't have escalated things.

"John told me what you said. You don't trust me. You sent him down this path, and now you're closing the deal for him."

"I'm trying to help you."

Murray shakes his head. He closes his eyes and grips his hair so hard it's like he's trying to exorcise some demon from his body. When he opens them, Rahmi sees pure desperation. He steps back, sensing a dangerous change in Murray. He wishes he had a straight shot at the door, but it's too late. Murray slams his fist down on the table, then grips it from underneath, flipping it over. The textbook that had been sitting on top shoots toward Rahmi, catching him under the right eye. The table crashes onto its side, slamming into his arm. He's knocked to the floor, and his back hits hard against the cabinet under the sink. Rahmi's dazed, but his panic is fading. Murray won't come after him, not now.

"Oh, Jesus, Rahmi?" Murray's voice calls in alarm from across the room.

Rahmi sits up. He blinks a few times and touches the skin under his eye. His fingers come back red.

"Rahmi, are you all right?" Murray's next to him, kneeling down.

"I'm fine," Rahmi murmurs, but as he moves his right arm, it sears with pain.

"Oh, fuck. Rahmi, I'm sorry."

Rahmi finds his glasses a few feet away, still intact, and puts them on. He looks around, disoriented by his view from the floor, by the overturned table and the scattered objects that once sat on top.

"I'm so sorry." Murray's crying. "I didn't mean to, I swear. Please believe me."

Rahmi nods, a little dizzy. He pulls his injured arm close to his body, the pain stronger now.

Chapter 48
Aftermath

There's a bitter taste in my mouth, but I can't throw up. Not now. Not while Rahmi's on the floor, his eyes weary and vacant.

"I'm so sorry," I say again. And again and again. But each time it sounds hollow. "I don't know what happened."

Rahmi's staring at the table, overturned in front of us. I slide a little closer to him, and see the cut under his eye. A thin trail of blood trickles down his cheek, like tears. My stomach drops and I reach my hand out, intending to wipe away the blood, maybe offer some intimate gesture of comfort, but Rahmi flinches a little. I close my eyes, a hopeless attempt to get away from this. From what I did to him.

"Rahmi, I'm a fucking mess," I say, rubbing my sore eyes. "I've let things get so bad. I'm sorry."

"We should pick the table up," Rahmi says, glancing toward the door, "before Grace gets home."

I watch him for a moment, then nod. "Okay."

I help him get to his feet, but he can't extend his right arm. He sets up a chair, but stays back while I pull the table upright and move the other chairs back into place. "Does that look all right?"

Rahmi nods, and I grab a cloth from one of the drawers and run it under the faucet.

"Can I?" I ask, holding it out toward his face.

He looks a little uncertain but nods again. He takes off his glasses. "Thanks."

As gently as I can, I press the cloth to his face and begin to dab away the blood. Rahmi stands there, but the way he shivers every few seconds lets me know he's still in pain. The cut underneath is long but doesn't look too deep. I sigh. At least he won't need stitches.

I run to the bathroom for a few Band-Aids and when I come back, Rahmi's stooped over, trying to pick up the books and other things that had fallen from the table.

"Let me get that." I rush to his side, grabbing the notebook he's reaching for. He straightens himself and leans forward to set the cracked beer bottle he's holding down on the table, but lets out an agonized yell and pulls his arm back.

"Fuck," he mutters, clutching his elbow and squeezing his eyes shut.

Seeing Rahmi in so much pain crushes me. I glance around the kitchen and it all feels like a dream. The furniture is back in place, the late-afternoon sun glints off the television like usual, and there's no sound in the apartment except for the ticking clock. For a second it is a dream and I can pretend it didn't happen. Until I look at Rahmi.

"Can I see?" I ask, indicating his arm. But I keep my distance.

Rahmi shakes his head, panic and fear returning to his face. "I think I might have broken it."

My heart sinks. *He* might have broken it.

In Rahmi's mind, it's just another thing he could have avoided if he'd been more careful. Tried harder. Stayed out of my way. That alone is enough to cement my self-hatred, but it's his expression that stops me—my thoughts, my breathing, everything. It's that look: that wary, calculating look he's giving me. It's changed his whole appearance. He seems like a child now. My eyes sting. I recognize it. I've felt every emotion that encompasses that look, and now I see the other part of my sick parallel in Rahmi. I see myself when I was young.

And I understand it was no accident that I broke his arm, just like it was no accident that my father broke mine when I was ten years old. I look back at Rahmi. He will never be able to let his guard down around me. A part of him will always be reading my face, my voice, searching for traces of anger that could lead to violence. And, I realize with pounding shame, a part of him will do that with everyone. He will never feel safe, and it's my fault. I've changed him.

Rahmi's looking down at his arm. He tries to move it again, but can't get more than a few inches before he stops, wincing.

"We need to go to the hospital," I say, my voice shaky. "You need an X-ray."

Rahmi frowns. "What are we going to tell them?"

I suck in my breath, jolted back to that day, twenty years ago. My dad driving me to the hospital, coaching me on the lie we would tell the doctors.

How did all this happen, Murray?

I shift my focus to Rahmi. He's watching me, waiting for an answer. Waiting for his lines—the right words that won't get him in any more trouble.

"We'll tell them what happened," I say, opening the Band-Aids I brought for his cut. "We'll tell them it was my fault."

Chapter 49
How All This Happened
Rahmi

They wait two hours before an older nurse shows them back to an exam room. She has tropical-print scrubs and Rahmi fixes his eyes on the palm tree sunset on her left shoulder while she takes his vitals. Murray sits in the chair in the corner, drumming his fingers against his leg. The nurse scribbles down a few more numbers, then takes the forms Rahmi had filled out in the waiting room.

"Looks like you hurt your arm," she says, reading his answers.

Rahmi nods, keeping his eyes on her shirt. "That's right."

Several voices rise and fall outside the door as a group moves down the hallway. The nurse looks up, flipping the pages over. She sweeps hair off her face and seems flustered. The ER is crowded and Rahmi's sure she's got a million places to be. "Well, there are a few ahead of you, but Dr. Greenbaum should be in to see you before too long," she says, looking up and smiling.

"Thank you." Rahmi smiles back, relieved he won't have to tell the story twice.

The nurse leaves and Rahmi lets his shoulders slump, exhaling. He adjusts his position on the paper-covered exam table and looks over at Murray.

"We should have brought dinner or something."

Murray smiles, but he looks sick. "We can go out after, if you want. Wherever you like."

Rahmi looks down, embarrassed by the obvious guilt offering. He doesn't want Murray to feel bad, but wonders if that's all he thinks it takes to buy back normalcy. He rests his forehead in his hand for a moment. His arm throbs. The right side of his face burns. And he isn't sure if Murray's presence will be a comfort to him at all.

"You don't have to do it, you know," Rahmi says, watching Murray tap his foot on the floor. "You don't have to say it was your fault. It was an accident."

Murray frowns and the tapping accelerates. "It wouldn't have happened if I hadn't lost control. Again."

Rahmi looks away. He sees Murray in pain and wants to give him a way out. Part of him believes it, too—that it was an accident. That a separate entity takes over when he gets angry, and does things the real Murray would never condone. But another part of Rahmi is more practical. More concerned with daily survival. That part just wants to say all the right things and smile through the chaos, in a desperate attempt to prolong their moments of peace. Because those moments get him through everything else.

"I don't know," Rahmi says with a slight smile, "I think we can still pin it on Noel."

Murray laughs. "Yeah, that'd be all right." He runs a hand through his hair and leans forward a little. "I really am sorry, though." His expression turns serious as he meets Rahmi's eyes. "You didn't do anything wrong, okay? It was me."

His eyes fill with tears again and Rahmi can't take it. "No, I shouldn't have brought up Cleveland. It w—"

"No," Murray says, getting up and walking over to him. He rests a hand on Rahmi's good shoulder and looks into his eyes. "This is the same shit I went through with my dad. He'd put me in the hospital and I would come away thinking it was my fault. I should have listened better, or acted better, or managed to calm him down." Murray shakes his head. "But nothing would have been good enough."

"You're not him," Rahmi says, his voice steady. "I know you're not."

"I sure as hell don't want to be," Murray says. "But look at me." His voice lowers. "And look at you."

Rahmi takes Murray's hand and moves to one side of the exam table, giving him room to sit down. They stay like that, holding hands, for a long time.

Murray is back on his blue plastic chair, drumming his fingers together while Rahmi reads the posters on the wall, when Dr. Greenbaum bustles in twenty minutes later. He's medium height, with curly brown hair and a full beard. And he's young—probably late thirties—which catches Rahmi off guard. They're all peers. Somehow that makes this harder.

"Hi, there. Rahmi, right?"

Rahmi nods.

"Good to meet you. I'm Sam Greenbaum." Dr. Greenbaum offers his hand, but Rahmi points to his arm apologetically. The doctor pulls back. "Right. I'm sorry." He turns to Murray. "Are you here for support?"

Murray nods. "Yeah, I'm Murray. His boyfriend."

Dr. Greenbaum nods and holds out his hand without missing a beat. "Nice to meet you, Murray."

They shake hands and the doctor moves to his stool, then grabs the clipboard of papers off the counter. "So, Rahmi," he murmurs, reading through the forms, "looks like you had a run-in with a table." He glances up and smiles, but Rahmi doesn't react. "Were you guys moving furniture or something?"

Rahmi swallows. "It wasn't a big deal," he says, his face heating up. "The table fell, and—"

"Rahmi." Murray's voice is strained. Rahmi looks over and he's shaking his head, his eyes wet. He opens his mouth like he wants to say more, but shakes his head again, and rests his face in his hand.

"The table fell . . . ?" Dr. Greenbaum says.

Rahmi watches Murray for another moment before turning back to the doctor.

"Yeah," he says, uneasy that he can't tell what Murray's thinking. "We were moving it."

"How did it fall on your upper arm?"

Rahmi glances at Murray but it looks like he's checked out. His expression is pained and his eyes are glazed, like he's watching a depressing movie projected on the wall he's staring at. Maybe he's remembering what happened. Whatever it is, Rahmi knows he won't be any help to him now.

"We were taking it down some stairs," Rahmi says. "I was at the bottom, and the top part just got away from him."

Rahmi's face is on fire now. He hates lying and is terrible at it. He stares down at his shoes, feeling Dr. Greenbaum's eyes still studying him.

"Huh," the doctor says, and when Rahmi looks up, he sees he's watching Murray. The previous warmth and humor are gone from his eyes. "Bet that hurt." He frowns, then writes a few notes. "And your eye?" he asks, turning back to Rahmi.

"I . . . I don't really remember. I guess I scraped against something sharp when I fell."

"Was any other part of you injured?"

"No."

Dr. Greenbaum casts a quick glare Murray's way before he scribbles a few more notes.

Rahmi sighs. They shouldn't have to lie. It was an accident. But Rahmi's clumsiness at deceit coupled with Murray's apparent paralysis already give them away. Dr. Greenbaum's a smart guy, and judging by his expression, he's dealt with this type of thing before. Now he'll frame his whole report in a way that makes Murray the bad guy.

"I'd like to do the rest of the exam in private."

Rahmi looks up.

Dr. Greenbaum's watching Murray. "Do you mind stepping out for a few minutes?"

Murray breaks his trance to give Rahmi an incredulous look. He frowns at Dr. Greenbaum. Rahmi looks away and rubs his forehead, ready for Murray to make this a lot harder than it needs to be.

"Is that necessary?" Murray says, a worried note edging his voice. "What do you need to do without me?"

"It's standard procedure to examine the patient alone."

Murray squints one eye. "Really?"

Dr. Greenbaum gives him a look. "Don't you usually go to the doctor alone?"

"What if Rahmi wants me here?"

The doctor turns to Rahmi. "You're welcome to have a nurse present, if you like."

"That's okay," Rahmi says, wishing the whole thing were over. He leans over toward Murray. "It's okay," he says, hoping the calmness of his voice gets through to him. "Just let him do the exam, then we can go home."

Murray sits back, eyeing Dr. Greenbaum. "Okay," he says. He stands up and puts his hand on Rahmi's back. "I'll be in the waiting room." He nods to Dr. Greenbaum before walking out.

Rahmi's breath sticks as the door clicks shut. He doesn't want Murray to leave, either, probably for the same reason. He doesn't want the doctor to say the things he's required to. He doesn't want this stranger, a man only a few years older than Rahmi, to feel sorry for him. But as he looks up and catches Dr. Greenbaum's sympathetic gaze, he knows it's already too late.

"What happened to your back?" he asks, setting the clipboard on the counter.

"What?" Rahmi frowns. "Nothing."

"When Murray touched you on the back just now, you winced. Like it hurt."

"I mean, I guess that's where I fell. Against the wall. It really doesn't hurt, though."

"Okay." He pulls on blue latex gloves. "Mind if I take a look?"

With the doctor's help, Rahmi takes off his shirt. He sits up straight, steeling himself for the feel of cold hands on his skin. But as Dr. Greenbaum presses down on his back, his touch is warm and light, and Rahmi can tell he's avoiding the worst parts.

"Looks like you hit something that was jutting out," he says. "Not just a flat wall."

Rahmi's stomach sinks. The handle on the cabinet. He closes his eyes. He doesn't want to do this, and the longer it drags out, the worse it will be for Murray. He knows the doctor is waiting for his answer—his excuse for how these injuries happened—but he doesn't have one.

"Rahmi," Dr. Greenbaum says gently, coming around to face him again, "why don't you tell me what happened."

Chapter 50
Another Hospital

My leg keeps shaking in the plastic waiting room chair, so after about ten minutes I get up and pace, my mind creating the worst possible versions of what's happening in that room.

I failed, again. All I had to do was tell the truth, but one look into the doctor's harsh eyes and I knew I couldn't. So I let Rahmi cover for me, like always, and now I can't pretend I'm any better than my father. I return to my seat and collapse, covering my face with my hands. I think about my doctor that day, twenty years ago—an older man with a Polish name I can't remember—casting my broken arm.

"How high up did you get?" he'd asked, not looking up from his work.

I stared at him. "What?"

"In the tree." He smiled at me before wrapping another length of red cloth around my arm. "Did you at least get to the top before you fell?"

I glanced over at my dad, standing a few feet away with his arms crossed and a grim look on his face. He wasn't going to answer. That was my job.

"Yeah," I said after a moment. "I got to the top."

The doctor laughed. "Good boy." He finished wrapping the cast, then sat back on his stool. "You know, it's the kids I see in here because they were exploring, taking risks—they're the ones who end up the strongest." He patted my knee and looked up at my dad. "Just keep him out of the tree for a little while."

My dad smiled. "I'll do my best."

And now I sit in another hospital, my eyes burning as I stare at my hands, unable to change the outcome. Unable to change anything.

I rub my eyes. At the time, I liked him—my doctor. Now I understand how grossly inept he was. He smiled and joked through my exam, more concerned with easing nervousness than assessing my injuries. He felt my arm, squeezed and extended it, but didn't ask about the red marks on my face. He had me remove my shirt so he could check my shoulder and collarbone, but didn't seem to notice the scars on my back. He didn't question anything my dad told him and didn't want to know more than the basic facts, such as they were.

I look toward the hall where Rahmi is being examined right now. My chest aches and I realize I want more for him. I want Dr. Greenbaum to see what's happening. I want him to tell Rahmi his story doesn't add up, and none of this should have happened. I want him to tell Rahmi it isn't his fault, because maybe then he'll finally believe it. I wipe the sweat from my palms onto my jeans. And he will. He's a good doctor. I think of the way he looked at Rahmi when he was explaining his injuries. Patient, understanding, but not about to let that bullshit get by him. I smile a little. If Dr. Greenbaum had been my doctor that day, maybe everything would have been different.

Chapter 51
Dr. Sam Greenbaum
Rahmi

"Well, the injuries to your back and your face are fairly superficial," Dr. Greenbaum says, giving Rahmi a reassuring smile. "Nothing we need to do for those."

Rahmi nods, wondering when he'll tell him to leave Murray. There has to be a script they follow, a model for how to tell patients like him that they're fucked.

"Now your arm," the doctor continues, "that might be a different story."

He stands in front of Rahmi and rests both hands on his shoulders. His expression is focused as his hands move down Rahmi's arms. Rahmi sucks in his breath when he gets close to the right elbow.

"Is that where it starts to hurt?" Dr. Greenbaum asks, lightly touching the spot on his upper arm.

"Yeah."

"And how far can you move it away from your body?"

Rahmi clenches his teeth and takes a deep breath, preparing for the pain. He slowly forces his arm outward, telling himself if he does a good job on this, maybe it means nothing's wrong and they can go home.

Dr. Greenbaum watches him with that same focused concern, but stops him when it's clear the pain is overwhelming. "It's all right," he says when Rahmi lets out a frustrated sigh. "You're doing fine."

"Maybe it's not broken."

"Maybe." He smiles a little. "Let me check it out a bit more, then we'll get you an X-ray."

Rahmi nods and Dr. Greenbaum takes his arm, letting the weight rest in one hand while he moves his other fingers over the top. His touch is so gentle and comforting, Rahmi almost forgets what brought him here in the first place.

"Tell me if any of this gets too uncomfortable. I don't want to hurt you."

Rahmi nods. As Dr. Greenbaum moves his hand back to his shoulder, Rahmi feels an increasing stiffness in his pants. His heart races and his ears burn. He shouldn't be feeling this. Not now. "That hurts," he says, just to get the doctor's hands off him.

"Okay," Dr. Greenbaum says, grabbing the clipboard and writing again. "We'll do the X-ray in a minute. I just need to ask you a few questions."

Rahmi frowns. "Sure."

"Do you feel safe going home?"

"Yeah, of course," he says, rubbing his feet together. "Like I said, Murray's not usually like that."

"What's he usually like?"

Rahmi pauses. "He's a good person. He's not what you think." He glances toward the door. "And he had a tough childhood."

"So, you feel bad for him?"

"No, I guess I just understand more where he's coming from."

"He grew up around violence?"

Rahmi nods. "His father."

Dr. Greenbaum looks up. "And now he's the same way."

"No," Rahmi says, his arm throbbing harder now. "This was an accident."

"All right." Dr. Greenbaum writes a few things down. "Has he lost control like that before?"

Rahmi shrugs. "Once or twice, I guess. But it wasn't a big deal."

"Were you injured those times?"

"No."

"But he tried to hurt you?"

"Listen," Rahmi says, "I know what you're getting at, but it wasn't like that. We figured it out, and we moved on. I never got hurt."

"Until now."

Rahmi's vision blurs. Greenbaum's getting this all wrong and it's making him crazy. Murray's a victim, too.

When Dr. Greenbaum breaks the silence, his voice is soft. "Do you want to get the police involved?"

Rahmi glares at him. "No."

"What about a therapist?"

"Murray has a therapist."

"Do you?"

Rahmi doesn't say anything and Dr. Greenbaum sets his papers aside, gazing down at his hands for a moment.

"Rahmi, it feels like you've heard all this before. Maybe you've been thinking about it yourself, trying to weigh your options. In the twelve years I've been practicing medicine, I've seen a lot of these situations, and it's my job to help you stay safe."

"Thanks, but I can handle it."

He nods. "I won't try to make you do anything you don't want to do, I just want to make sure you see what's going on." Dr. Greenbaum adjusts his position on the stool. "It sounds like things have been getting worse—that Murray's violence has escalated. He probably spent a lot of time early on showing you his good side, and now it's hard to separate those feelings from what's happening now."

Rahmi fights the impulse to argue, knowing the doctor won't listen. Murray's good side isn't a performance; it's who he is. The other part is a bad side effect from a horrible childhood. It's a weakness, but one he's working on.

"You need to think about what staying in this relationship will cost you," Dr. Greenbaum says, studying Rahmi's face. "Every time Murray crosses a line and you don't stand up and say, 'Enough,' the line moves a little bit. And he knows it. He knows just how far he can push you and still get away with it." His dark eyes burn into Rahmi's. "I've seen it again and again, and these guys, they don't get better. They only get worse."

"Murray's not like them," Rahmi says. "He found therapy on his own. He's trying to get better."

"What's his motivation to get better if you stay with him no matter how abusive he becomes?"

Rahmi bristles. "That's not how it is. You don't know him."

"You're right," Dr. Greenbaum says. "All I know is you came in with injuries sustained after a fight with your boyfriend. And all I can do is advise you on how to proceed." He leans forward. "Let me just say this, Rahmi: You don't deserve what happened today. You shouldn't have to pay for temporary stretches of happiness with hospital visits. My advice is to make a plan for leaving." He pulls a card out of a drawer and hands it to Rahmi. "There are trained counselors who can help you if you make that choice."

Rahmi looks at the card. He can't stand the thought of Murray being lumped in with all the other guys they deal with.

No.

Rahmi shoves the card deep into his pocket. This is not who they are.

He blinks a few times, then looks up at Dr. Greenbaum. "Can I get the X-ray now?"

Chapter 52
Alone Together
Rahmi

Murray won't sleep in their bed. After they got back from the hospital, he told Rahmi he'd take the couch. Rahmi said it was unnecessary, that he didn't need to punish himself anymore, but Murray insisted.

As Rahmi watches him cover the grungy couch with a sheet and blanket, he considers telling Murray the truth—that he just doesn't want to be alone. But it would make him sound weak.

It turns out Rahmi's arm isn't broken. After the X-ray, Dr. Greenbaum diagnosed it as a bone bruise and said it would take a few months to heal. Rahmi had felt a rush of relief and hoped the news would lessen Murray's guilt, but he remained somber all night, only mumbling a few superficial sentences before they'd gone separately to bed.

And Rahmi knows they won't sleep.

He lies in their bed, running the events of the hospital through his mind, revising his reactions, admonishing himself for not insisting that Murray stay in the room. But then he thinks about Dr. Greenbaum, and the concern in his eyes. He went beyond the script. His intensity, his desire to protect Rahmi was genuine. Rahmi's face heats up as he recalls the exam and the doctor's gentle touch. His low, calm voice. He frowns, and a wave of shame washes over him. What kind of boyfriend is he, getting an erection from the touch of another man? Rahmi shakes his head, but he can't dispel the memory of Dr. Greenbaum. Sam. And he can't help wondering what it would be like to hold his hand. Hear him laugh. A man who thinks he deserves better. A man with such a low propensity for violence he can't even understand it.

Rahmi sits up in bed, glancing around the room and doing his best to clear his thoughts. Murray always supports him with school, even helps with his homework. He was there for him when Seda got married, and when his mom had a stroke. Rahmi thinks about Coney Island and smiles.

For as compassionate as he was, Dr. Greenbaum doesn't know them. He doesn't know how much they can overcome.

A little before six a.m., Rahmi hears a soft knock at the door. He's still awake, but the sound startles him.

"Come in," he says, sitting up. His arm is throbbing and the cut under his eye is making the right side of his face ache. He swallows a few pain-killers from his nightstand as Murray walks in. Rahmi smiles. "I thought it must have been Grace. Why did you knock?"

Murray shrugs. "In case you wanted to be alone." His eyes are red and bleary, and he hasn't even changed his clothes from yesterday. "I couldn't sleep."

Rahmi nods. "Me neither."

Murray walks over to the bed. "Is it okay if I sit?"

"Yeah, of course."

Rahmi frowns, unsettled by Murray's heightened formality. Two days ago he'd have run into the room and launched himself onto Rahmi while he lay in bed, just to be funny. But today he asks if he can sit.

"I'm sorry," he says, shaking his head. "I shouldn't have let you lie about what happened."

Rahmi tries to speak but Murray holds up his hand.

"I lost my nerve when I saw Dr. Greenbaum. The way he was watching me . . . he already knew. And I was too scared to say it." He sighs. "But then I understood: he's the doctor I needed as a kid. And I'm glad you got him."

Rahmi rubs his forehead. "But he doesn't think we should be together," he says, trying to understand. "He wants me to leave."

Murray nods. "I know."

"Then why are you defending him?"

"Rahmi," Murray says, unable to meet his eyes, "I love you."

Rahmi's muscles relax and his chest lightens, like part of their dark-ness dissolved in that moment. He smiles, then leans over and touches Murray's face with his good hand. He kisses him. But as he pulls away, he sees Murray's not smiling, and his eyes are clouding with unhappiness. Rahmi takes his hand. "What's the matter?"

"I love you," Murray says again. "And that's why we . . ." He takes a long breath and rubs his face. "We can't be together."

Rahmi sits back. The pain in his arm is worse. He closes his eyes. Murray's ending things. After all they've gone through, he wants it to be over. Rahmi's body feels heavy, like his clothes are weighted, and his mind won't focus. Not with his arm on fire.

"You want to break up with me?" Rahmi asks.

"No, I don't want to," Murray says, looking down. "I have to. I put you in the hospital."

"They didn't admit me."

"I need to get real control over this, or I will end up hurting you again." Murray looks Rahmi in the eyes. "I can't let that happen."

Rahmi's breath quickens. "But I can help you."

"You've given me too many chances."

"No." Rahmi's eyes sting. He starts to hate Dr. Greenbaum for getting between them and for making Rahmi care about him. "So many times, Murray, it wasn't your fault. Like with John, and Noel." He sounds desperate now, but he doesn't care. "Even yesterday . . . I shouldn't have suggested you leave. I want you to think this through. You need support."

Murray wipes his eyes. "Believe me, if there was a way for us to stay together, I'd jump at it, but it would be out of selfishness."

"But what if I want you to stay?"

Murray's gaze rests on the bottles of painkillers on the nightstand. "Rahmi, you can't cover for me anymore."

"What?" Sickening heat rises from Rahmi's stomach to his chest, and anger hardens his voice. "I'm not covering for you."

"You do it all the time. You tell me it's John's fault, or Noel's fault, or your fault. You tell people I hurt myself cooking when I have a bandage on my hand. You tell the doctor we were moving furniture when you got hurt. You tell me you're okay when you're not. And I've always wanted to hear it, until now." Murray stares at the floor. "I can't keep pretending this isn't my fault."

"It's not always your fault."

"Rahmi, listen to yourself," Murray says, rubbing his forehead. "You just told me I'm not to blame for nearly breaking your arm, because you suggested I go to Cleveland for a while." He shakes his head. "How bad does it have to get before you tell me to fuck off? Do you think you deserve this?"

"I just want to help." The words catch in Rahmi's throat. He lowers his head. Murray's right. He makes excuses all the time, and he's doing it right now. He's part of the problem. He gives Murray a way out when what he really needs is someone to stand up and say, "Enough." But he can't think about that now, not while he's losing his boyfriend. As long as they stay together, they can work on their problems. He's not ready to give up.

"You can help," Murray says, resting his hand on top of Rahmi's. "You can let me leave. I need to." Murray's voice is firm. He's made up his mind. And his confidence, his uncharacteristic calmness, agitates something in

Rahmi. He's made the decision for both of them, and he's making it look easy.

"I guess you've got it all worked out," Rahmi mutters.

"It's not what I want. But it has to be this way."

"So, you've decided for the both of us?" Rahmi drags his fingers through his hair. "I would've liked to have a say in that."

"I'm sorry." Murray's ears redden. He never likes it when a conversation gets away from him. "But I know what you would have said."

"You don't, because you didn't ask," Rahmi snaps.

"Rahmi," Murray says, with a slight smile like he's humoring a child, "come on, I—"

"No, just stop!" Rahmi yells, sitting up straighter and wincing. He rips his glasses away and rubs his eyes with his sleeve. "How can this be so easy for you?"

"It's not," Murray says, his voice rising. "It's killing me."

Rahmi laughs. "Well, Jesus, man, I've never seen you so in control. I guess you're getting the hang of it."

Murray leans forward on the edge of the bed with his elbows on his knees. He breathes in and out. He's trying to keep his head.

After several seconds he looks up, and his eyes are softer. "I ran this conversation through my head a thousand times last night," Murray says in a voice so sad and gentle it makes Rahmi's throat tighten. "And I was never happy with where it went. But a few times, I let it play out differently. I imagined you were so devastated by the idea of me leaving that I changed course. I said let's try it again. And I made promises." Tears brim over Murray's eyes but his voice doesn't change. "I said I'd be different, and I'd never do anything to hurt you again." He shakes his head. "But it's just a fantasy. We both know those promises never last." Murray looks up and the pain in his face obliterates the last traces of Rahmi's anger. He squeezes Rahmi's hand. "I have to leave," he says. "And you will be happier."

Rahmi can't hold himself together anymore. He lets his body feel the grief his mind has been holding onto, trying to suppress. He cries, not with a few stoic tears, but with the unrestrained flood of misery he's needed to release for months. His shoulders shake and Murray moves to comfort him. He holds Rahmi but doesn't say anything. It feels like hours pass, but Rahmi can't stop. And for all the shock and misery and denial inundating his mind, the underlying constant is relief. Murray's right. And Rahmi doesn't want to be afraid anymore.

"Where are you going to go?" he asks after a few minutes.

Murray smiles. "There are flyers all over NYU looking for sixth or seventh roommates."

Rahmi nods. "I just . . . ," he begins, blinking the remaining tears from his eyes, "I love you, too."

Murray pulls Rahmi in again and holds him, tighter than before. But Rahmi knows it's not a plea for him to stay. It's a definitive, final gesture. It's a goodbye.

Chapter 53

Give Up

New York, Four Months Later

Something's wrong. Noel always shows up at the Grab&Go a little after nine-thirty on weeknights, buys a marked-down hot dog and a Red Bull, then heads to Jemma's place. I check my watch. It's ten o'clock.

I rub the bottom of my shoe against the lamppost I'm standing next to, scraping the remains of somebody's gum onto its worn metal base. Ten o'clock. I frown, glancing down the street. I thought I knew this fucker by now.

After another fifteen minutes, I'm about ready to leave when he shows up. I hear him before I see him. I'm looking the other way, trying to make out the faces in this group standing outside a bar, when I hear his laugh. It's a strained, irritating sound, different from his unreserved drunk laugh, or his derisive, dangerous laugh. It's a performance. I turn, not too fast, and there he is, across the street in front of the Grab&Go. He looks sharp, as always—his clothes business casual, his hair gelled and combed. Everything about his appearance is a lie. He's with some girl, young and pretty, but she has a dirty, desperate edge that makes their connection add up. I've seen it before. He's got a type, but they never seem to last. Except Jemma.

I turn a page in my guide to New York, illuminated by the streetlight, and try to make out what they're saying. They seem happy enough, so I'm guessing it's early in the relationship.

Noel glances down at his watch. "Fuck," he says, turning away with his hands on his head.

"What?" the girl asks.

He walks back to her and says a few words I can't make out. He points to the Grab&Go, with his eyebrows raised like he wants her to agree to something. Her eyes dart around, but she nods and they both walk into the convenience store.

I close my eyes and lean against the lamppost. I think I know what's going on, and when they walk back out six-and-a-half minutes later, I'm sure of it. Noel's holding his tinfoil-wrapped hot dog and Red Bull, blinking rapidly. The girl didn't buy anything but is holding a tissue. She rubs her nose with it every few seconds. Noel just uses his sleeve. He squeezes the girl's arm and gives her a schoolboy smile.

"Next time," he says. He kisses her and turns away, toward Bleecker Street. She stands there a moment longer, watching him go, then turns and walks the other way.

I give it a minute before I follow Noel. I know where he's going, and every night as I walk in his shadow, I wish he would turn on a different street. Find a new goddamn neighborhood. But he never does. He makes his way down Sixth, sometimes whistling or humming to himself. Three nights ago, an older man walking ahead of him tripped on the uneven sidewalk and spilled his groceries. Noel stopped and helped him. He asked if the man was okay. And the man smiled, even shook his hand. I had to stumble into an alley to regain control of my breathing and cool my overheated body. But it was part of my education. In the seven weeks I've been watching Noel, I've come to realize that the shittiest people you could meet spend most of their time looking just like everybody else.

By the time I arrive at the apartment building, he's already buzzed Jemma and is leaning against the brick wall with a cigarette in his hand. I stay in the shadows of the construction dumpster down the street, rubbing the sweat from my palms onto my shirt. I'm always afraid I'll run into Rahmi—that he'll see me like this and think nothing's changed. I adjust the Indians cap I'm wearing. But it's not like that. I'm just looking out for Jemma.

Noel takes a long agitated drag on his cigarette. His other hand's on his hip, fingers tapping against his belt.

"Come on, Jemma," I murmur, looking up at the apartment and understanding each second takes a dangerous toll on his patience.

By the time she trudges out the door, Noel's cigarette is so low that he lets it fall onto the sidewalk and crushes it under his shoe.

"Took your damn time, didn't you?" he says.

Jemma glares at him. "You're the one who was late."

Without warning, his hand shoots out and grips her arm. "You get three minutes next time, okay?"

She shakes her arm free but doesn't say anything. My heart pounds as I study Noel's face for clues about what he'll do next. His expression is hard and his hand still hovers in the air, like he might need another try to get his message across. I think about how his face looked just a few minutes ago— the laugh, and the innocent smile he pulled on that other girl. I guess when you've spent months wearing somebody down, you don't need a charming veneer anymore.

And over these weeks it's become clear that's what Jemma is: worn down. I've seen it play out in real, excruciating time. She's given up. There are still traces of the real Jemma there, but she doesn't fight his dominance like she used to. She comes down when he buzzes her, she lets him pick the bar or the nightclub or the strip joint, she rarely tells him to fuck off anymore. I follow as they head up Bleecker. If Lamar were here, he'd tell me everything's a choice, and this was hers. This is how she gets what she needs.

I expect them to stop at Rusty's, the dismal little hole with black light and synth music they've gone to the past few nights, but they walk on by. They walk a couple more blocks, then turn left on Sullivan, but at this point Jemma's dragging her feet. I get the feeling she's not up for whatever they're about to do, but Noel keeps urging her on. They stop outside Hard Candy, a gaudy strip club with neon signs boasting barely legal nude girls. I stop a few doors down, in front of a Laundromat. Noel lights another cigarette and squints up at the bright signs. He looks at his watch and motions for Jemma to go inside, but she shakes her head. Her face is like stone and she won't even look at him when he yells at her. But he should understand. On the eleventh day of following Noel, I learned Jemma works here. She's a dancer—maybe more, but I've never been inside. Noel usually comes here on his own, at odd times like Sunday mornings, when no one's around but the owner he deals with.

"Don't fuck this up for me," he says. His hand is on her shoulder now.

She doesn't move. Her eyes are on the ground and I wonder if she can even hear him anymore. My skin prickles and the blood pounds faster through my veins. It's the way she's shutting down, and the way he's so intent on getting her inside. I take a long breath. He offered the guy something only she can give.

Noel's leaning in close now, talking low. I stare at Jemma, willing her to push him away and run. But it's not that easy. He has guns and knives and any kind of confrontation could prompt him to use them. But he can't get away with this. I crack my knuckles and move a little closer.

Noel must have crossed a line with something he said because Jemma looks up, the fire back in her eyes. She snarls something I can't make out, and he hits her. A swift, well-practiced backhand that instantly does its job. She doesn't speak again, and won't look at him. He growls one final remark, then leads her inside by the arm.

I step out of the darkness and stand on the sidewalk, my eyes stinging. It's different, seeing him do it. I've felt the urge to handle Noel before, to put myself between him and Jemma, because I know what he's capable of. But until now I hadn't seen it. And now I want to kill him.

I walk a few steps to the bench outside the club before the nausea forces me to collapse. I sit and cover my eyes, trying to remember what I'm doing here. I thought if I knew where he was, what he was up to, I'd feel better. I shake my head. I'm an idiot. I wanted a service project—a way to get my mind off Rahmi and everything else, and maybe help Jemma. But I'm no more effective than a shadow. I tried to prove to myself I could keep tabs on Noel without losing control, but I've just confined those impulses to my mind, indulging in a loop of violent fantasies. I don't feel better, and I'm sure as hell not helping Jemma.

My hands shake. They could come out at any time, and what would I do? My ears are hot. I'm doing it again. I think about waiting at the side of the building, waiting for Noel to walk away. I think about slipping up behind him, grabbing his throat and pulling him into an alley. I'd get in a few solid punches before I pulled one of his weapons on him. He'd still be stunned, trying to figure out what was happening.

No. I stand up and take deep, raspy breaths, pacing in front of the club. I'm not helping anybody. I wipe my eyes and trudge to the payphone. I pump the change in, my heart hammering. I'm doing what I said I'd do. I pick up the receiver and dial the police. I glance toward the club. Jemma will run. She'll clear her stuff out of the apartment and I'll never see her again. As the phone rings, I squint to see them through the dirty glass of the front window. Noel is talking and laughing with one of the dancers. Jemma is gone, doing his work for him. I stand a little straighter. She'll run, but anything has to be better than this.

Chapter 54
Ghosts

It's still hot and the air is oppressive when my shift ends at seven p.m. I pour water on my face and rub it into my hair. I gaze down Prince Street, watching the sun sink lower in the orange sky.

My supervisor, Justin, calls out to me as I start walking home, telling me to have a good night. I wave, thinking about the offer he'd made earlier, after scaring the shit out of me by telling me we needed to take our lunches together.

"So, Murray," he'd said, sitting next to me on the curb in front of the old warehouse we're renovating, "you signed on for three months, right? Seasonal work?"

My shoulders fell. I couldn't even last that long. I nodded. "That's right."

"Well, you're doing a good job," he said, looking past me. "And we've had a lot of turnover this year."

I nodded again, still unsure where this was going. "I like it," I said. "I haven't done construction before, but . . ." I looked away, across the street. "I don't know. It's a good fit."

"Glad to hear it." Justin unwrapped the gyro he'd bought from a stand down the street. "We've got a permanent position, if you're interested."

I looked at him. "Really?"

"Yeah," he said. "Nothing fancy, just what you've been doing. General labor–type stuff." His eyes focused on mine. "But we need somebody who can make a commitment. More than a few months, anyway. A year, at least."

I looked down. A commitment.

The sounds of the street intensified, pulling me away. Another year in New York, building and tearing down. Another year of walking past Rahmi's place on my day off, my chest tight. Another year of four roommates in an asbestos-filled apartment on Greene Street. I glanced up, watching people pass under the mammoth skyscrapers, feeling their urgency. I closed my eyes and forced my breathing to slow before I turned to Justin.

"Can I think about it?"

I've been writing a lot of letters lately. Another to Dani, three to Rahmi, one to Emma, and one to John. I try not to make excuses in them, but it's hard. I still find myself distorting reality, twisting our narratives to rationalize my behavior. So I never finish them.

I turn my desk lamp to shine on the empty page of my notebook. I pour another glass of whiskey from one of the bottles my roommates keep. I glance at the clock. It's nearly midnight, but I find it's easier to start late. I'm doing what Lamar suggested in one of my first sessions with him: I'm keeping a journal of my emotions. I write about times I was losing control, and how I handled myself. I write about deep breathing and visualization. I write about using my work in construction to channel physical impulses. I write about my attempts at meditation. And as I think back through the days, I'm always astounded by how many times my temper flares. I write quickly, the heat rising in my body as I'm faced with how insignificant these triggers are. But I don't leave anything out, and soon the page is filled. It's always filled.

I end by writing to Rahmi. Nothing as structured as the letters I can't finish, but rather fragmented thoughts that won't leave my mind. Today I write about how I heard someone laugh across the street and, for a moment, thought it was him. I finish the glass and pour another. I write that I miss him most at the end of the day, when everything's quiet. I write about how I hate living with other people, even though I've kept them strangers. Then I write that I still love him, but I won't try to win him back. I close the notebook.

The light flickers, bringing me back. I move to turn it off, but something catches my eye as I lean over the desk. A file folder sticks out from under a box in the corner of the room. I know what it is, though I'd forgotten about it. I down the rest of the whiskey and shine the light in the direction of the corner. I walk over, sitting down on the stained taupe carpet. I pull out the file and feel the instant stinging in my eyes. It's Mr. Everett's file on me—the one Chase gave me at his funeral. The tab says "Henderson, Murray (19)" in faded pencil. I take a long breath. I've only looked at my file three or four times in the past ten years, and I could never read it for very long. I look down at my fingers, resting beneath the cover. Every sentence brings an instant rush of memory, so many I wish I could erase. But I don't want to erase him.

I open the file. I see the forms I'd filled out, questionnaires and psych evals, and I still remember the questions I'd dodged, the answers I had spun to make myself seem normal.

His notes begin as quick phrases he jotted down. The first: *timid, fearful, polite*, then: *stomach issues.* As I read on, I remember the progression of our sessions. *Concerned with normal, gaps in memory, self-harm.* That same wave of fear rises in my stomach, but I keep reading. *Traditional family, anger, abusive toward girlfriend.*

As he got to know me, his pages began filling with detailed paragraphs about what I told him. I still can't read it all. I catch snippets as my eyes dart over the lines. *Memory gaps coincide with injuries. Parents had to tell him what happened.* I turn another, but I won't last much longer. *Murray believes his pain is his fault. That he deserves it. He lashes out at anyone who threatens to expose this pain.*

"I wouldn't put too much stock in that."

I whirl around, wiping my eyes. Standing only a few feet away, leaning against the doorframe, is Mr. Everett. He's smiling, but looks tired. Just like I remember.

"It was a long time ago."

I taste acid in my mouth and sweat springs from my skin. Everything about his appearance is the same as I remember: his dark, chaotic hair, his wrinkled button-down shirt and khakis, his kind smile and sad eyes. I stand, my heart slamming.

"Mr. Everett?"

"It's really good to see you, Murray. You're not the kid I remember, though; you're all grown up."

My head pounds and I blink a few times, trying to clear my vision. I glance around the room, embarrassed for him to see me like this. To see my life in this state.

"You look the same," I manage to murmur.

He laughs. "Yeah, I'm afraid so." He crosses his arms. "So, New York, huh?"

"Yeah. I mean, I hope it'll work out." I'm still not sure what's happening, but the strangest part is it feels right for him to be here. And it doesn't feel like any time has passed.

"Law school and the East Coast," he says with a smile. "I remember those were the things you wanted. I'm proud of you for going after them."

"Thanks." My face burns. "I've made a lot of mistakes, though. It hasn't really gone the way I wanted."

He nods. "I know."

"You remember Roger Maldonado?" I ask suddenly. I didn't know I was going to ask him that at all.

"You don't need to worry about Roger," he says, with that gentle, easy manner I'd missed so much. "Let him try what he needs to. It's not hurting anybody."

"That's what Chase said."

"I know it's harder on you guys," he says. "You and John and Austin. And I don't expect you to just let it go. But it's okay." He smiles again. "I promise."

I nod but I can't reply. And for the first time since moving out here, I miss Cleveland.

"And really, it's not like I was qualified," he says, nodding to the file still in my hands. I look down at the faded pencil. "I actually studied art history." He tilts his head a little. "Did I ever tell you that?"

"No," I say. "But John did, after . . ."

Mr. Everett nods and walks into the room. "He and I were in the same boat, back in college. We both studied what we loved, with little hope of making money." His smile falters. "At least John made a difference."

My eyes burn. "You made a difference."

"That's nice of you to say." He sits on the bed. "You were a real bright spot in my life, Murray. I'm glad I got to know you."

I frown. It's like he's saying goodbye—leaving all over again. "I mean it," I say, a knot rising in my throat. "The time I had with you meant everything. You helped me."

He sighs. "I nearly got you killed, telling you to go back to your father."

I shake my head. He's wrong, and it wasn't his fault. He sees I'm going to tell him this, though, and he stops me.

"You're a good kid. I'm just sorry I was so bad at counseling. I wasn't a doctor, and it turns out I was pretty shitty at acting like one."

I don't know how to answer him, what to say to the man I would have given anything to talk to again. My heart rate won't slow down and I just want to know where to start, how to tell Mr. Everett how much all his effort meant to me. He leans forward, studying my face, like he's putting together what's going on in my mind.

"What are you hoping to find?" he asks, nodding again to my file.

I shrug. "I just want to get better."

He lowers his eyes. "Nothing in there is going to help you, and I'm sorry for that. It will only hold you back." He looks up again and his eyes are wet. "If I were you, I'd destroy it. Forget your time at the museum. At least try to. None of it worked, and none of it mattered."

I laugh a little in surprise. His manner, his voice, changed so fast. It's like the whole room has darkened. "How can you say that? How can you say it didn't matter?"

"That file," Mr. Everett mutters, "is bullshit. It was my selfish attempt to fix problems I had no business interfering in."

I'm unnerved by the note of anger in his voice. He was never like that. And he always believed in the museum. But the way he can dismiss it all so easily makes my whole body shake.

"You know why I still have it?" My confidence is coming back because I see my role now, and I have something to defend. "You know why I need this file?" I ask, holding it up. "Because it shows that even at nineteen I was this way." I wipe my forehead, my vision jumping. "I was hurting myself and a lot of other people because of the pain you helped me uncover. And since you left," I say, my voice wavering, "I've been trying to cover it back up. I couldn't stand living with it." I look Mr. Everett in the eyes, trying to make him understand. "My file reminds me that I've been here before, and I can't keep taking the easy way out. I need to face it. And ...," I trail off, glancing down, "it's the only thing I have that was yours."

Mr. Everett is quiet for a moment. "You shouldn't think of me like that," he says, shaking his head.

"Like what?"

"Murray," he says, smiling slightly, "you're angry with everybody. Every single person in your life you're mad at, except me. And I'm the one who really fucked you over."

My skin starts to tingle and my head's spinning, so I set the file on my desk and sit in the chair across from him, rubbing my temples.

"You're not angry with me," he says, "because I'm not here. And I can't let you down again. It's another fantasy." The concern in his eyes instantly takes me back to our sessions. To the museum he wants me to forget. "It's why you keep that file but never read it through," he continues. "You know I failed, but you want someone to look up to."

"You didn't fail." I wipe my hands on my pants. "You just didn't let anybody in."

His brow furrows. "Are you letting anybody in?"

"I'm trying. It's harder than it used to be."

"Listen," Mr. Everett says, running his hands over his face like he's gearing up for something, "I am not anyone's hero. I took your problems and made them ten times worse. I set you on a course of violence and grief, then left you to do it alone." He narrows his eyes. "Do not romanticize my memory. I'm not worth the effort."

My stomach pitches and I blink rapidly, hoping to stall the tears. "You know what I always thought?" I say, fragments of memories shooting through my head. "I should have asked you something—anything—about your own life." I wipe my nose with my sleeve. "I think about that all the time. I mean, I guess I'm just really sorry that I never did."

The hard edge is gone from Mr. Everett's voice when he speaks again. "You were nineteen years old, Murray. And dealing with trauma I couldn't begin to understand. I never would have put my problems on you."

"But what about John? He told me the same thing. That you wouldn't let him in. And he was your best friend."

"It wasn't his job to fix me."

"But he wanted to help," I say, my voice rising. "He would have given anything to help you."

"You don't know John like I did. He takes everything to heart. I told him more than most, but I could sense his limit. I wouldn't do that to him either."

I sit back and cross my arms. I'm sure my ears are bright red. "Austin thinks you just didn't trust anybody."

He shakes his head. "It wasn't like that."

"Then what was it like?" I yell, unable to hold back anymore. "Why couldn't you take care of yourself the way you took care of everybody else?" My vision clouds again. "And you still think you're a failure? I will never understand that."

Mr. Everett watches me carefully for a few moments, and I can't tell what he's thinking. His eyes are red and watery, and his face is drawn. I worry he's going to leave, and the last thing I'd have said to him would have been in anger.

"Okay, Murray," he says finally. "I'm going to let you in." He lets out a long breath, then leans forward. "I had a son. He died ten years before I met you, and it was my fault." His hands tremble and I see him glance at the bottle on my floor. "I was distracted, and I lost track of him. And then when I saw you at the museum"—he shakes his head—"the resemblance was striking. And your mannerisms, your timid kindness . . ." His eyes well up and I think maybe he can't do this, but after a moment he continues. "You're the closest I ever got to having him back. So, when I saw this strain between you and your father, I thought about how I'd give anything to repair things with my son." Mr. Everett looks away. "And I proceeded to give you the worst advice I'd ever given, out of selfishness." He wipes his eyes, then looks back at me. "How can you reason with a man like that?"

I'm not sure if he's talking about my father or himself. But I'm starting to understand the level of pain he was dealing with during the time I knew him. "I'm really sorry, Mr. Everett."

"Thank you."

"But what happened to me wasn't your fault."

"Murray," he starts, anger building in his voice, "it wasn't just you. Do you know what I told Austin?" I shake my head and Mr. Everett cracks his knuckles. "I told him he wasn't feeling his pain enough—that he wasn't letting go in the rooms. I told him to go crazy in there. Do you know what that advice got him?"

My stomach sinks and I wish there weren't more coming. I wish I could make him see that he did help people, even as he stacks up evidence against himself. I shake my head again.

"He had the worst flashback of his life during that session. And it didn't end there." He stares past me for a moment, like he's reliving something, too. "I can't go into it, but . . . it was terrible."

"There's more to Austin's issues than that," I say, unable to handle the defeat in his eyes. "Maybe you made some mistakes, but Jesus, at least you were trying."

"They were more than mistakes, Murray, th—"

"No, it wasn't your fault," I yell. "We all made choices, and we all fucked up."

"Not like—"

"Ash, listen to me!" I rise from my seat, the blood pounding in my ears. "I killed somebody—do you get that? And you can't tell me it was your fault or anybody else's. It was me." Between the tears in my eyes and blinding pain in my head, I can barely see him. "I shot my father in the chest with his own gun, and it wasn't an accident. It may have been self-defense, but even then I made a choice. I could have aimed for his leg or his shoulder, but I didn't. I needed it to be over. I needed a guarantee that I'd never see him again." I rub my eyes roughly and walk over to Mr. Everett. I take a breath and sit next to him on the bed, unsure what will even happen if I get this close to him. But as I turn to face him, I understand he's just the same as he always was. "It was me," I say again. "And I won't get better thinking my problems come from anybody else."

Mr. Everett looks down at his hands and nods. "I understand, Murray. I'm sorry you had to go through all that." He meets my eyes again. "And I know you're worried for me to see you now, that I'll think you haven't changed. But I see you trying. I see you doing the work now." He smiles. "You'll get there."

"I have to," I say, trying to smile back at him.

"Hey," he says after a moment. "You finally called me Ash."

I laugh. "Yeah. But it didn't feel right to me."

"I know." He rubs his forehead and glances at me sideways. "Can I tell you something? One last piece of advice, I guess."

"Of course."

"Don't give up on yourself."

I raise my eyebrows. "You're one to talk."

"Good thing this isn't about me."

I study his face, feeling a rush of the old fondness along with renewed sadness that he's gone. That he'll never see himself the way we did. I look down at the half-empty bottle, my empty glass. I frown. Could he even change his mind if he wanted to? Or is it set with the thoughts he had when he died? I glance at the clock. Will all this evaporate anyway when the sun comes up and the alcohol is out of my system?

Mr. Everett stands and moves toward the door. I get up, too, panicked that he's leaving even though I know he has to. He turns back to me.

"I wasn't much of a therapist, but I still loved you, Murray. And not just because you reminded me of him. I'll always care about what happens to you."

"Mr. Everett," I say, with an edge of desperation because I'm just trying to keep him here a little longer. I swallow hard. This is my last chance. "Is there anything I can do for you?" I feel the tears brim over again. "Is there any way I can still help?"

He smiles but shakes his head. "No." My head is hazy and the air between us is thick. "But it's really nice of you to ask."

Chapter 55
Hard Distance

I get up early with a sickening headache and call Lamar's office. He's not in, but I take his soonest appointment, this Friday. I hang up and glance at the clock. I don't have to be at work until ten, but I can't stay in the apartment.

The hazy morning light gives the already crowded streets a ghostly feel. I walk twice around the block before I head to the corner payphone. I inhale the cool, damp air, wondering if I have the guts to follow through.

I slow my pace, running through possible outcomes, but I can't stall anymore. I know I'm responsible; I admitted it to Mr. Everett. And I said I'd make things different. Now I have to see if my convictions still hold up in the light of day.

"John?" I cradle the phone against my shoulder and wipe my forehead. "It's Murray."

"Murray? Hey." He sounds surprised, but I'm encouraged to hear a note of relief in his voice.

"Listen," I say, "I know you might not want to talk to me, but this won't take long." I take a slow, deep breath. "John, you were right. I have a big problem, and I can't keep ignoring it. I can't keep letting myself lose control."

He's silent for a few moments and I try to put myself in his head. He's heard this all before. To him it's just another dodge, another way for me to try to win back a second chance.

"I'm glad you called me."

I lean my back against the booth and close my eyes. Part of me really believed he was done with me.

"But you have to tell me the truth," he says. "What happened to Rahmi?"

"What?" My eyes open.

"Did you hurt him? Did he leave you?"

Heat pounds through my veins. I breathe. This isn't John's fault. And he's not wrong.

"I broke up with Rahmi, a few months ago," I say, careful to keep my voice neutral. "And I moved out. I didn't want him in the middle of this anymore. He deserves better."

"Okay."

"I did hurt him. I flipped a table and nearly broke his arm. And after all that, he still wanted to make things work. He wanted to forgive me." Tears sting my eyes. "I guess that's when I finally understood where I was. I can't be with anybody. Not for a long time."

After several seconds, John sighs. "Are you seeing your therapist?"

"I'll see him on Friday."

"How is this time going to be different?"

"What?"

The hard distance in John's voice is throwing me off, slowing my momentum.

"How are you going to make sure your anger doesn't take over again?"

I lean forward, letting my forehead rest on the cold glass of the booth. I squeeze my eyes shut against the miserable ache in my head. I see Mr. Everett, like he's still in front of me, smiling with all his pain locked behind his eyes. Believing everything was his fault. "I don't know," I say, rubbing my sleeve across my face. "I don't have it worked out yet, and I'm sorry. But I can see it now. I understand what I'm doing and where I'm going, and . . . it's terrible." I grip the phone a little tighter. "I need help."

"Are you coming back to Cleveland?"

I shake my head. I was ready for that. "I'm sorry, John; I can't. I want to give New York another try." I wind the cord around my finger. "I've been working for a construction company. My supervisor just offered me a permanent spot if I can commit to a year." I pause. "I'm going to tell him yes."

"Then how can I help you?" John asks, and for the first time I wonder if he's hurt that I'm not coming back. That I don't need him the same way I used to.

"Well, I was thinking, I could get Lamar to release everything to you and Austin. What we talk about, my progress, everything. If I skip a session, you'd know."

"So, you want accountability?"

I run my hand over my eyes. "Yeah, I guess. I just know I'm going to need more help if I expect to really change. And nobody knows me better than you."

"Are you doing this for Rahmi?"

"What do you mean?"

"Do you want to change so you can get him back?"

"No." I straighten my posture and focus on the graffiti covering the walls of the booth. "I know I can't do that."

"Okay." John's voice is softer again. "Well, I'm glad you've been working."

"Yeah." I release my breath. "It's been good."

After a few seconds of silence, John clears his throat. "Of course I want to help you, Murray."

"Really?"

"I just wish we were in the same city."

"I know," I say, touched by the emotion in his voice. "I do, too." I pause. "But you understand why I can't be there, right?"

"Yeah," John says after a moment. "I get it."

"Thank you." I intend to say more, but can't find the right words. I'm overcome by his loyalty, his willingness to take me back. "Thank you," I say again, rubbing my forehead.

"Of course, Murray." He clears his throat again. "And I've been running it over in my mind, too—how things went when I was there. I'm sorry I was so hard on you. I'm not that good at seeing my kids go through tough times, I guess."

I smile.

"Call me after your appointment Friday, all right?"

Chapter 56
While I'm Away

Lamar leans back in his chair, studying the ceiling as he processes what I've told him.

"When does your boss need an answer, about the job?"

I shrug. "In the next week or so. I wanted to talk to you first."

"Sounds like you're confident, though," Lamar says. "It sounds like you want to stay."

I nod. "I do. And now that I've talked with John, I feel good about it."

"I'm glad you reconnected with him."

"Yeah." I sigh and slump against the back of my chair. I had no idea how bad I was taking our separation until I talked to him again.

"And where did you leave things with Rahmi?" Lamar's voice is harder now. He's still mad, and I don't blame him.

"He helped me move out," I say, my eyes starting to burn. "It took some convincing, but he knew we needed to break up, too. He was set in his own pattern, making excuses for me, and . . . I was making him a wreck." I shake my head. "But, I mean, we love each other. It just sucks, you know?"

Lamar nods. "I think you made the right choice. Both of you. I'm sure it wasn't easy."

I sit for a minute, staring at the floor. I still find myself fantasizing about where we'd be now if I had been different. How we'd plan for the future—maybe get a place of our own after Rahmi graduates. Think about finally telling his family.

"Murray?"

I look up. Lamar's watching me. "Yeah?"

"Is that okay?"

I rub my face. "What?"

"I'd like to go back to Noel for a minute. Is that all right with you?"

I push my thoughts away. "Sure."

"Okay." Lamar's eyes are focused. "How long were you stalking him?"

I flinch. *Stalking.* I don't like the way that sounds, like I was the predator. "Almost two months."

"Every night?"

I pause. "Most nights."

"But you never confronted him?" Lamar sounds matter-of-fact, like he's ready to believe me either way.

"No. I was getting too riled up. When I thought about attacking him, I called the police instead."

"And what happened?"

"I don't know, but I stopped seeing them after that. Hopefully he got arrested."

Lamar nods, but I can't tell what it means. He was obviously disappointed to hear I injured Rahmi, and maybe the Noel thing is making it worse. I just hope he can see that I'm ready to work now.

"Murray, I don't condone stalking, and I can't say this obsessive type of behavior is ever justified." He pauses. "What's encouraging, though, is you were able to respond, rather than react." He sits up straight and folds his hands together. "You recognized your anger building, threatening to turn into violence, and you found another outlet—in this case, getting the police involved. That's a big step forward."

I nod, cautious about what might follow this praise. Sure enough, Lamar gives me a quizzical look.

"I'm curious, though; why did you keep it up for so long?"

"Following Noel?"

"Right."

I pause. I thought that part was obvious. "I was trying to help Jemma."

"True," he says, but with rising, doubtful inflection. "You didn't think about calling the police earlier?"

"It was kind of a last resort."

"Okay." Lamar picks up his notebook for the first time today. "How did you feel, when you were following him?"

"I don't know ... I guess helpful, at first. Like I was doing something."

Lamar writes a few words, then looks at me. "Like you were in control?"

I sense a psych trap and don't respond.

"There's no wrong answer," he says with a smile.

I shrug. "I guess. I didn't want Noel to be in control, that's for sure."

He nods. "About how many nights would you say you felt your anger building?"

I laugh a little. "With that guy? All of them."

"And how did it resolve?"

I pause. "It didn't, I guess. I'd just talk myself down, or cut through a different street for a few minutes so I wouldn't be around them."

Lamar jots another note. "Would you feel better?"

"Eventually."

"But you kept it up, every night."

"Almost every night," I correct him. "And I told you, this was about Jemma. It doesn't matter how I felt about it."

"It matters a great deal how you felt about it." Lamar caps his pen and crosses his arms. "Okay, I see two things at work here," he says, with that glint of satisfaction he gets when he's about to put some of my shit together. "On one hand, you have your altruistic goal: helping Jemma. You keep an eye on her, you circumvent the ethical concerns around stalking Noel, and it gives you a sense of purpose."

I nod, sensing the second thing won't sound as nice.

"On the other hand, you have your rising anger. You know Noel will trigger that anger, but you still put yourself in the same situation again and again. Yes," he says, cutting off my protest, "you're doing it for Jemma, but I also think you want those feelings triggered."

I frown. "Why?"

"Two reasons," he says, clearly glad I asked. "Anger, for you, Murray, is a constant state. It's latent some of the time, but it's always there. I suspect it's one of the few constants you've had in your life since childhood. That makes it comfortable, familiar, and a feeling you seek out, even if it's unpleasant."

My brow stays furrowed.

"But," Lamar continues, the corner of his mouth twitching into a smile, "you're starting to navigate those feelings without a violent release. That's the second reason you want your anger triggered: you want to practice. Every night following Noel has been an exercise in feeling anger without letting it control you. And the final exam, the moment that would have had you seeing red a few months ago, was when Noel hit Jemma in front of you. You could have given him the brutal beating that would have satisfied your anger and your desire to protect Jemma—while maybe getting you both killed in the process—but you chose a different path. You chose to call the police, and calm your feelings internally. Murray," he says, his smile broadening, "this is progress."

I take a deep breath. It sounds real, all laid out like that. It makes me feel like I can do it. "You think I can get better?"

"You *are* getting better. The important part now is to keep working, keep practicing, even when there are setbacks." He glances down at his notes. "You need to avoid these types of unhealthy situations, though. Stalking…"

He shakes his head. "It's part of the cycle you're trying to break. You can get plenty of practice in everyday life. Any argument you have with a coworker or friend, any unfair demand your boss puts on you, is a chance to respond thoughtfully. You will still feel angry, and sometimes you will still react in ways you regret later. Don't let that discourage you. You know what success looks like now. You have some tools that work for you in the moment. Just remember that progress isn't a straight line."

I nod, energized by his confidence but also overwhelmed. I wish I could have Lamar with me out in the world, coaching me whenever I get into trouble. Telling me I'm about to cross a line.

He leans forward. "Don't feel like you need to have everything figured out today," he says, as if reading my thoughts. "We have plenty of time."

I nod again and smile. *We.*

Epilogue

New York, Six Months Later

Walking down Bleecker Street doesn't bother me as much anymore. I've done it enough during this last project, replacing the drywall in Fiore's Pizza. I walk down to the Grab&Go on my breaks, letting the wistful ache settle in my stomach but not cloud my mind. My life in this neighborhood isn't a time I want to go back to. I still miss Rahmi every day, but I have moved on. I hope he has as well.

I throw away my trash from lunch and turn back onto Bleecker. Light snow is spitting, and I pull my gloves back out of my pockets. By the end of the week, this job should be done. Then we'll be on to a new street, a new block, away from these old ghosts. I shake my head. I couldn't stay in Cleveland because the whole city became a bad memory—now I'm crossing off neighborhoods in New York.

When I walk past our building, I look up toward the old apartment, like I always do, wondering if Jemma's gone for good. She's the one on my mind when I pass, so I don't even see Rahmi standing outside the building.

"Murray!" I hear him call out, and turn around. He's in his same shitty winter coat and hat, attractive as ever, smiling at me. A hard knot rises in my throat, but I can't help smiling back. It's so good to see him.

"Hey," I say, walking over. I worry about how I should approach him—offer my hand for him to shake?—but he opens his arms. I hesitate a moment, then hug him, and at once a flood of emotion pounds back through my veins. When we move apart, I see he has a cigarette between his fingers. "You've taken up smoking?"

He shrugs. "It comes and goes."

I nod. "How have you been?"

"Pretty good," he says.

I study his face for a moment. I believe him.

His eyes are clear and animated again. He stands taller than he used to, and his voice is steady. "Are you still over on Greene?"

"Yeah." I laugh. "They're driving me crazy, though." I glance up at the apartment again. "How's Jemma?"

Rahmi's face turns serious. "Remember that asshole, Noel?"

I nod, my heart racing.

"The cops busted him. Jemma came back here and grabbed some stuff, then left. That was"—he pauses and narrows his eyes at the sky—"five or six months ago, I guess."

"I hope she's better off."

"I'd have to think so." Rahmi takes a drag of his cigarette.

"You coming up on graduation?"

He smiles. "I transferred to City College. They've got the English program I really want. My parents are helping me pay for it."

I raise my eyebrows. "That's great. I'm really glad you're going for it."

"Thanks." He lets the cigarette fall to the sidewalk and grinds it with his shoe. He turns back to me, but this time his face is solemn. "I've been seeing somebody," he says.

I stare at him for a moment before my mind catches up to his words. My face burns and the sting in my eyes is unbearable. It hadn't occurred to me that he might be dating again. I don't know why; he's smart, warm, funny, incredibly sexy . . . I look down at my shoes. I guess I assumed when I stopped dating, the world did too.

I take a few breaths before I bring my eyes back up to Rahmi. He's watching me, not with the nervous, placatory gaze I'd gotten so used to, but with calm self-assurance. He's giving me the time I need with this.

Sweat collects under my arms despite the cold and my breath is still coming fast, but I'm starting to see the bigger picture. If choosing not to beat the shit out of Noel was my final exam, then this is Rahmi's. Moving forward, attempting a new relationship, and telling his violent ex about it . . . he deserves some kind of medal. I let another long breath out.

"Is it serious?" I ask, taking a half step back so he doesn't feel crowded.

"No." Rahmi smiles. "It's only been about two weeks." He looks back at the apartment. "It's the guy who took Jemma's room, after she left."

I follow his gaze and nod. "I guess no roommate is safe with you."

He turns back to look at me, maybe to read my face, and starts laughing when he sees I'm smiling. He shoves his hands in his pockets. "It seems like you're doing well. I'm really glad."

"Yeah." I glance down the street. "I think I am."

He nods and squints back up at the sky. "Snow's picking up."

I stand with him and watch. After a minute, he turns to me with a broad smile.

"Remember Coney Island?"

I laugh. "Of course. Best date I ever had."

"Yeah." He gazes past me at the swirling snow. "Me, too."

"You know, I never got to ride the Cyclone."

"Really?" Rahmi raises his eyebrows. "You've lived here over a year. That's fucked up."

I shrug. "It's not easy finding a good tour guide."

He looks down but he's still smiling.

"Maybe I'll get there this summer," I say.

Rahmi looks up. His eyes are glassy and he looks like he wants to tell me something more—to go beyond superficial conversation and talk like we used to.

I smile, letting him know I'm here, but I won't push any more than that.

We stand outside our building, looking at each other, unable to articulate the meaning of this moment I'd bet neither of us thought would ever happen. I'm about to say something—an inane bit of conversation just to break the silence—when Rahmi adjusts his glasses and stands a little straighter.

"I've really missed you," he says, like it wasn't something he expected. He looks distressed and I have to fight the impulse to move in and comfort him. It's not my place anymore, and that understanding hurts more than anything else.

"I've missed you, too." I glance down at the cement between us. "But that's a huge understatement."

His eyes shift back toward the apartment. And I realize, I have to know. I have to know if this plan—my insistence that we separate in order to break our dysfunctional pattern—even helped him. Everything about Rahmi seems stronger and healthier, but he's good at putting up a front. "Can I ask you something?"

He nods. "Of course."

"Are you happy?"

He stares off into the distance again, but I can tell by the way he squares his shoulders that he already knows the answer. "Yeah," he says, meeting my eyes. "For the most part." He studies my face. "Are you?"

"I'm getting there." My chest aches just looking at him. I take a breath. "Knowing you're all right—that helps."

His expression turns a little sad. I should leave, but to pull myself away, knowing this could be the last time I see him, is a pain I'm not prepared to handle. Then I think back to our last fight. To Rahmi's misplaced loyalty and Dr. Greenbaum's serious eyes. I think of my father's hand on my shoulder as he drove me to the hospital.

"I should get to work," I say, looking down the street so I don't lose my composure.

Rahmi nods. "All right."

Again I consider extending my hand, offering that formal, lifeless gesture to the person I care most about. But when my gaze returns to Rahmi's face—so kind and gentle and genuinely tortured—I forget to be stoic. I forget my place and just need him to know I wish things had been different. I open my arms and he looks relieved. He moves forward and pulls me in close, just like he used to, and we hold each other. I feel him sigh. I close my eyes and breathe him in one more time. It's not long enough, but after a few more seconds I let go, knowing it would only get harder.

He blinks and wipes his eyes. "Take care of yourself, Murray."

I nod and squeeze his arm. As he turns and walks back to his apartment, I continue down the street, wondering what he'll say to his boyfriend. And I smile because I realize it doesn't matter. He might have already told this new guy all about us, and I hope he did.

I take my time walking back to work. I watch the snow collect on the sidewalk and street, on cars and buildings. I see a little girl, maybe five or six, with her older brother, trying to play catch with a snowball. Every few throws, it disintegrates and they have to make a new one. I watch them for a minute, until I can no longer put off going to work.

A gust of wind blows from behind, urging me on. I glance at the buildings as I pass. New York is my city now. It's not perfect, but it's right. I want to be in a place that pushes me to change, not one where I let shadows hold me back. I want to keep working with Lamar. I want to run into Rahmi again someday. And I want to see Coney Island in the summer.

Justin's crew is up ahead, unloading the truck. I look over my shoulder before I join them, and catch one more glimpse of the little girl. Her brother watches as she throws snow in the air, smiling as it lands all around her in a shimmering haze of white.

About the Author

KATE KORT was born in St. Louis, Missouri, in 1985. She studied English and world literature at Truman State University. She currently lives in a suburb of Portland, Oregon, with her husband and four children. Some of her favorite authors include Salman Rushdie, G.K. Chesterton, Carl Hiaasen, Mikhail Bulgakov, Andrei Bely, and Arundhati Roy.

She is the author of three novels: *Glass* (2015) and its sequel, *Tempered* (2023), as well as *Laika* (2017).

CPSIA information can be obtained
at www.ICGtesting.com
Printed in the USA
JSHW080826110423
40171JS00002B/183